Final Refrain

Music. Mayhem. Murder.

Robin Gohsman
with: Tammy Fruits

PublishAmerica
Baltimore

First printing

ISBN: 1-59129-860-1
PUBLISHED BY PUBLISHAMERICA BOOK PUBLISHERS
www.publishamerica.com
Baltimore

Printed in the United States of America

Dedications

I dedicate this book to my wonderful, loving and beautiful wife, Mary. Without her support, encouragement and understanding, the words you will read shortly (and hopefully enjoy immensely) would ring hollow.

My hope for everyone is that they too may have a friend, love and soul mate as uniquely special as mine.

I thank God for Mary, and I thank Mary her for her patience, love and unfailing confidence. Just as with everything else in my life, all that is good is a reflection of her wonderfulness.

Mary, thank you and I love you.
Robin Gohsman

I dedicate my efforts on this book to my son Chase, who truly has taught me the meaning of unconditional love.
Tammy Fruits

Acknowledgements

With grateful appreciation to: Kristen Mueller, Thea Keane, Meg Galin, Buck Tilton, Brandon Tushkowski, Christine Gaspardo, Dave Zemlicka, Tom Luhman and Patty Motta whose uniquely special talents and contributions have made this work possible.

A special thanks to Kristy, Jenny, Robin, Tommy, Jimmy and Andy: I love you and I am extremely proud to be your father.
Robin Gohsman

~~~~~~

With gratitude to the pioneers of the concert business who I am proud to call my mentors: Irv Zuckerman, Steve Schankman. Greg Hagglund, Dave Lucas and Chris Fritz. With special thanks to childhood friends, Cat and Janelle; also thanks to Candice, Johnny C, Dollhead and Elbe, the friends who I picked up along the way.
Tammy Fruits

A Special Note

If you enjoyed this book, please pass along the word to others so they may share your delight. If you didn't like the book, please buy five copies and send anonymously to your enemies, thus extracting revenge as they too suffer through hours of reading torture which you already so nobly endured.

Chapter One

In her luxuriously appointed suite atop London's prestigious Connaught Hotel, Angel nestled her head into the shoulder of her lover. Wrapped in the security of love, Angel mused about all that had happened in the previous eight months – the meteoric rise of her band, the murders that hauntingly followed them, the ominous clouds of doom that had been cast over the lives of so many, and the recent rays of happiness that were only so slowly emerging. But emerging, nonetheless.

Angel was the mysteriously beautiful lead singer of the phenomenal band The Ungrateful. More accurately, Angel was still beautiful, she was still a singer, but The Ungrateful was a band no longer.

The newly found fame for The Ungrateful had been, ironically, a mixed blessing. *USA Today*, in an uncharacteristic journalism scoop, first broke the story of Angel's teen years. Curiously, the barrios, the gang affiliation, the drugs, the short rap sheet and the time in "juvie" combined to make the allure of Angel all the more compelling.

Time Magazine, in a feature article accompanying the cover shot, had called The Ungrateful a "sensation that defied classification," and glowingly referred to Angel as "the most beautiful woman in the world."

Angel was, indeed, truly stunning. Angel's mother was Puerto Rican and her father was, well, her father's heritage was anybody's guess because he disappeared shortly after Angel's conception. Her mother had only referred to him as that "dirty, rotten bastard." The irony of the "bastard" reference was never lost on Angel.

Anyway, her genealogical question marks seemed to enhance the universal appeal of her beauty.

Her wide, almond eyes had the haunting quality of a two-way mirror. Angel's eyes sparkled, but never revealed even a fleeting glimpse into her soul.

A smile creased Angel's full ruby lips as she recounted her first appearance on MTV's *Total Request Live*, her interview with Carson Daly, her rise to the top of the rock and roll world, the sell-out concerts, the magazine covers, her glamorous life as a superstar, her rapid ascension to join Cher, Tina, Madonna,

Aretha and Whitney as single-named rock and roll diva icons.

No doubt about it, Angel knew both the depth and the power of her beauty. But she thought that even Carson went a little over the top when he referred to her as "More sensual than Tina…more erotic than Madonna."

Angel's smile quickly faded as she unsuccessfully fought to ward off the haunting memories of the eight fans who were murdered at her concerts. Fans who unceremoniously and irreverently became known as "The Ungrateful Dead." She wondered what the future would hold for Tommy, Morgan and Ace, her forever friends and former band mates.

Angel's anguish and mental hell were interrupted as her lover softly caressed her olive brown skin, then gently kissed her high cheek bones and softly tossed her shoulder-length, lightly curled onyx black hair.

Angel's breathing became heavier with each soft, delicate touch of her body. Fading into blissful pleasure, she and her lover kissed tenderly and then wandered – tentatively at first – and then furiously into a loving expression of oneness. Their passion culminated with intensifying waves of pleasure that totally satisfied both of their desires.

A short time later, Angel quietly rose and softly kissed her sleeping lover's hand. Angel stood in front of the large picture window overlooking metropolitan London and slowly opened the drapes. A brilliant sunshine filled the room.

Chapter Two
(Months Earlier)

Morgan Chino glanced furtively from her computer and subconsciously rolled her eyes. Morgan's father had e-mailed her another one of his never-ending pleas.

Morgan was eternally grateful to her father for her privileged upbringing, but the yoke of his involvement, requests, and expectations had become unbearable.

Dr. Fujimaro Chino was a scattered-brained and brilliant, but somewhat misguided, chemist. Born in Japan, Dr. Chino met Morgan's mother, another Japanese student, during post-graduate school at the University of Chicago.

After a night of revelry, celebration and over-indulgence at Chicago's popular Flapjaws, a local favorite known mostly for its hot wait staff, friendly ambience, and for its generously-sized, juicy and delectable burgers, the chemistry between the Japanese graduate students resulted in their daughter's conception and their hastily arranged marriage.

Determined to assimilate into the American way of life, the Chinos shunned their proud Japanese heritage. Almost pathetically, they foolishly clung to the misguided notion that by ignoring their ancestry they would seamlessly be woven into the fabric of their newly chosen cultural preference. And so, Morgan was named.

After graduation, Dr. Chino patented a long-chain carbohydrate/herbal combination that was "guaranteed to help you lose ten pounds in ten days or double your money back."

In addition to the weight loss product, Dr. Chino invented scores of other concoctions promising to help women everywhere "get shapely hips, rippled abs," and "make them look ten years younger." The brilliance of Dr. Chino's work was widely known to insomniacs everywhere. For $29.95 (plus shipping and handling), Dr. Chino's formulations would also "effortlessly remove hair – even from highly sensitive places;" "smooth out creases and wrinkles," and "restore youthful vitality to your sex life."

Shortly after graduation, Dr. Chino incorporated the American Pharmacal Company, which annually grossed millions of dollars. The Chinos lived on a near-palatial estate in Lake Forest, IL. And the majority of the nouveau-riche fortune was dedicated to help ensure that Morgan would have all the best that America had to offer.

Ballet, voice, violin, modern dance and then gymnastics. Morgan's adolescence consisted of going from one private lesson to the next, all in the comfort of either her mother's Mercedes or her father's Lincoln. Her destiny as a child prodigy was, indeed, carefully orchestrated and seemingly, divinely predetermined. Luckily for all, Morgan possessed incredible natural talent.

Only as Morgan blossomed into womanhood did her gymnastic career prematurely end, but her greatness as a musician was all but guaranteed.

After graduating high school as her class valedictorian, Morgan's sheltered world of parental oversight was altered unexpectedly and tragically when her beloved mother died of a massive stroke.

After her mother's death, Morgan realized just what a loving buffer she had been between Morgan and her father. With each passing day, Dr. Chino's oppressive and slightly maniacal nature became more evident.

Morgan enrolled as a classical music major at Northwestern University in Evanston, IL. For Morgan, the short distance between Evanston and Lake Forest grew longer each day.

During an early fall expedition into the city, Morgan ventured into a coffee shop on the fringes of the "loop." Just across from the aptly named Division Street, where the distant worlds of the Cabrini Green projects and Chicago's Gold Coast intersect, Morgan and Angel first met.

For whatever the reason, Morgan instantly connected with Angel. Over time, Morgan's and Angel's personal and professional lives became interwoven for reasons Morgan never really understood, or cared to understand.

Maybe, in part, it was Angel's ghetto swagger; maybe, in part, it was because Angel represented some of the things Morgan so missed about her mother. Or maybe it was just Angel's stunning looks and engaging personality.

But Angel helped Morgan develop her own sense of identity. For the first time, Morgan was able to enjoy life on her own terms, not her father's, nor those of her many teachers, coaches or private instructors.

Morgan thoroughly enjoyed the freedom from her father that The Ungrateful allowed. More importantly, the emotional emancipation was both exhilarating and empowering, and she found the prospects of fame were extremely alluring.

Morgan closed the cover of her laptop, and lay on her bed. Drifting off into semi-consciousness, her mind raced furiously as she contemplated her future life as a star, a lifestyle that was so intriguing and appealing to Morgan.

Chapter Three

Tommy Puccini always thought that he was born and raised in a traditional Irish/Italian family. In reality, the only thing traditional about the Puccini family was that both mother and father were present at his conception.

Tommy's formative years were a testimonial to the indomitable spirit of the human race to endure and survive seemingly insurmountable obstacles.

Tommy's mother, Kelly O'Malley Puccini, emigrated from Dublin twenty years ago to either escape the ravages of religious conflict or avoid a near-certain lengthy prison term. Kelly's attempts at an intercontinental escape from reality were not nearly as successful as her escapes fueled by various chemicals and mind altering substance-induced travels. From the time Tommy toddled, Kelly was stoned, drunk, zonked or in transition between highs.

Tommy's father, Tomaso Vincent Puccini III (a.k.a. "Tommy Three Sticks") was a proud third generation Italian-American with a heritage deeply rooted in family, religion and crime. Tommy's grandfather was rumored to have an indirect connection with an East Coast crime syndicate. Despite sporadic government observation, no evidence of any wrongdoing or other nefarious activity was ever uncovered in the Puccini family's wholesale liquor business. While Kelly drank herself into a daily stupor, Three Sticks worked. And gambled.

Beginning early in his childhood, Tommy accompanied his father on his daily round of the taverns and clubs in Chicago. Tommy's presence with Three Sticks was as much a manifestation of his father's love as it was a temporary father/son diversion from his mother's drunkenness.

Eventually, Tommy was "adopted" by a loving network of tavern workers and performers who, mysteriously, provided a nurturing environment to counterbalance the dysfunctionality during Tommy's formative years. Not surprisingly, Tommy developed a strong affinity for the musical genre predominant in the Chicago clubs controlled by the Puccini family liquor empire – the blues. More specifically, the wailing, hopeless, "there's never gonna be a tomorrow, no hope blues" sung by black legends like John Lee Hooker and Muddy Waters.

Tommy's emulation of the blues came through an often-played Gibson acoustic guitar given to him by an aging black musician. And pick. How Tommy learned to pick. The guitar became an extension of both his fingers and his heart. Tommy Puccini lived the blues. Tommy Puccini loved the blues. Tommy Puccini played the blues. Six strings. Twelve strings. Slide. Bottle. Electric. Whatever.

Tommy made human despair real. Just as human despair made Tommy's blues real. And Tommy began to love the people who brought his blues "out of the closet."

Slowly, to the chagrin of both his Irish mother and his Italian father, Tommy Puccini's ethic affinity changed. The transformation caused his father to derisively refer to him as "Tommy Oreo."

And so Tommy practiced. And practiced. From his grade school days at the ever-so parochial St. Mary of the Angels to his indoctrination to the ways of the Jesuits at St. Ignatius Loyola College Prep, Tommy played his "axe" till his fingers bled and his heart soared.

High school ended, and Tommy drifted from his strict Catholic upbringing. In the place of dogma, memorized prayers, clerical hierarchy and catechism principles, Tommy substituted a blend of Southern Baptist, evangelicalism and social awareness. Though his religious affiliation defied characterization, the habit of attending weekly church services never left Tommy. After playing at smoke-filled blues clubs early into the Sunday mornings, Tommy would venture out exploring various churches in an ongoing quest to experience many different religious services, each hopefully characterized by the presence of a revivalist spirit.

Chapter Four

Ammanuel C. Ezure was born in Kingston, Jamaica on a sweltering August morning. The son of beach merchants, Ammanuel soon became known as simply "Ace."

Ace grew up on the beach and soon was charming tourists in this tropical paradise with his Rastafarian wit. Despite a laid back "hey mon" countenance, Ace possessed a desire that was as hot as the island's noonday sun to escape the fate of his parents. Ace, more than anything, wanted away from the Jamaica that only the natives knew.

And soccer provided his passport to freedom.

From the time he could walk, Ace spent all of everyday playing soccer on the beaches while his mother hustled high priced, worthless trinkets and baubles to memento seeking tourists. From sunup to sundown, Ace relentlessly mastered the soccer ball.

At night, while his father was smoking ganja, Ace was practicing as a steel drum percussionist and perfecting the mesmerizing beat peculiar to the reggae bands.

Soon, the soccer ball was as much a part of his body, as music was part of his soul, as his desire for escape was of his spirit.

As Ace's sand soccer ability grew, so did his body, and he became an extremely impressive physical specimen. By the time he was seventeen, Ace was 6'1" and 165 pounds of muscle and sinew encased in a shiny, ebony skin, framed with flowing Marley-like dreadlocks.

Combining the speed of a gazelle, the determination of a bull and the guile and cunning of a leopard, Ace's ability to score goals landed him on the Jamaican National Soccer team.

It was in Chicago's Soldier Field that the Jamaican National Team played the United States in the final qualifying match for the North American berth in the World Cup.

All eyes were at mid-field as Ace stood with ten of his teammates, three referees and the 11 from the United States side. Sixty thousand fans stood, and with a growing excitement, sang the *Star Spangled Banner* led by a beautiful vocalist who accompanied her vocals with a violin.

Ace stood and rocked uneasily. His excitement grew, too, as he thought about the stunningly beautiful and incredibly talented musician performing.

Soldier Field was resplendent in a sea of patriotic colors. Red, white and blue bunting surrounded the field. The American flag was patriotically presented throughout the concourses of the venerable venue.

Within the stadium, the multi-ethnic fabric of Chicago's melting pot was woven throughout the stands.

In the eastern-most lower grandstand, the Polish contingent loudly bellowed an unrecognizable, constant and consonantly dominated chant.

Nearer the mid-field, a large group of enthusiastic Hispanic soccer aficionados sported red and green colors and a contagiously happy attitude.

The Jamaican group was small, boisterous and highly visible.

Their international compatriots outnumbered the American fans, yet the home fans enthusiastically chanted, "USA! USA!" and intermittently tried unsuccessfully to engage the crowd of nearly sixty thousand to participate in the wave.

Just before the game's regulation time expired, Ace scored an amazing goal that propelled the Jamaicans to highly improbable upset of the heavily favored Americans.

The goal was truly magical. Ace's "manager," Stewart Lindsey, pumped his fists repeatedly into the air. Visiting dignitaries and scouts from professional leagues smiled reservedly as they furiously scribbled notations. The international fans were temporarily stunned in silence by Ace's brilliance, and then erupted. Even the dejected American fans were somewhat solaced by the fact that they had witnessed one of the greatest goals ever scored in soccer's storied history.

The goal set off a frenzy of excitement amongst the Jamaican throng and was wildly cheered in island celebrations that ran far into the Caribbean night.

After the match, Ace felt less like celebrating with his teammates, and more like exploring the beautiful city of Chicago. Leaving his downtown hotel, Ace walked in amazement down Michigan Avenue's "Magnificent Mile." Turning away from the bright lights and glitter of State Street, Ace wandered a while and followed the sounds of laughter into an unassuming place called "Flapjaws." It was there that Ace noticed a beautiful young woman who looked vaguely familiar. Maybe it was her presence, maybe it was her beauty, or maybe, just maybe, it was her violin case, but a smile creased Ace's face as he recognized Morgan from the *Star Spangled Banner* performance earlier that evening. He sauntered over with an engaging and illuminating smile and introduced himself.

In an irony neither would ever understand or appreciate, Ace and Morgan sat and spoke for hours in the same booth that was shared by Morgan's parents more than twenty years earlier. Unlike Morgan's parents that long-ago night, their conversation was marked by sobriety, highlighted by sincerity, filled with laughter and tantalized with an innocent flirtation.

Chapter Five

Becky Rose grew up in the small town of Oregon, Wisconsin. When Becky was 16, her mother's insatiable sexual appetite resulted in a string of affairs and culminated when Becky's mother left the family for her latest stud du jour.

For Becky, it didn't matter. She had grown up without her mother's love, and her physical presence would hardly be missed.

Becky soon became the homemaker, cook and surrogate matriarch for her heart-broken and devastated father and older twin brothers, Josh and Jake.

Since early childhood, Becky had grown closer each passing day with her brothers and father. Hunting, fishing or shooting, Becky was almost "one of the boys" but was always feminine and demure   even when dropping a whitetail from seventy-five yards or flawlessly filleting a 26-inch walleye.

The Rose boys were two of the finest athletes ever to strap on a jock for the Panthers of Oregon High School. Three sport stars, the Roses soon attracted the attention of a never-ending stream of college and professional scouts.

Friday nights in Oregon were typical of "football Friday" nights in small towns across America. With the exception of the limited presence of national chains, all the local businesses like dry cleaners, barbers, printers, salons and diners closed early so their owners and employees could watch Oregon's march towards another state play-off berth.

As the fall winds blew the leaves off the trees and winter's chill entered the air, all of Oregon turned its attention to basketball. Jake Rose threatened to break the state's single season scoring average of 33.2 points per game. The combination of Josh's passing skills, family affinity and Jake's deadeye marksmanship was promising to fell an enduring Wisconsin prep record, and Becky provided the normalcy to a home life that was constantly challenged by recruiters, well-wishers and scouts.

When the harsh Wisconsin winters succumbed to the gentle breezes of spring, the Rose boys turned their attention to baseball. This time, roles slightly reversed and Jake was a flame-throwing pitcher and Josh a rock-steady catcher.

In one of the most celebrated signings ever, the Rose boys each signed lucrative professional baseball contracts with the New York Yankees and were assigned to Triple A ball in Rochester, New York.

Becky's senior year in high school was largely devoted to study in hopes to gain admission to the prestigious Division of Biological Sciences at the University of Chicago. Despite Becky's stunning, natural beauty and a seemingly endless stream of potential suitors, her focus remained on nurturing her father and studying.

Becky turned eighteen shortly after she earned the prestigious distinction as valedictorian at her high school graduation. On the Fourth of July, Becky's father died.

The coroner's report listed heart attack as the official cause of death, but Becky knew differently. The funeral was typical for a small town. Nearly all of the locals paid their last respects at the funeral home. The Rose family refrigerator and freezer were soon overflowing with casseroles, brownies and other homemade offerings of condolences. Curiously, the only thing the events surrounding the funeral lacked was a genuine sense of loss and sorrow. Becky, Josh and Jake realized some time ago that their long-suffering father died the day their mother walked out the door.

As the boys returned for a hopeful late summer call-up to the "big show," Becky prepared herself for the rigors of undergraduate school in anticipation of her eventual admission to the Pritzker School of Medicine at the University of Chicago.

Chapter Six

It was at the First Baptist Church service in a dilapidated brownstone storefront across from Cabrini Green that Tommy first heard the music of God.

Tommy was convinced that he was hearing heaven's own singing. Front and center, in a flowing purple gown, was Angel.

Angel sang the music that was in Tommy's heart. She sang the music that Tommy only thought flowed from his fingers and made his guitar come alive. Made his soul come alive.

After the service, Tommy met Angel at the social and they instantly connected on a variety of fronts – social, intellectual, emotional, spiritual. They talked – about anything and everything – growing up alone, the unbridled joy of performing. They shared thoughts, fears, ideas, hopes, and aspirations. Most of all they shared their love of music and their vision for the future.

For Tommy, it seemed that he and Angel shared a similar soul and an identical passion.

"Make music, make money, make good," Angel said to Tommy as she talked about her life's dreams, "to be able to touch others with my music or because of my music." It was obvious to Tommy that he shared Angel's passions and her social conscious.

Tommy Puccini and Angel connected that afternoon. They connected as soul mates. They connected as friends. They connected as two people who were intent on changing the world for the better and believed they could do so. And they established a strong relationship that would serve as the foundation for their future as band mates. For Tommy, the afternoon was intellectually, spiritually and emotionally exhilarating.

After this afternoon of sexless passion with Angel, Tommy returned to his walk-up to prepare for another night of picking and wailing in a smoke-filled club.

Greeting Tommy at the door was his roommate, who met Tommy with a hard kiss on the lips and roughly led him into the bedroom. Minutes later, their clothes were strewn about the room, and their bodies were meshed in the throes of passion, a passion much different from his earlier encounter with Angel.

"I love you," Tommy said, his body drained from the cumulative effects of his exhaustive emotional and physical encounters.

"I love you too," said Becky. "I always have, I always will. Our love is the reason for my being, and I will always be here for you. For us."

Becky lightly stroked Tommy's cheek and whispered something in his ear that made them both giggle.

Angel invited Tommy. Angel invited Morgan. Morgan invited Ace. And four people sat, talked and invited fame and fortune. No, not quite invited fame and fortune. Demanded it. Willed it. Worked for it. Oh how they worked for it.

From early in the morning to late at night they relentlessly practiced and refined a sound that was uniquely their own. A sound borne out of their divergent backgrounds. A sound borne out of their massive, collective talent. A sound borne out of their musical creativity. A sound borne out of their youthful exuberance. A sound borne out of their unbridled passion.

A sound sired by many parents, with a singular appeal to a wide variety of tastes. "Mass market eclecticism" was how Tommy characterized their music.

"Self-absorbed, pompous, pseudo-intellectual ass," was Ace's retort, greeted by good-natured laughter and mirth from all.

For as good as they were becoming musically, so too were they becoming good friends – who genuinely liked and respected each other – for their differences and for their similarities.

After one particularly grueling session, Angel's childhood friend, Reggie Beasley, wandered in. Angel introduced him to the group and, uncomfortably, asked a favor.

"You know, sometime soon we're going to start getting real gigs, and we're going to need sort of a manager. Someone to book the gigs, collect money, help promote us, transport our equipment – stuff like that. Reggie and I go all the way back to Cabrini, and I wondering if he can be our manager."

"Yo, welcome aboard, dude," Ace replied, "Now what the fuck you standing around here for? You better be getting that black ass of yours out and start hustling us up some gigs."

"And what you be calling yourselves?" Reggie teased, good-naturedly.

Choosing the name "The Ungrateful" was actually, quite quixotic.

"What should we call this sorry-assed collection of misfits?" Ace asked.

"What do you mean 'sorry-assed'? We've got talent. We've got each other. Never forget that you ungrateful son-of-a bitch," Angel laughingly replied.

And thus they became "The Ungrateful." And did The Ungrateful ever become popular.

A small, lucky and appreciative crowd who knew that they were fortunate to be experiencing something truly special witnessed their first appearance in the smoked filled backroom of a tiny Chicago tavern. And each subsequent appearance found a larger, ever-growing and increasingly awe-filled audience of devotees.

Fortunately for Ace, Morgan, Tommy and Angel, Reggie's hustling of gigs soon became unnecessary, as the requests for appearances for The Ungrateful soon exceeded days available. New foreign words like "venue" and "capacity" became a part of The Ungrateful's vernacular. Curiously, they actually understood their meaning.

Unfortunately, Reggie Beasley was stoned, drunk or high and only tangentially associated with The Ungrateful's sweeping successes.

Chapter Seven

Jordan Taylor rose from the meeting with the vice president of touring and felt slightly light-headed and greatly enthused that she had won the assignment she had hoped for, prepared for, but never thought that she would get.

Jordan regained her composure and steadied herself in a manner to belie her child-like excitement before she addressed her staff.

"Our record of accomplishment, attention to detail, and professionalism has been noticed, and our team has been selected to produce the reunion tour of The CDs. I'm proud of our selection and confident that we'll successfully manage all aspects of what promises to be one of the largest commercial concert tour ventures of all time."

Jordan's professionalism was apparent, and both her appearance and demeanor contrasted with the casual and laid-back attitudes of her subordinates. Jordan detailed the concerts cities: Boston, New York, Philly, Washington, DC, Cleveland, Chicago, Kansas City, Dallas, Phoenix, Las Vegas, Los Angeles and San Francisco.

Jordan assertively handed out assignments to her staff. After nearly eight exhaustive hours of intense, detailed planning, the activities of the band, the booking agency, the record label, the local promoters, the radio stations, the venues managers, the artist managers, the security manager, the merchandise manager, the stage manager, the tour accountant and even the bus driver were choreographed with the anal precision Jordan was infamous for.

"Any questions?"

"Yeah, like why is a complete unknown like The Ungrateful opening for one of the most famous bands of all time on one of the most-hyped tours ever?"

"Don't know, but I'm going to find out. I'm leaving for Chicago in the morning."

Jordan's flight to Chicago's O'Hare airport was, thankfully, uneventful. "The travel gods were with me today," Jordan thought, "a first class upgrade and an adjacent empty seat." The three-hour flight from LA allowed Jordan sufficient time to catch up on some long-lagging e-mail correspondence and review, for the umpteenth time, the details of the tour.

Jordan's town car took her directly to where The Ungrateful was supposedly rehearsing. "Let's see if we can beat the traffic on the Kennedy," Jordan urged her driver, in hopes that she could catch the final set of The Ungrateful's practice gig before she met the band.

Jordan entered through the unlocked front door and immediately knew that the reverberating sound that she heard for the first time was truly something special.

As she cautiously made her way through the darkened hallways to the doors opening to the stage area, Jordan found herself both smiling and gyrating to a musical sound she didn't quite recognize but knew that she already loved.

Finding a seat in the back row, Jordan marveled at not only what great individual musicians she was hearing but how they seamlessly melded together a variety of musical genres into a coherent and highly enjoyable sound. Jordan thought to herself, "and people think I'm anal," as she watched in amazement as The Ungrateful, time and again, went back to perfect some imperceptible nuance or nanosecond differential in timing.

Jordan was not only amazed by the band's work ethic and professionalism, but she was equally impressed with how they related to one another. Playfully. Respectfully. Friendly.

The practice set ended and Jordan approached the stage to introduce herself to The Ungrateful.

"Yo, yo," Ace laughed at Tommy, "da bitches brought on reinforcement to outnumber us."

"Whatever dudes," chided Angel, "come here and rub my back 'cause I be sore from carrying your sorry ass selves and making you look good for the lady today."

"Can't we all just get along?" Tommy replied, facetiously imitating Rodney King.

Ace told Jordan that, "the thought of singing in Boston had him on edge, crabby, irritable, emotional and slightly bloated."

"Could it be," Ace asked Jordan, "that I'm suffering from pre-minstrel syndrome?"

And so it went.

Ace told Jordan how he came from Jamaica, "made some beautiful music with Morgan and decided to make some more music with the band."

Angel relayed how she brought these "misfits together and cracked their asses into shape."

Tommy smiled silently as Morgan discussed their musical philosophy of "begging, borrowing, stealing and to make tunes that sets the soul a healing."

Jordan emerged from the orientation impressed, excited and a little bit afraid of the incredible talent that was opening for one of the most popular groups in the history of rock and roll.

Chapter Eight

Mickey Delaney caught himself reminiscing, "Thirty-five years of doing anything is a long, long time. Thirty-five years atop of the rock and roll world is an eternity." When the band originally formed, Mick Jagger was monogamous, Keith Richards was lucid and only occasionally dabbling in drugs and Michael Jackson was years before the first of his many cosmetic surgeries. Hell, Michael Jackson hadn't even been born when Mickey and the boys originally got together.

Mickey thought back to the day, more than thirty-five years ago, when they stood before practice in the garage attached to his parents ranch home on the tree-lined streets of suburban Detroit.

The band had just arranged their first paying gig and they needed a name – quickly. The Motown sound was hot in town and they toyed with "Mickey and the Detroit Tunes." Waves of Brits came across the ocean but "Mickey's Men," "The Mickey Delaney Five," "The Bugs," and "The Immovable Rocks" were all rejected as too similar to what was already out there. Sometimes imitation isn't the highest form of flattery. Sometimes it's just a lack of creativity

With no other alternatives for a name for the band, Mickey Delaney, Charlie Rice, Brad Doucette, Jimmy Crowe and Bill Dalton combined the initials of their first and last names and settled on "The CDs."

Mickey had always hoped he was smart enough to predict what a fortuitous selection the band's name turned out to be. Hell, if Mickey was even remotely that clever, he would have gladly settled for the "LPs," or "The Eight Tracks" or even "the Cassettes."

But Mickey was just plain fucking lucky.

Partly because of their wildly popular music – and partly because the band was the first listed when anyone surfed the net for music – The CDs' discs had become the largest selling musical group on the internet. So pervasive was the band's name, internet filtering devices to block their records were suddenly appearing on pop-up screens throughout cyberspace, and a federal lawsuit was filed by a competing label to formally require all businesses selling music over the internet to eliminate initials and only use the words "COMPACT DISCS."

And now, thirty-five years later, Mickey was ready to lead The CDs on their long awaited and much anticipated reunion tour.

All nineteen thousand seats of Boston's Fleet Center were filled and pulsing with excitement for the debut of the reunion tour of The CDs. Over the past thirty years, The CDs had become the third largest selling musical group ever. The CDs last toured in 1995, largely due to the cumulative effects of twenty-five years of excess.

The CDs had come to represent all the excess that was inherent in the rock and roll business. The band had consumed and ingested enough controlled substances to be eligible for entry into the pharmaceutical hall of fame.

The sexual exploits of the band members were legendary.

Customarily, prior to a gig, The CDs sent the production crew and road dogs into the audience to scout "talent." When these road dogs spotted a potential nominee for conquest, they signaled the committee on stage. If the nominee was accepted, the drummer would spin his drumstick and point to the lucky lady, and she would then be presented with all-access back stage passes. With such a complicated system in place, it was amazing that The CDs's live sets were as tight as they were.

What was even more amazing was their success ratio, as their gaggle of groupies could fill the better part of the Fleet Center by themselves.

It was facetiously suggested when The CDs' drummer entered into rehab in 1996, a prominent Kentucky distillery reduced its workforce by 10% to compensate for the anticipated decline in volume. (Upon further investigation, it appears that the actual lay-off was only 5%.)

The most notable change in The CDs over the years may have been the dramatic changes in their tour rider. For many years, The CDs worked extremely hard to develop, protect and enhance their reputation as rock's bad boys. Simply put, the boys could throw it down.

Prior to 1996 gigs, all dressing room catering requirements on the band's tour rider included provisions for:

4 One Liter Bottles of Jack Daniels
2 One Liter Bottles of Johnny Walker Black Label
2 Bottles of Opus One
1 Magnum of Moet Chandon
1 Carton of Marlboro Red

3 Boxes of assorted condoms
2 Tubes of Johnson & Johnson KY jelly
5 Cases of Heineken
3 Bottles of Extra-Strength Tylenol

The Fleet Center gig included:

96 Bottles of spring Water
24 Bananas
1 Massage therapist
Assorted raw vegetables
12 oranges
1 Box of Kleenex
1 squeezable container of honey
12 skinless, free range chicken breast grilled over a hardwood fire

The preparation for the Fleet Center debut was immense and befitted the record $250 average ticket price. Just as before, The CDs went big. This tour was a twenty-five truck show, with enough "pyro" to entertain a small city on the Fourth of July.

The logistics were complex. The roadies, hangers-on and support staff numbered 125. In addition to the tour manager; there was the production manager, stage manager, lighting director, lighting crew, sound director, sound crew, the all-too-important pryo-technician, and a prop director. Additionally, a carpenter was always present to ensure that all was on the level, and a wardrobe director was on board to accessorize outfits consisting mainly of t-shirts and blue jeans. And, of course, the video director. All in addition to the local crew consisting of loaders, up riggers, down riggers, stagehands, spot ops, etc.

Opening for The CDs was a new music phenomenon – The Ungrateful. The Ungrateful's music defied classification, but the band's magnetism was both engaging and expanding – exponentially.

The Ungrateful's unique sound represented the ethnic diversity of the band members; Jamaican, Mulatto, Japanese-American and Irish/Italian American. They were audacious, exciting, riveting and played good-humored music. The Ungrateful was a cultural collage exuding talent and unbridled energy.

It was a little blues, a lotta reggae, with a strong classical influence, a

27

dash of funk and some boogie-woogie; all woven into virtuoso music performed by extremely talented and passionate musicians.

As the curtain rose, a throng of humanity pressed forward in anticipation. The stage scrim framed the view in an almost surreal fashion.

The backlit stage highlighted the sensuous shimmers of two lithesome and scantily clad almond-skinned women. Almost eerily, the sweet percussion of Ace's steel drums laid down a beat that unified thirty-eight thousand clapping hands and gently stamping feet.

Stage right, in a white flowing gown that contrasted with her jet-black hair, Morgan Chino stood with a violin in one hand and a bow in the other, separated by a tantalizing hint of cleavage.

Stage left, in well-worn jeans and a plain white T-shirt, Tommy Puccini's fingers danced over the strings of an amplified acoustical guitar, adding a huge dose of unneeded adrenalin to the charged mass.

Energy. Thy name is Ungrateful.

Back in the mix location, the lighting director anxiously anticipated his cue. And when Morgan stroked her first delicious note, a simple haze of smoke arose and a solitary spotlight shone on the stunningly beautiful Angel.

Simply, the chords of Ungrateful's soon-to-be chart topping, smash hit *More* resonated; Ace, Morgan and Tommy meshed in a collective effort that was so overpowering it, ironically, was subdued, highlighting Angel's mysterious vocals and haunting lyrics:

You take her home, kiss her goodnight
Say you love her, but it's a lie
Deep down there's something else you need
You want it so bad, it makes you bleed

Tommy, Morgan and the gracefully gyrating backup singers harmonized on the chorus:

You come knockin' at my back door
Beggin' More. More. More
My love's your drug, and you gotta score
You need More. More. More.

Angel throatily, sweetly, yet dynamically sung:

Tell her so-long, You know it's me you want
It's not the kill, Baby it's the hunt
I drive you wild, make you insane
You make her cry, and honey I'm to blame

You're wantin' me bad, darlin I can tell
Follow this dark angel, to the pleasures of hell

You come knockin' at my backdoor
Beggin' More. More. More.
My love's your drug, and you gotta score
You need More. More. More.
Feel me in your veins
More. More. More.
I'm driving you insane
More. More, More.

Nineteen thousand patrons cheered The Ungrateful wildly. Stomping. Clapping, Yelling. Screaming.

And somehow in the din, the commotion of a concertgoer being led by the staff EMTs from the first aid room to an awaiting ambulance went unnoticed.

The curtain closed on The Ungrateful to the chagrin and disappointment of the charged and stoked audience.

When the curtain arose a short time later for The CDs, the crowd's energy had noticeably waned.

Inside the ambulance speeding towards Boston General hospital, the EMTs worked feverishly to save the life of the young woman who collapsed at the concert. The ominous wailing of the siren filled the night's air as life slowly drained from the woman, despite the valiant efforts of the rescue team. She was pronounced dead on arrival at the hospital.

The desk officer at the Boston Police Department quickly glanced at the file. The only thing even remotely out of the ordinary at the Fleet Center concert were the conflicting reports of the description of a middle-aged gentlemen who questioned will-call about the tickets supposedly left for him by his daughter, Angel. No tickets were left for the gentleman, and mysteriously appearing, long-lost relatives of band members seeking free tickets are common place occurrences at major concert events. What was perplexing to the desk officer were the radically different physical descriptions of the man by the only two people who interacted with him. The woman on duty during the morning shift described him "medium build, goatee with a slight English accent." The woman handling will-call requests during the afternoon shift described him as, "clean shaven and ruggedly handsome."

The desk officer made notations of the description inconsistencies, and also thought how the death of the young woman was unusual. Unusual in the sense that the vast majority of reports of young adult deaths that crossed his desk involved drugs, gangs, guns, motorcycles or alcohol, or some combination. Overworked, he kept his speculations to himself and passed the file on to the medical examiner for the expected confirmation that the woman's premature exit from this world was nothing more than unfortunate.

Chapter Nine

FBI Special Agent Sloan Dillard sat at her desk and scanned the entertainment section looking for a review of last evening's concert. For fifteen of Sloan's twenty-eight years, The CDs had been a part of her life. In junior high school, Sloan and her girlfriends had each selected a band member as their "special love." For Sloan, no doubt, it was Mickey Delaney. In her mid-teen years, The CDs' posters plastered the walls of the bedroom Sloan shared with her sister.

Sloan's senior year in high school marked her emergence from what she humorously referred to as her "nerd cocoon." Sloan had come to accept herself for what she was – highly intelligent, athletically ungifted but "cool" in her own way. Sloan partially credited The CDs for assisting her through that sometimes-painful journey from adolescence to young adulthood.

Due in part to the incredible number of hours Sloan spent studying with the music of The CDs playing in the background; she graduated from high school as her class valedictorian. Despite coming from a family with limited financial means, Sloan's academic grades, SAT and ACT scores qualified her for full scholarship at a number of prestigious universities.

Sloan's choice of college surprised many, and disappointed a few, namely her mother and father. Eschewing prestige and size for feel, Sloan rejected scholarship offers from some of the nation's top schools and enrolled at a small Midwestern liberal arts college.

Sloan's junior year was spent abroad in Spain, and when she returned for her final year of school as an accounting major, Sloan was fluent in both English and Spanish. Upon graduation, Sloan's brilliance, charisma and personality landed her job offers from the nation's "Top Five" accounting firms.

For reasons that were never quite clear even to her, Sloan rejected the security of guaranteed income and a well-established career path in public accounting and pursued acceptance into the accounting entry program with the Federal Bureau of Investigation.

Sloan was accepted and began training as a Special Agent at the FBI's training facility in Quantico, Virginia. For the most part, Sloan excelled at the various aspects of her training. Despite her self-acknowledged lack of physical coordination and agility, Sloan passed the New Agent Training program; though, at times, she felt like Private Mayo's special project in *An Officer and a Gentleman*.

Upon graduation, Sloan was assigned to the FBI's Boston field office. Under the tutelage of veteran FBI agents, Sloan quickly learned the ins and outs of life as a FBI agent. What Sloan couldn't be taught, and had to learn through sometimes painful and sometimes humorous experience, was how to deal with the oppressive male chauvinists who tried to make her entry to the male bastion's exclusive club impossible.

Sloan had heard that her internal moniker had become "Special Agent Titties." To cope, Sloan worked even harder, and gained a certain sense of individual satisfaction in conjuring up nicknames for her mean-spirited and less-than welcoming male co-workers, referring mentally to her top three nemeses as "Special Agent Wee-One, Special Agent No-One, and Special Agent One-on-One" for their collective lack a female companionship.

Sloan spent some time rotating through various assignments for the administrative services division, the counter-terrorism division and the criminal justice information services division. In four years that seemed like an eternity to Sloan, she persistently overcame gender bias and was eventually promoted to her current position as the Special Agent in charge of the Bureau's Washington, DC Criminal Investigation Division.

Sloan read the review of the concert and wondered if the reporter had an axe to grind with one of the greatest rock and roll bands of all time or if The CDs had really slipped as far as the writer suggested.

Sloan's training and normal skeptical demeanor prompted her to wonder what propelled the seemingly meteoric rise of this new band called The Ungrateful, and her compassion and empathy temporarily saddened her as she read about the unfortunate death of one of the concertgoers.

Chapter Ten

Twenty years in an Irish prison has the very real potential to significantly change a person. However, twenty years in the brigade had only changed Paddy O'Keane a "wee bit." Paddy still retained his passion-filled love for Kelly. And his passion for his deeply beloved Ireland. Passion for her deep heritage. Passion for the future of Ireland. Tasting his first breaths of freedom in over two decades, Paddy realized that he still desperately needed two things – Kelly Maureen O'Malley and money for the cause.

Paddy viewed his incarceration as a detour off the noble and righteous path that God had designated for him. And Paddy was determined to make those responsible pay dearly for interrupting God's will. If there was one thing staring at four cement walls did to Paddy, it was to intensify each of his many passions and to strengthen his resolve to rectify the inequalities inherent in his beloved island.

Fortunately for Paddy, his network continued to operate for the two decades since his departure. Not only did the network continue, it actually flourished with now well-developed sectors on both sides of the Atlantic and strongly entrenched pockets of support in certain American cities.

Paddy breathed deeply, knelt down and kissed the soil, then departed in a car that rumbled off into the pastoral Irish countryside.

Within hours, the key members of Paddy's alliance had assembled in a rustic Irish pub. Pint after pint, the resolve intensified, the cause became more grandiose and divinely authored, and Paddy's visit with his American compatriots was confirmed. And his quest for money for the cause became international.

Chapter Eleven

Kelly Puccini poured a full glass of Crown Royal and contemplated her sagging breasts, now-massive derriere, graying hair, hopeless future and the flickering remembrance of a long-lost love, religious persecution and insurgence, her political activism, involvement in "the cause" and the transcontinental flight caused by the untimely detonation of a pipe bomb. Fourteen British soldiers and Protestants perished that day in County Down in 1979. Ten Republicans subsequently fasted themselves to death in prison in 1981. And Kelly bore the full brunt of the deaths of twenty-four people, only ten of whom mattered to her.

The souls of those deceased Irelanders left a void in Kelly's life that she desperately tried to fill with liquor. But neither liquor nor time could erase the memories of her native Ireland and her forever-beloved Paddy O'Keane.

Kelly often wished that she were one of those who died for the cause, and more often wished that she could gaze but once again into the emerald green eyes of Paddy.

But Kelly also knew that sometimes the sacrifices for the cause were of both an undetermined length and an unknown outcome. And those two thoughts were the only thing that kept even a small flickering flame of life and hope burning within Kelly. Her marriage was more of a sham now than it was twenty years ago when as a fiery redheaded beauty she stole the heart of a black-haired and stick figured Italian stud.

Oh, Kelly loved Three Sticks and Tommy enough to play the role of a loving and dedicated wife for the years after Tommy's unexpected birth. But now that Tommy was, unfortunately, gone and Three Sticks was, fortunately, never home; Kelly was free to submerge herself in self-pity and wallow in the wonderment of what never was.

The shrill ring of the telephone startled Kelly and interrupted her agonizing, ritualized self-torture.

"Would the lovely lady of the house be home?" Paddy asked in his unmistakable and forever memorable brogue.

Kelly felt herself slowly come to life with the sound of Paddy's voice. Figuratively and literally, shaking the fog that had dulled her senses and her mind, Kelly stammered, "Paddy, Paddy, Is that you? Oh, God, please let it be you?"

"Sure enough is, my love. Live and in person. Right here in the beautiful United States of America. And hopefully, soon to be in the arms of one beautiful little Irish lass."

Twenty-two years ago, Kelly Puccini's world was instantaneously shattered and changed forever by the untimely detonation of a bomb. Kelly's slowly returning instincts warned her that her seemingly unalterable life was again going to change – a thought that both excited and frightened her. For there was a certain, pleasurable sense of security her nearly catatonic life provided her. But the exhilaration that she remembered with Paddy was alluring.

Chapter Twelve

Stewart Lindsey presided over the meeting as the Jamaican Soccer Federation was deliberating, in a sweltering, smoked filled room. Some time ago, Stewart had signed a personal service contract with Ace's parents that guaranteed Stewart would receive eighty percent of Ace's future soccer earnings.

From the time that Stewart first saw Ace on the beach, he knew the kid was something truly special. And it wasn't difficult at all for Stewart to ingratiate himself with Ace's mamma and pop. A couple of doobies for the old man, some costume jewelry for the old lady; and Stewart had Ace's and his parents' signatures on a contract that indentured the budding international superstar to Stewart indefinitely. If Stewart benefited from the association prospectively, Ace garnered benefits immediately.

First and foremost from Stewart's perspective, Ace was "rescued" from his cavalier life on the beach and placed into a structured junior apprentice soccer program. Secondly, Ace learned to play in official games. And oh, how he did play. From the first time he laced his soccer boots and stepped onto the baked mud pitch, Ace played a game that was dimensionally different from any of the other twenty-one players on the field. Faster. More intense. Faster. Stronger. Quicker. More productive. Ace possessed the rare ability to score goals, seemingly at will. And Stewart owned both his contract and his soccer future.

Based largely upon his phenomenal performance in Chicago and his unlimited future potential, Stewart had finalized a contract for Ace to play with England's prestigious Manchester United for $21,000,000, and was anxiously awaiting receipt of his money.

Ace's decision to stay in Chicago and play music had made the likelihood of Stewart's financial bonanza uncertain. For Stewart, the potential impact of losing the record transfer fee of $21,000,000 was devastating. Stewart had a problem. More succinctly, Stewart had twenty-one million problems. Ace's decision to leave soccer and "fucking beat drums for a bunch of wackos and freaks;" had not only postponed, but threatened to permanently eliminate Stewart's long-awaited, and desperately needed, payday.

No doubt about it, Ace's newly found choice of careers needed to be revisited. If Stewart had his way, and he eventually would, the only music Ace would be making would be the sweet sound of the soccer ball ripping the back of the net just beyond the outstretched arms of the soon-to-be dejected goal keeper.

"Drastic times call for drastic measures," Stewart bellowed to the Federation. "I want my fucking money, and I wanna see Ace fucking playing soccer. Now! I don't give a flying fuck how we do it. Just fucking get it done!"

The meeting adjourned when Stewart cleared a pile of papers off the desk with a sweeping motion of his arm. As the papers fluttered in the air, the terrified members of the Federation scurried for the door. Stewart slammed his clenched fists onto the table and buried his balding head into his massive hands.

Reluctantly, he dialed the private number and reported his failure to procure the necessary money. Miguel Zabala was not pleased, to say the least.

Chapter Thirteen

Dr. Fujimaro Chino sat and pensively stared into the distance. Silently, intuitively and painfully, Dr. Chino mused about Morgan – his lost daughter and only living family member, his lost business and his lost future.

Dr. Chino wasn't overly surprised when the FDA finally discovered what he had known for so long – an unlabeled, mysterious ingredient in his special diet formula. Hell, he had known for over twenty years what was just now surfacing, and he was somewhat surprised that things had gone on undetected for so long.

Since the early days of his operation, Dr. Chino had included a secret ingredient he procured from South America in his diet formula. Dr. Chino rued the day he made that first decision – after an affable Venezuelan graduate student somehow persuaded him to test his secret ingredient. But the subsequent test results were so impressive, and the lure of making it for real in America so tantalizing, that Dr. Chino altered his patented formula and included the secret ingredient. The young Venezuelan, Miguel Zabala, had established an American base for his burgeoning international empire and a lock-hold on the business and soul of Dr. Fujimaro Chino.

The subpoenaing of his business records, the seizure of all inventory, and the padlocking of American Pharmacal was expected. The looming charges of murder weren't.

Bravely attempting to manifest the great American entrepreneurial spirit, Dr. Chino tried valiantly not to let the FDA's investigation break his resolve to carry on. Initially, he retained a prestigious Boston firm to either head off the investigation or minimize the scope of the inquiries.

Just as Silicon Valley had become a Mecca for computer companies, the East Coast, Northeast and Washington, DC had a concentration of some of the country's most successful pharmaceutical companies. And like summer follows spring, a cadre of legal firms followed the cash rich and litigious-prone drug companies. Naively, Dr. Chino was hopeful that the reputation of one of the nation's most prestigious and well-respected pharmaceutical law firms would help deflect pressure, insulate and protect him from the FDA.

As Dr. Chino read, and then reread, the FDA's charges, he realized that what he needed was not a pharmaceutical law firm, but the best criminal defense firm money could buy.

The FDA charges alleged that it was the addition of trace amounts of methamphetamine into Dr. Chino's patented "long-chain carbohydrate/herbal combination formula guaranteed to help you lose ten pound in ten days or double your money back" product that was responsible for the weight loss. And the recent deaths.

"Skinnier maybe, but dead definitely," Dr. Chino sarcastically thought to himself as he contemplated the forthcoming criminal charges.

Dr. Chino realized that he had an immediate problem that needed to be solved; the FDA had collaborated with the FBI and had frozen his assets. Because of the complexity and severity of the FDA's case, the prestigious criminal law firms he had contacted requested retainers in the $500,000 range.

Morgan was the only one he knew with access to that kind of money. And she had largely ignored him since she had left for school a long, long time ago. He desperately needed to get her attention. And her money.

Chapter Fourteen

Reginald Beasley fidgeted nervously as he snapped the band and searched for a vein. Reggie grew up in Cabrini with Angel and through it all "had her back." From early on, Reggie was there – first for Angel, and then for The Ungrateful.

"Fuck," Reggie thought, "I became their manager when they were a sorry-ass collection of misfits who sounded like dogs coupling. I did fucking everything for them; managed the group, booked their gigs, worked the mix location, verified the drop count so the slimy tour promoters kept the settlement straight."

"Fuck," Reggie said out loud to no one, "I was a fucking multi-tasker before the word was even fucking invented."

Angel's words still rang through his ears like the juice ran through his veins; "No more drugs, Reggie, none. Or you're through. You're fucking us up. You're fucking your life away. We'll get you help. But you got to want to help yourself. I've seen it too many times. Heard the screams at night. Saw the widows in the morning. Watched the babies cry as the their daddies got cuffed and led away. You're done or we're done."

"Fuck 'em, fuck all those mo' fos," Reggie thought, as his eyes rolled back and gold rushed into his veins. "I'll get 'em. Just you wait and see. Don't be fucking with Reggie Beasley. Or your sorry ass gonna pay. Pay back's a mudda fucking bitch! You wait and see. Specially you, Angel. Fuckin'ho!"

Reggie's euphoric rush morphed into a nonplused, horrific panic when he answered the telephone. Though the drugs pulsing through his veins further clouded his overcast mind, Reggie recognized the unforgettable voice of Miguel Zabala. Under the best of circumstances, contact with Miguel was ominous. Under these circumstances, even Reggie's altered mindset could sense the eventual doom.

Kelly O'Malley Puccini waited nervously at the international arrival gate at Logan Airport. The combination of lying to Tommy Three Sticks and the anticipation of seeing Paddy O'Keane tumbled Kelly's stomach and sent her pulse racing.

Kelly had pleaded with Three Sticks to let her go to Boston for Tommy's debut. She was shocked that he consented and even arranged for her to meet up with him in New York.

In a hotel overlooking Boston's historic Patriot Hill, Paddy O'Keane and Kelly Puccini released twenty-five years of frustration and pent-up passion as intercontinental waves of pleasure pounded their changed bodies, united in spirit and flesh.

While Kelly basked in the after-glow, Paddy ironically noted the similarities between the "cause" and the Boston patriots and the freedom fighters more than two hundred years earlier. Just as the political turmoil resulting from "taxation without representation...," motivated a group colonial insurgence against the British Crown, so too could Paddy's cause change the world.

Paddy had the passion. Passion for the cause. Passion for Kelly. All Paddy lacked was money. And Kelly was the link to solve his money woes. Or Tommy Three Sticks. Or Tommy the musician. For Paddy it didn't matter, the color of their money was the same. And his favorite color. Green.

Paddy's official itinerary didn't call for this rendezvous with Kelly, but "Hey," Paddy thought, "when in America, why not do an American?"

Only Kelly was really Irish and not an American, but "It's the best of me lines so far," Paddy chuckled under his breath.

Tommy Three Sticks slammed down the telephone at his suite at New York's Plaza Hotel and nervously paced the room. Three Sticks was less than two hours removed from his Central Park meeting with certain New York "business associates."

Tommy knew that the clock was running out and he desperately needed help. His "business associates" had been patient. Too patient in their minds, but not patient enough in his. And now the inevitable would occur unless Three Sticks could either hit a five-team parlay, or a rich relative would bail him out. Neither of which had a high probability of occurring. Three Sticks was already seven hundred-fifty thousand dollars behind, mainly due to "sure thing" parlays. And the likelihood of even finding a book who would take his action was remote. His daily "vig" alone was over "ten large." And Three Sticks had broken so many promises to Tommy, that his own son ignored him. Three Sticks was, in his opinion, simply fucked.

Three Sticks sat nervously on the bench and pondered the massive New

York skyline. "If only," he thought. "If fucking only."

Three Stick's thoughts were interrupted as three of his associates suddenly appeared out of, apparently, nowhere.

"Hey, kinda warm for topcoats."

"Sit down and shut the fuck up and listen," ordered the slightly built younger man.

"Sticks," said the heavy set man, "I'm sorry. We go way back. Back to Chicago in the late sixties. Back to when we fucked with the democrats at the convention. Back to when we fucked those doped out hippie chicks. But that was then, and this is now. Sticks, you of all people, know the rules. I've done all that I can. It's out of my hands."

"You can do it for me," Three Sticks pleaded. "Just a couple of weeks, I've got the money all lined up. Just a little time. Just a fucking little time!"

"Shut up and listen, fuckhead," said the slight one. "Your whiney-ass pleas ain't worth shit. Two weeks. That's it. No money. No more Three Sticks. Capiche?"

Kelly Puccini stepped out of the shower and delicately dried herself off. Standing in front of the full-length mirror in the hotel bathroom mirror, Kelly let the towel drop to the floor and shyly inspected her completely nude body. First full front. Then a side view. Then the other profile.

Kelly smiled. For whatever reason, her breasts seemed fuller and less droopy. Her eyes brighter. Her hair a little less gray, and a little redder. Her nose smaller, her stomach a tad bit tighter.

Kelly smiled again, feeling alive. For the first time in over twenty years.

Paddy watched her secretly and found himself coming alive again with excitement.

Chapter Fifteen

Sometimes, it can be tough to safely score in a foreign city. Fortunately for Reginald Beasley, there's a frightful, yet reassuring, commonality uniting the hood in cities across America. And Boston was no different. Neither was New York.

It was payback time for that fucking bitch Angel and her sorry-ass collection of fuckin' poser-wannabes. Reggie had paved the way for their impending stardom. And the motherfuckers stole his future from him.

Reggie scored and waited impatiently for the magic of nirvana to run from his veins, sending those all-too familiar pleasure sensations to what was left of his brain.

The Ungrateful was entirely unprepared for their New York City reception. The term "artistic freedom" was transformed to "artistic whoring" as the record label reps and the artist management team worked their "magic."

The CDs' envy and jealousy slowly transformed into a somber recognition of the unexpected.

For The Ungrateful, part of it was exciting. Part of it was exhilarating. Part of it was demeaning. But all of it was way over the top for this eclectic group of musicians who were each struggling in Chicago not too long ago.

Angel on MTV.

Morgan at the cover shoot for *Glamour*.

Tommy live on Howard Stern.

And Ace – The Ungrateful's publicist was quite sure that even Letterman had never experienced anyone or anything quite as unique as Ace.

But this was New York, and Ace was equally comfortable and confident performing in front of a nation-wide television audience as he was on the soccer field in front of sixty thousand screaming fanatics.

Letterman announced the evening's guests to the muffled applause from a studio audience not quite sure what to expect. On this very stage, more than thirty years earlier, a similar musical phenomenon met the American public for the first time. Just as the Beatles captured the hearts, minds and souls of America on their debut on the *Ed Sullivan Show*, so to did Ace with

Letterman. This time, however, it was slightly more unconventional. But equally controversial.

Ace's entire life had consisted of facing obstacles and overcoming them. Although Ace knew his dreadlocks, his heritage, his background and his occupations were not obstacles, he was keenly aware of the prejudices that preceded him. And Ace loved to both debunk preconceived notions and showcase his devilish sense of humor.

Letterman assumed his customary, show opening place in front of his desk and engaged the audience in an irreverent and whimsical repartee about the day's happenings.

Just as Dave was about to launch into his infamous daily "Top Ten" list, Ace appeared from stage left. A look of total surprise and mild shock came over Dave's countenance as Ace, barefoot and dreadlocks flowing, led Dave to the couch. Ace grabbed Dave's mike while the stunned cameramen and film crew stood motionless and mesmerized.

"Hey mon, it's all good," Ace drolled with both a hint of sarcasm and a much-needed air of reassurance. "Just keeping it real," he added.

Ace started easily, breezily and with confidence:

"The Top Ten reasons you wouldn't want your daughter to marry a rock star:

10. Son-in law hangs with "homies" named, P Diddy, Snoop and Slash; while your daughter's friends are Missy, Buffy and six Jennifers.
9. Son-in-law is upfront about all past lovers and has computer space storage issues when listing them.
8. While your daughter celebrates important sentimental dates like births and weddings, son-in-law's important firsts include: first acid drop and first arrest.
7. Son-in law's standard pre-nuptual agreement specifies that he gets all distribution rights to any sex videos he makes with your precious daughter.
6. Realizing your grandchildren will likely be named 'Zeus' and 'Moonchild.'
5. Rehabilitation costs are included in the monthly household budget.
4. Knowing that your son-in-law's hair and make-up makes him more attractive than your daughter.
3. Son-in-law has gotten it more in the last month than you have in the last decade.
2. Columbians celebrate National holiday in recognition of your son-in-law's contributions to the local economy.

And the Number One reason you wouldn't want your daughter to marry a rock star...

1. Son-in-law realizes that it takes two to make a marriage work, but an occasional three-some really keeps it exciting."

Tears streamed down Letterman's cheeks. The audience howled wildly. The camera crew was doubled over in laughter.

Ace sat down, plopped his bare and calloused feet on Dave's desk, pulled out a cigar-shaped fatboy, and toked up on live television.

Morgan Chino never considered herself beautiful. Attractive maybe. Distinctive, definitely. Five feet eleven inches. One hundred fifteen pounds. Jet-black hair. Pleasing. But beautiful? Never.

Somehow though, Morgan's beauty was enjoying a cult-like reverence. And since the "untimely" photo of a slightly exposed Morgan was posted on the Internet, the legend of Morgan's beauty grew.

Carpe diem.

The publicist knew she had lightning in a bottle, and it was time to generate some electricity. She touted Morgan to glamour rags as a hot, new talent, certain to set newsstand sales skyrocketing. And more importantly, fuel The Ungrateful buzz train that was rumbling across America.

She pitched Morgan as someone without the classical beauty of a Nikki Taylor, but a unique look like Gisele or Naomi. And *Glamour* bit, hard.

"Make love to the camera," the photographer implored. "Yeah, that's it. Work, with me. Work it baby; gimme your best. Just you and me baby. C'mon. C'mon. That's it. Oh yeah, you're beautiful. Feeling beautiful. Looking great. More. More. Smile. Seductively. Demure now. That's it. Don't give it all away. Not just yet. Yeah. Oh yeah."

Morgan's excitement was palpable. Despite the hot lights and the mass of people – make-up, hair stylists, wardrobe, lighting, runners, 'gofers' and posers – Morgan found the entire scene significantly surreal and slightly arousing.

Morgan's now famous breasts were tantalizingly, but tastefully, highlighted by a scoop-necked top. The photographer snapped photo after photo quickly, with a growing appreciation for both the beauty and professionalism of this first-time model.

Morgan smiled "spontaneously" on cue and soon realized what difficult work modeling actually was.

The magazine's design staff was extremely confident that the shot finally selected for the cover would be, undoubtedly, bold and audacious.

Somehow, amidst all the activity, the record label rep had surreptitiously snapped unauthorized photographs. Morgan was chagrined, the *Glamour* contingent was outraged and millions were further tantalized, when the pirated photos of Morgan appeared later that day on the Internet; posted, undoubtedly, by the enterprising representative of the label.

Morgan Chino just joined Britney, Christina, J Lo and Alicia in the fantasies of young men everywhere.

The CDs were stoked by both the expected New York hype and the Big Apple's considerable energy. Just as The Ungrateful opened for them on stage, today they "opened" for The CDs on a special live appearance on MTV's *TRL*. Warming Carson and the crowd, so to speak.

Not that anyone really needed to be warmed up, the special *TRL* gig was MTV's tribute to The CDs and a historical indoctrination to a generation who was toddling when the band first started rocking.

Today, The CDs ruled. Twenty-five thousand hard rocking fans cheering wildly. For a friggin' television appearance.

Yesterday's doubts and the juvenile, self-conducted "popularity polls" were distant memories as the Times Square crowd swelled. The Ungrateful was in attendance, but the crowd noise for The CDs was unmistakable and deafening.

As Carson interviewed the band, their ever popular videos streamed in the background. The phone lines buzzed, and the e-mails whirled at a dizzying pace.

Below, amid the flurry of activity in Times Square, an unfortunate fan found herself, unexpectedly and tragically, in traffic just feet in front of an oncoming, speeding New York taxi.

Her hysterical screams were muffled by the cheers for The CDs. The screams carried her last breath.

The Ungrateful's reception at the Madison Square garden concert was unprecedented and unexpected.

In addition to the sold-out house, the streets leading up to the legendary venue were lined with enthusiastic admirers of Ace and Morgan. An equal number, but decidedly more vocal, group of protestors were present searching for the inevitable media spotlight following The Ungrateful in hopes of calling attention to a wide variety of causes: legalizing marijuana, preventing cruelty to animals, stopping the exploitation of foreign workers, and reaffirming the right posses firearms. A spontaneous counter-protest ignited when one placard appeared calling for the right to "arm bears."

Interspersed within the crowd was a smattering of surprisingly invisible white supremacists who "hated the mother-fucking attention this group of fuck-head foreigners and half-breeds was enjoying."

Any false hope and flickering notion that The CDs held of whom actually was the event's event were permanently and forever erased at the Garden that evening.

The Ungrateful, quite simply, blew the audience away. But they kept coming back. Again and again. Five encores for the opening act. Angel tantalized, Morgan mesmerized, Ace energized and Tommy, Tommy flat out kicking ass in a never-to-be-forgotten performance. So drained was the crowd from the emotional and physical energy they expended during The Ungrateful's set, that seats were empty by the time the curtain rose for The CDs. $250 seats, nonetheless.

The emergency room at New York & Presbyterian Hospital annually treats more than 120,000 patients, many of those drug related.

The girl being wheeled in by EMTs on the gurney was quite unlike any previous suspected overdose.

Despite the visible effects of a racing heart and sky rocketing blood pressure, the young lady didn't look "druggie-like" – whatever that was. Even with sweat pouring off her forehead and streaming down her face, the remains of a fashionable hairdo and a tasteful application of make-up were apparent.

The ER doctor ripped opened her designer blouse and furiously moved his stethoscope in an attempt to locate an ever-faintening heartbeat. Suddenly, her body stiffened, and the effects of a massive stroke were evidenced.

Despite the heroic efforts of the best emergency room personnel on the entire East Coast, the young lady was dead. Unbeknown to the attending doctor, the deceased bore a striking physical similarity to some other, equally unfortunate, women who had shared a number of common characteristics, including an appreciation for the emerging musical greatness of The Ungrateful.

Each day, the population of New York City ebbs and flows like the tide – births, deaths, immigrants, emigrants, travelers in and out. With rare exception, little significance is attached to the comings or goings of the masses.

The Times Square precinct of the NYPD is perhaps, its busiest. Eight million people seemingly pass through its jurisdiction hourly. The NYPD investigators are constantly faced with the inevitable conflict arising from the tension caused by limited resources, massive expectations and an unwavering commitment to service and professionalism.

The Times Square "accident" was cursorily reviewed at first. Bringing closure to any case was always the objective, and it was too early to sacrifice expediency for efficiency. And when the junior lieutenant located the Jamaican-born cabbie, the investigation became "live."

Usually, the journey through the police bureaucracy is a laborious and time-consuming one. Last night's death in the emergency room at New York & Presbyterian Hospital was an exception.

In less than twenty-four hours, the New York Police Department's Mid Town Precinct had moved the case from missing persons, to vice, to narcotics, to the coroner.

It was now officially classified as an overdose of methamphetamine.

The file was sent to homicide.

The Jamaican cabbie was scared. Very scared. His past was behind him, and he suspected that his future was too. His expired visa, illegal gypsy cab, broken English and now an impending "homicide by reckless use of a vehicle" charge combined to form an oppressive sense of eternal hopelessness.

"She was pushed, Mon!" the Jamaican cabbie proclaimed again, "I swear on the mother fucking bible she was pushed!"

The case was transferred to New York homicide.

Two mysterious deaths in New York, with perplexing similarities.

Chapter Sixteen

The fallout over Ace's antics on the *Late Show* was significant, yet manageable and slightly serendipitous. As always, the publicist was quick to pounce on the opportunity to keep the band on the front page – not that they needed any artificial assistance.

In a "jointly issued" statement read in front of the Liberty Bell, both Letterman and Ace confirmed that the toking was a hoax.

Tommy Puccini lay back in bed as Becky's head rested gently on his shoulder. A delightful afternoon of love, with both of them "arriving" at the same wonderful space of pleasure together, had left Tommy completely satiated.

"I love you," Becky murmured. "My dream has come true in you. Please always be you and always love me."

Tommy softly replied, "I love you Becky; you are my inspiration and my life."

Just then Tommy's cell phone rang and he lazily checked the caller ID, then unceremoniously shut off the telephone without answering.

"Tommy," Becky implored, "You've got to talk to him sooner or later. That's more than five times today alone. He's your father, and besides me, your family is all you've really got."

Tommy rolled his eyes and gently kissed Becky. Again and again. All over her still charged body.

Sometimes, you just get lucky. Sometimes, not.

It's really just a matter of perspective.

The undercover Philly "narcotic officers" were chilled to the bone on the corner of 10th Avenue, when Reggie Beasley tried to score some meth.

In accordance with all of the judicial rights born in from the blood of the freedom fighters, Reggie was ceremoniously read his Miranda rights, and then led to the district patrol office for booking. As usual, technical glitches abounded, but Reggie was eventually led to a holding cell that reeked of stale urine and fermenting vomit.

After spending the night in custody, Reggie's familiarity with bondsmen worked to his advantage, and he was released. Shortly thereafter, the computer system of the Philadelphia Police Department was back on line, and the e-mail marked "urgent/high priority" was transmitted.

Sometimes, you just get lucky. Sometimes, not.

It's really just a matter of perspective.

First Union had hosted some kick-ass concerts before. Springsteen's reunion with E-Street. U2. Madonna. The Stones.

Collectively, the excitement generated by those icons of rock and roll would have to be doubled to approximate the electricity flowing through the crowd when The Ungrateful left the stage. Juiced. Stoked. Over the top. Even more so than New York.

Unfortunately for The CDs, they again "headlined" after The Ungrateful's opening. The Ungrateful's "opening" for The CDs was destined to take its place in history along side "jumbo shrimp" and "military intelligence" as a few of the greatest oxymorons of all time.

Anti-climatic would be an overstatement to describe The CDs that evening – both their performance and the fans' reaction.

The majority shouting and clamor involving The CDs that night was post-show in their own dressing room, muffled only by the shrillness of the sirens outside.

After the curtain had mercifully dropped and the post-concert lights went on, the lifeless body of a young female was discovered stage left, in an area just vacated by a maelstrom of mayhem.

The perfunctory police interviews of The CDs/The Ungrateful tour entourage were, as expected, inconclusive. Neither the artists, nor the tour management, nor the roadies, nor the hangers-on, nor the stage manager, nor the lighting crew, nor the sound crew, nor the video crew, nor the tour's security detail had seen or experienced anything significant or out of the ordinary. Out of the ordinary for a rock tour, that is.

The local promoter sarcastically urged the police to add The CDs to the victim list, because, "they're already fucking dead."

The tour was cleared by the Philly police to move on to Washington, D.C. Entourage members were encouraged to recall any unusual events. Ace wondered aloud if the time he witnessed the gorgeous backup singers in the throes of passion on the tour bus was "unusual." "Unusual in the sense that I was lucky enough to witness it," Ace added wryly.

The Philadelphia medical examiner's report was simple. Twenty-two year old Caucasian female. (Previously) apparent excellent health. No evidence of drug use. No alcohol in system. No evidence of recent sexual encounter. Death by strangulation.

Chapter Seventeen

In the Washington, DC suburb of Rockville, MD, the Food and Drug Administration operates under the auspices of the United Sates Department of Health and Human Services. "Omnipotent" is how the FDA was described by Dr. Chino's criminal attorney. "Omnipotent and omniscient" he added, for effect.

The FDA's allegations, if proven true, were serious. So serious, that if proven, the next sentence usually read:

"Life, without parole."

The FDA alleged that Dr. Chino's illegal addition of trace amounts of methamphetamines in his diet formula was a contributing factor in the deaths of three diabetic dieters.

Dr. Chino was confident that, if money were no object, he would be able to exonerate himself. Unfortunately, money, or more correctly – the lack thereof, was presently a significant object.

Inevitably, there comes a time in a rocker's career when the past can no longer carry the present. The secret is to recognize that time before it is too apparent to others.

The CDs knew that being a "has been" was infinitely more preferential than being "never was." However, the key now was to rescue dignity and respect from the embarrassment of the previous nights.

And Jordan Taylor had just the right spin. Jordan knew, ever since Chicago, that this day would come. She just never anticipated that it would come this quickly.

The meeting convened, and everyone connected with the tour was represented; Jordan, The CDs, The Ungrateful, artist management, the booking agency, two record labels, the promoter and a gaggle of hangers-on.

If she could escape with a consensus from this group of egomaniacs, she actually might be as good as others thought. "Brass balls," Jordan thought to herself, "show 'em all you've got brass fucking balls."

And she did.

Jordan's plan was simple, and she conscientiously avoided any reference to the over-used "win/win" scenario so popular in today's lexicon that the phrase has been rendered meaningless.

"We will announce to the press that the MCI Center date will be the final live performance for The CDs," Jordan proclaimed in a bold voice that belied her trembling nerves. "We will record the performance live and then release the 'Last of The CDs,'" she added, all the while silently strategizing the negotiations of an HBO live broadcast special.

"Hopefully, the energy of The Ungrateful will be able to carry the rest of the tour as a solo," Jordan concluded; without anyone detecting the massive sarcasm her brass balls camouflaged.

Surprisingly, a consensus was reached and the plan was universally supported.

A fifty-something man apprehensively entered the United States Department of Justice Headquarters on Pennsylvania Avenue. "I'd like to report a series of crimes," he calmly stated to the FBI receptionist.

"The real crime is that I have to deal with a series of loonies like you every day," she thought to herself.

"All the agents are currently busy," she informed the seemingly nervous gentleman. With a slightly discernable disdain in her voice she added, "but I'm certain one will be available shortly."

"May I tell them your name?" she dutifully inquired.

"Mercedes, John Mercedes." He answered in tone that reflected his annoyance with her lack of professional decorum.

"Please have a seat, Mr. Mercedes," she replied, "and someone will be with you shortly."

As the receptionist returned to buffing her nails, she failed to notice that Mr. Mercedes had quickly walked past the seats in the waiting area and had headed down Pennsylvania Avenue in the direction of the White House.

Walking around the MCI center, the lyrics of Lou Bega's hit were subconsciously embedded deep within the killer's twisted psyche:

A little bit of Monica in my life,
A little bit of Erica by my side,
A little bit of Rita is all I need,
A little bit of Tina is what I see.

Yes, indeed, tomorrow's concert was time for Mambo #5!

As they had at each of the previous tour stops, Angel and Morgan divided the group in half. Angel took the women into the large room, while Morgan used her considerable persuasion to separate the children from their mothers.

Angel started, just as she had in Boston, New York and Philly, with a prayer.

The women at the shelter were skeptical at first. Being in an abusive relationship with children is enough to make anyone skeptical. But as Angel continued to talk, their skepticism gave way to a slight glimmer of hope.

Angel talked of power. The power of prayer. The power of belief in yourself. The power of hope. And the women listened intently.

Angel finished, and Morgan came forward. And while Morgan discussed money, and lack of money, and what can be done about it; Angel read to an enraptured audience.

Angel and Morgan left as anonymously as they arrived. The only remnants of their visit were a newly empowered and hopeful group of battered women and a $25,000 check to the shelter.

Morgan had spent her entire youth programmed and disciplined. She was now thoroughly enjoying the freedom her emancipation with The Ungrateful offered. Acting on wickedly naughty impulses was completely foreign to Morgan. Hell, acting with any degree of spontaneity was something that had only gradually and recently crept into Morgan's life. Old habits die hard, especially ones that were ingrained so thoroughly. But there was something about Mickey Delaney that Morgan found irresistible.

Ever since she first laid eyes on Mickey, Morgan had wondered just how true all of those stories actually were. Stories of sexual prowess of mythical proportions, which, if even remotely true, convinced Morgan that the thrill of discovery would be a thoroughly enjoyable journey.

Morgan knocked on his door. When he answered, Morgan opened her kimono and showed him what millions had squinted at a nineteen-inch computer monitor to discover. Beauty from the land of the rising sun, by way of Chicago, Illinois.

Mickey's 55-year-old physique rivaled Ace's, and a smile creased her moistened lips as she recalled her introduction to Ace months earlier.

Riveting blue eyes and unruly, jet-black hair, just past the shoulders, provided the frame for an interesting, though not classically handsome face. It was the drop-dead smile that previewed a delicious naughtiness that so intrigued Morgan. That and his reputation.

Morgan touched his shoulder and trailed a finger down his chest to his taut stomach and beyond. She stared deep into his eyes and wondered if this was a still a good idea. When she saw the glint in his eyes, the smile creasing his lips, and his growing excitement, she know it was time for the condom.

Time passed in a slow, sensual blur. And the last encore for The CDs' Mickey Delaney turned out to be a memorable one. For Mickey, and especially for Morgan.

So the next time Morgan would see Mickey Delaney and The CDs would be on VH1's *Where are they now?* show. So what. Morgan felt rewarded for her explorations and thoroughly satisfied. "Yep," she chuckled, "his reputation was certainly well-deserved. A veritable rock legend."

The Jamaican embassy in northwest DC is always a flurry of activity. Nothing in the past, however, compared to the whirlwind of activity and commotion surrounding both the coming and going of Stewart Lindsey and the Jamaican Soccer Federation.

Their protestations and pleas for assistance went unheeded. Stewart's desperation grew.

Ace wouldn't listen. Ace wouldn't even talk to him. The bank wouldn't listen. And now his own fucking embassy had turned a deaf ear. Twenty-one million and just beyond his grasp. Hell, the interest alone on that kind of money would solve at least a portion of his problems. Clearly, the time was now to heighten efforts to change Ace's mind.

The reporter for *Rolling Stone* was, oddly enough, the first to hint that the recent deaths might be related, somehow, to the concert tour. The quick changes in locales from Boston to New York to Philly and now to DC had impeded the enforcement cooperation amongst the various jurisdictions.

Sloan and her team had joined the investigation at a less-than-ideal time. Time was not an ally, and the competition for a potential collar for the locals complicated an already fragmented investigation

In the interview, Ace glibly deflected the reporter's question about the possibility of a serial killer; "I had both Captain Crunch and Tony the Tiger in my plain sight each evening," said Ace wryly, "and I can guaran-fuckin-tee that we're not dealing with a cereal killer."

"I humbly suggest that you consider Colonel Mustard, in the library with the candlestick," Ace added in a perfectly affected accent of an English nobleman.

As was their custom, Tommy and Becky walked hand-in-hand to the concert. Somehow the walk, the fresh air, the lack of screaming fans, the talks and the love flowing between them, provided a much-needed sense of normalcy to their relationship.

"Thanks for always being here for me," Tommy said, as he lightly kissed her cheek.

"I always will be," Becky answered. "Always."

As they approached security at the back stage door, Tommy and Becky heard the shouting of an all-too familiar voice, "Tommy, Tommy please, for Christ-sakes I'm your goddamn father, and now you're too much of a fucking hotshot even to talk to me."

Tommy and Becky scurried within the confines of the MCI Center, as the security guard earned his entire $7.50 hourly wage by preventing Tommy Three Sticks from entering the building.

They were way too cowardly to wear their infamous uniform this far from their home in Tennessee. Nonetheless, the six young men, two whose heads were skinned and four sporting the ever-so hideous "mullet," formed matches into the shape of crosses, and unceremoniously torched them. After nearly two cases of beer consumed in a DC drive up motel, their confidence level matched their hate.

The crew scurried about to finalize the MCI Center for The CDs's "swan song." Since tonight's performance was going to be broadcast live as a special tribute on HBO as well as taped for a farewell VHS/DVD, the logistics were more complex than usual. One camera was positioned on the overhead boom, two handhelds were in the barricaded pit area, one camera was on a stick at the mix, one handheld was to work both the pit and on stage, and one wireless was going to rove the entire center. Additionally, coordination between the video control center, the teleprompters and six monitors mounted in boxes placed around the stage was exacting.

The rigging crew, ground support and lighting crews collaborated to correctly position the house spotlights, the truss spotlights, the ancillary lighting and the video and audience lighting.

As a tribute to their many years on the road, the accoutrements in The CDs' dressing room were slightly changed for their grand finale at the MCI Center. In place of mineral water and fruit, were liquor and drugs. Stoli,

Kettle One, Grey Goose and neat little rows of blow shimmering on the prone mirror.

Hell, a going away party should be a party to remember. And besides they had the rest of their lives to rehabilitate. Again.

The "deal" brokered by Jordan, now known as "the balls-of-brass tour producer" was simple: The Ungrateful would play only one song. One song, not one set.

The record label dudes for both The Ungrateful and for The CDs loved the idea for completely different reasons; for The Ungrateful, the focus on the new release would accentuate the already significant hype, for The CDs, the less time The Ungrateful was on stage, the better.

Since the tour would be significantly changed after tonight's event, the preparation for the MCI gig was "over-the-top," even by the excessive standards common on the rock 'n' roll circuit.

The majority of twenty-five truckloads of special effects and props would go back in the packing crates and then into storage – unless they could somehow be incorporated into tonight's performance. No sense in being parsimonious with the special effects tonight.

The pyro coordinator was given carte blanche to make tonight's finale one to remember for the ages. More. Bigger. Brighter. Louder.

Security tonight was tighter than usual. The normal security contingent consisted of the tour security manager and a huddle of linemen from the local college football team, supplemented by the local ushers. Bad-asses, the ushers were usually not.

Tonight was a different story. Partly because of the interest surrounding The CDs' final performance, partly because of the live recording, but mostly due to the death in Philly, security was airtight.

The football contingent included both the offensive and defensive lines, along with the linebackers and the special team lunatics. Joining them, also wearing tight fitting t-shirts with "SECURITY" emblazoned across the chest, was the entire collegiate club rugby team.

DC police surrounded the MCI's perimeter. K-nine patrolled the Center's concourse, and it was anybody's guess how many undercovers had infiltrated the crowd, though their badly trimmed goatees and earrings unwittingly gave a few away.

Final preparations were nearly complete, and the MCI staff, the production execs, the artists' representatives, the local promoter and the tour producer were meeting to ensure everything for tonight's performance would be perfect.

In the background, the sound check featured the familiar repeats of, "testing, one, two, testing..." while the house lights were synchronized and the pyrotechnicians double checked their settings and reviewed their cues.

The house lights dimmed, and the crowd grew mysteriously still. The curtain rose and a single light shown brilliantly down on the center of the stage. The very, very vacant center stage.

The stage manger panicked. The tour security manager scrambled and muttered gibberish into a crackling walkie-talkie. The band manager and the production manger looked at each other quizzically. Security tightened its ring around the front of the stage. And the police started moving in.

A single light again panned the stage. When it returned, it illuminated four people holding hands at center stage.

Angel. Morgan. Tommy and Ace.

Ace took the microphone and addressed what was now the most silent crowd in the history of live rock and roll. Simply and eloquently.

"We are honored to have shared the stage with these legends. We are humbled when we think of their accomplishments. We are hopeful we can someday approach a fraction of their greatness."

Ace reached down, picked up a soccer ball and kicked it high into the audience.

The four circled tightly. "To The CDs," Tommy said. "And Jordan, sorry, we've changed the song."

Without accompaniment or backup they sang, with emotion-filled, strong but slightly quivering voices the lyrics, from Rod Stewart's *Forever Young*. From the opening lines, "May the good lord be with you down every road you roam" the crowd swayed from side to side in unity.

As the song continued, the crowd's emotion, sentimentality and appreciation for the incredible musical accomplishments of the CDs built to a crescendo. Though Ace, Angel, Tommy and Morgan were singing a cappella, they were not singing alone.

Nineteen thousand voices joined with them in singing the last stanza:

...But whatever road you choose
We're right behind you, win or lose.
Forever young, Forever young.

The lights went dim. The stage went bare. And once again The CDs prepared to face an emotionally drained audience.

The CDs assumed their stage positions, and waited impatiently for the extravaganza to begin. The noise of the crowd was deafening. The blow stoked their juices. Their emotions ran the gamut as they realized this would be, indeed, their last encore.

The special effects started. A dry-ice fog arose and encircled each band member. The curtain rose. And massive booms of fireworks heralded the beginning of the end for a living rock legend.

Two single gunshots, synchronized perfectly with the thunderous eruption of the fireworks went unnoticed by all but two of the audience. Two unfortunate young women, whose temples were shattered by the well-timed and well-placed bullets, lay dead in their front row seats at the MCI Center.

The house lights went up. The crowd screamed. The CDs stood dazed. Security scurried. The venue's unrehearsed "state of emergency" plan clumsily unfolded. Amidst the chaos, descending from the catwalk an unseen individual retreated and seamlessly blended into to the crowd rushing for the exits.

The concert ended prematurely. Just as the lives of six young women had already.

And the overmatched police immediately narrowed the suspected murderer down to one of nineteen thousand.

Chapter Eighteen

The metro DC police responded to the call from the motel's manager. While the older officer cautiously surveyed the corridor, his partner peered into the slightly cracked door of the motel room, which precipitated the manager's 911 call. She immediately drew her weapon and radioed for backup.

Within seemingly nano-seconds, the motel was swarming with police in full-riot gear. But they had greatly overestimated the intelligence of the room's inhabitants.

Six young men, in various stages of drunken stupors, sat on the motel's threadbare carpet. Two with skinned heads were passed out adjacent to a duffel bag containing automatic weapons. Scattered around the room were various messages of racial hate and white supremacy.

Homemade explosives that were so crudely constructed as to be completely un-detonatable surrounded the four mullet-heads. The arrests were uncomplicated.

As she filed the post-arrest paperwork, the officer remarked to her partner; "The infinite stupidity of the human race never ceases to amaze me."

FBI headquarters were a flurry of activity. Computers spit out volumes of information. Almost a billion dollars worth of computers simultaneously pointed to the same conclusion (a day too late for two young women from DC) that the *Rolling Stone* reporter surmised the previous day; young women were getting murdered on the tour.

The young graduate from Georgetown University's journalism school read the reporter's article profiling the string of deaths. "Headline writing is an art," she thought. "An act of unbridled creativity."

"THE UNGRATEFUL DEAD" screamed the headlines of the Morning Edition of *The Washington Post*. "Move over Woodward and Bernstein," she mused braggadociosly.

For once in her career, Jordan was flustered: visibly and physically. Emotionally, she was a complete fucking wreck. Ever since she volunteered, no demanded, to produce the entire tour, the pressure was immense.

Now, the unfolding debacle found her across the table from two FBI agents.

Two FBI agents who wanted answers to some questions that she didn't know the answers to, and some questions that she couldn't answer.

"For the record," Sloan inquired, "your name, please."

"Jordan...Jordan Taylor."

"For some reason," Jordan thought, "this FBI bitch doesn't scare me, but she intimidates the hell out of me."

Jordan thought that Sloan's insistent requests were unreasonable and potentially overwhelming. Just the first one would have Jordan and her staff busy for almost an eternity – the names, addresses and phone numbers of everyone associated with the tour.

"Fuck," Jordan thought, "that's over 150 people – not including the local hires: two bands, two band managers, tour manager, production manager, two merchandise managers, the stage manager, the tour accountant, the bus drivers, twenty five truck drivers, the booking agency, the record label dudes, the venue managers, roadies, posers, stage hands, electricians, carpenters, family members and various other hangers-on.

"Payroll," Jordan chuckled, "payroll's a good starting point."

The second request, if it were not so damned fucking ludicrous, Jordan ruminated, was laughable. "All known people who had contact with either band since the tour's opening night." "Including 'known' groupies," Jordan mused, "the list is actually quite manageable." "Groupies, by their very nature, are unknown."

And so it went. Jordan was expected to procure the answers to a laundry list of Sloan's queries and one question, if ever fully answered, threatened to reveal Jordan's closely-guarded secret.

If ever anonymity was blissful, today was the day. Unfortunately, members of The Ungrateful were now famous. And their newly found fame hadn't allowed time for them to become wise to the ways of an unscrupulous and blood thirsty media.

The paparazzi descended upon them unmercifully. Flashbulbs popped. Cameras rolled. Tape whirled. Microphones gurgled.

And the tabloid headlines were both predictable and pejorative:

"UNGRATEFUL INTRODUCES NEW MEANING TO THE TERM 'DEADHEADS'"screamed the *Globe*.
"KILLER PERFORMANCE AT THE UNGRATEFUL CONCERT" shouted the *National Enquirer.*

"DROP DEAD GORGEOUS NOT A GOOD THING FOR UNGRATEFUL FANS" blared the *Mirror.*
"CURTAIN FALLS ON THE CD's CAREER AND TWO UNLUCKY FANS' LIVES" blasted the *Observer.*

The FBI interviews were exhaustive. If nothing else, Sloan was thorough. Each member of The CDs was interviewed individually. Then collectively. The same questions were asked, again and again. Alone. Together. In groups of twos. Threes. Fours. Then the groups' members were randomly shuffled and interviewed again. And again. The questions centered not around whom, but around why. Why would anyone follow a musical tour and randomly, yet apparently selectively, commit murder?

What possibly could be the motive?

Drug deals gone bad? Invidious groupies? Vengeful roadies? Resentful family members? Jealous lovers? Scorned never-lovers? Envious business associates?

The CDs had scattered enough remnants of vice over the last twenty-five years to occupy a cadre of full time agents pursuing live leads: spectacular drug and alcohol abuse left a legacy of assorted debris and vengeful vermin, legendary exploits with groupies criss-crossing the country resulted in an unknown number of unplanned pregnancies, unwanted venereal diseases and unhappy memories, outraged moral fundamentalists vowing to end sins of Sodom and Gomorrah; the list went on and on with each lead more nefarious than the previous.

Conversely, the relative youth and "inexperience" of The Ungrateful made the FBI's search for a motive decidedly less sensational but exponentially more problematic.

Sloan decided that her best strategic option would be to postpone interviewing the band members of The Ungrateful. Since they were performing when the murders had occurred, it was doubtful that they themselves were suspects. Since they were so new to the scene, it was improbable that they had already engendered the intense hatred that was a prerequisite of a mass murderer. Sloan's initial focus would be on the family members and associates who accompanied, or followed, the band on the tour.

Individually, Sloan segmented The Ungratefuls' family members accompanying them on the tour.

Angel: no known father, mother back home in Chicago, and no siblings.

Tommy Puccini: both father and mother placed in Boston, New York, Philadelphia and Washington at time of slayings; girlfriend also in Boston, New York, Philadelphia and Washington, no siblings.

Morgan Chino: mother deceased, father in Boston, New York, Philadelphia and Washington at time of murders, no siblings.

Ammanuel Ezure: both parents presumed to be in Jamaica, no siblings.

"What do you think the odds of four only children working together are?" Sloan thought to herself.

It would be an understatement to describe the last couple of days as "difficult" for Dr. Chino. The FDA allegations hinted at possible murder charges being filed, and now he was about to be interviewed by a youthful looking female FBI agent about six additional murders.

Dr. Chino's apprehensions were slightly allayed when Sloan entered the room. Most likely it was the combination of her warm smile, friendly handshake, pleasant, non-threatening demeanor, and her almost-gracious hospitality and congeniality that helped put Dr. Chino at ease and temporarily softened his skeptical and protective nature. "If only the FDA investigation could go this smoothly," Dr. Chino thought to himself as he slowly sipped the piping hot coffee from the ceramic mug that Sloan had kindly offered.

"Let's go back to where you were the night of the concert in Boston," Sloan started.

Dr. Chino cooperated, somewhat reservedly, as Sloan meticulously recorded his recollection of every passing moment since he first arrived in Boston.

"Dr. Chino," Sloan concluded, "I thank you very much for answering the questions I have asked. That will be all for today, but I want you to keep me advised of where you will be should I need to contact you for further questioning."

Dr. Chino left, relieved. As the door closed behind him, Sloan extracted a 3x5 pastel index card from her desk. Carefully selecting an appropriately colored magic marker, Sloan wrote Dr. Chino's name in large bubble letters. Sloan placed the notated index card in the large Zip-lock bag which held the finger print laden ceramic coffee mug which Sloan had so generously offered Dr. Chino.

Tommy Three Sticks was, actually, quite comfortable being questioned by Special Agent Sloan. Maybe it was genetics, maybe it was the moment's respite from his oppressive gambling debts, maybe it was because the thought of him offing anyone was completely ludicrous and highly humorous, he didn't know. And didn't much care. What he cared about was coming up with some large ones. Now.

"Mr. Puccini," Sloan began, "I thank you very much for coming in today. I have some simple questions that I would like to ask. I do not want to be long. So let's get right to it."

Tommy Three Sticks was appreciative of Sloan's forthrightness, and willingly answered the seemingly innocuous questions focused mainly on establishing his whereabouts and proximity to the recent murders.

"Thank you very much, Mr. Puccini, I now have some questions for your wife."

Sloan's keen instincts were alerted to something curiously suspicious about Kelly's demeanor. She wasn't quite sure what, but Sloan noted her hunches and entered follow-up possibilities into her ever-increasing spreadsheet.

Kelly Puccini fidgeted uncomfortably in the straight back plastic chair. Kelly felt completely disingenuous. Holding Three Sticks' hand didn't feel right, but she needed the reassurance.

Kelly sat, almost trance-like and provided Sloan with perfunctory answers to her questions. As Sloan's questions wound down, Kelly's spirits picked up appreciably. The question that Kelly had dreaded never came.

Not mentioning Paddy wasn't really honest, but this was an inquiry into murder, not infidelity. And Sloan never asked. What Kelly wanted was to be with Paddy. Now. And forever.

As Sloan finished her inquiry, Tommy Three Sticks slowly drained the last drops of coffee from the ceramic mug, which Sloan had so graciously provided, and Kelly Puccini finished the last drops of the refreshing water that had soothed her apprehension and parched throat.

Sloan watched Mr. and Mrs. Puccini walk, hand-in-hand towards the elevator. As they waited for the elevator, Sloan watched their charade of oneness evaporate.

Sloan returned to her office, snapped on a pair of latex gloves, and carefully placed the appropriately identified and Zip-locked drinking receptacles next to Dr. Chino's in the bottom left hand drawer of her desk.

Becky Rose wanted Tommy to be with her, just as she always wanted Tommy to be with her. Becky replayed, for Sloan, her and Tommy's day of concert routine: "After sleeping late and some special 'close time'," Becky said with her cheeks flushing crimson, "Tommy and I eat a late room service lunch. Tommy showers, we change and walk around the city, and then onto the venue. I kiss Tommy goodbye at the backstage door, wish him well, and I then head back to the hotel," Becky concluded.

"When do you go back for the show?" Sloan queried.

"Usually never," Becky replied. "I'm about to start my first year of graduate studies at the Pritzker School of Medicine at the University of Chicago. While Tommy's playing, I'm studying."

"Always?" Sloan asked.

"Almost always," Becky rejoined. "But my brothers are playing Triple A ball for the Yankees farm team in Rochester. I met up with them in Boston."

Sitting nonchalantly behind the receptionist's desk at the FBI Headquarters on Pennsylvania Avenue, the young woman applied a purplish colored polish to her impeccably manicured nails while she scanned the morning paper. The now notorious tour was all over the paper. Stories about The CDs abounded. Their colorful history was chronicled; groupies interviewed, drug excesses recorded, record sales celebrated, musical talent saluted and personalities profiled.

The stories about The Ungrateful were less plentiful and scandalous. Band members' names listed, hometowns – mostly boring stuff.

"Fuck, fuck, fuck," the receptionist thought as she scanned the bios of The Ungrateful and remembered the earlier and unconcluded visit of John Mercedes.

Paddy O'Keane left the meeting at the pub with a sense of accomplishment. "It's nice to know that you've got friends from back home abroad," Paddy thought. "It's even nicer to know that they'll support my cause, with both money and supplies," Paddy reflected, as his mind now wandered to Kelly and the life that they could have together. "If only. If bloody only."

DC United was getting thumped by the Chicago Fire before a sparsely filled RFK Stadium. Four members of the Jamaican Soccer Federation were huddled in the last rows of the lower grandstand. Their attention was riveted, not on the field, but was focused exclusively on an English lad with a guttery brogue. His teeth were crooked, his smile was deceiving, but his plan was fiendishly simple. Stewart Lindsey smiled broadly.

So intense was Stewart's and the Federation's attention to the unfolding plan, that they failed to recognize Ace as he sauntered by with a box of popcorn in one hand and Morgan Chino on his arm.

Angel was shrouded beneath a floppy hat and very wide and very dark sunglasses. She casually entered Starbucks and was instantly beguiled by the beautiful woman behind the counter. Angel ordered a coffee and whimsically speculated that the marketing genius who came up with the sizes "tall," "venti," and "grande" was a diminutive white guy in Seattle with serious self image issues.

"And how do you want it?"

Angel was tempted with the cleverness of various replies, but simply answered, "Room for half 'n half, please."

"Gladly, and have a day as fantastic as you," she countered with her reply.

Angel took her coffee and went to a back table. As the music played softly in the background, Angel started writing the lyrics to another song.

Danger

You're on fire, you want her so much
She plays you, withholds her touch
Living and loving, loving and living
But it ain't just love that's she's giving

Danger.....
You better beware
Danger....
Don't let her take you there
Danger.....
The girl gets around
Danger.....
She's gonna bring you down

Never again that's what you vow
Next minute you're beggin, now, now, now
You're all mixed around, torn up inside
And still you let your passion ride

Danger....

You better beware
Danger....
Don't let her take you there
Danger....
The girl gets around
Danger.....
She'll bring you down

You're in your house, but not at home
And it's killing you, these times alone
She'll do what you ask and play her part
But you've always wanted a piece of her heart

Danger...
You better beware
Danger....
Don't let her take you there
Danger....
The girl gets around
Danger....
She'll bring you down.

Danger....
She's a stranger to love.

Angel put down her pen and reread her lyrics and she wondered where she got the inspiration to write so passionately.

"More coffee?" Angel never looked up.

The brass around Jordan's balls was slowly returning and her confidence, though somewhat feigned, was heartening for The Ungrateful.

"People," Jordan stated, "you've got a decision to make. Either you cave in to this psychopathic mother fucker, or you get on with the most publicized tour in the entire history of rock and roll." She continued, "I have spoken frequently with Sloan and the FBI, and we're cleared to move on to Cleveland. They assure me that security will be 'presidentially' tight. I've got a phone growing out of my goddamn ear from all the conversations I've recently had; the booking agency reports that the entire rest of the tour is sold out. Scalpers are getting over $500 per ticket. The record label is stoked. The CD's sure to go platinum. The promoter and venue manager in Cleveland haven't been this naturally high in years. Besides," Jordan noted, "we're not even sure that we have anything to do with this. Despite all the 'Ungrateful Dead' bullshit in the papers, fingers logically point to some badass fall-out somewhere in The CDs' past. So, whaddya wanna do?"

Angel spoke first; "Growing up in Cabrini, I saw it all go down. Bangers offin' ballers, crackwhores selling their sorry ass selves for the next fix, gangstas, pimps, you name, I saw it. Never stopped me before, it isn't going to stop me now."

Tommy was next; "This is a total tragedy, man. I really feel bad for the chicks. But don't we owe it to our fans; fuck, don't we owe it to ourselves to keep on keeping on?"

Morgan followed, "Ever since I was young, people were telling me what I could or couldn't do. This time, we control our destiny, not some fucking freak who gets his rocks off killing. Word out. I'm rocking on."

Ace began speaking.

"In a poor Jamaican funeral home, a young man in traditional green tunic lay dead. 'Please,' his widow said to the Jamaican mortician, 'my husband's dying wish was to be buried in a white Rastafarian tunic.'

"'Fine,' said the mortician, 'just bring in the tunic.'

"Weeping uncontrollably, the widow replied, 'Impossible, he never had a white tunic and I have no money.'

"The next day the widow returned for the funeral and her husband was ceremoniously attired in a clean, white Rasta tunic.

"'How did you do it?' she excitedly asked the mortician.

"'It was easy,' he replied, 'a man died yesterday wearing a white Rasta tunic. His widow said he desperately wanted to be buried wearing green to represent the beauty and vegetation of his native Ethiopia. He was about the same size as your husband. He was in white, wanting green. Your husband was in green, wanting white. Then, it was just the matter of switching the heads.'"

Tommy, Angel and Morgan gasped. Jordan laughed loudly, and soon the entire group was laughing hysterically for the first time in way too long.

But Ace wasn't finished. He said; "Mon, in me deigh, I've sen evrytin. If ya whan a know bout det, yar in da rite place. We keep on singn, we keep on rockin, and we keep on jommin to da beat. Dey aint seen nuttin yet. Jamn on!" And with a sudden switch of dialect, Ace ended with, "Rock on Dudes."

Jordan reached into her pocket for her cell, placed a call and confirmed the tour was on to Cleveland, home of the Rock and Roll Hall of Fame.

In twenty-plus years of driving the bus on various rock and roll tours, the driver was pretty sure that he'd seen everything that could be seen, until tonight.

For obvious reasons, the sight of three agents in blue windbreakers with the bright yellow letters "FBI" stenciled in block was one he was unaccustomed to seeing. Seeing the agents "chatting up" the members of The Ungrateful made the whole scene a little more surreal.

He recollected the strangest bus scenes his fading memory could conjure up – the famous rapper bedding a succession of almost twenty five women (many sporting wedding rings) in less than one and a half hours, the requisite day-of-departure strippers (usually outfitted as police officers), coke being snorted off the rock hard (and sometimes decidedly not rock-hard) bodies of a variety of sexually oriented musicians and groupies, colorful drug busts (and feeble attempts to 'stash the hash' in the not-too obvious spots like the bus' closets and toilets), the moving "show me your breast" contests conducted up and down America's freeways, the various bra and panty collections, the drug or alcohol induced trashing the bus that became so frequent it's now considered passé (except for some gangsta rappers), the few times the bus rolled on when the lead singer was still back in the dressing room rocking some groupie, the get out of town quick escapes when the band left the stage early and the crowd got ugly, the too-many arrests, the roadies posing as band members and entertaining unknowing, dim-witted, but amply endowed groupies; and the "progression" of drugs - from heroin to LSD to acid to methamphetamines to cocaine to crack to crystal to speed, and now on to ecstasy. And always weed. Sometimes supplemented by the musicians' traveling pharmacies with amply stocked medicine chests featuring quaaludes, barbiturates, anti-depressants and sleeping pills.

"Curiously," the driver thought to himself, "this is the first tour in quite a long time when methamphetamines were around."

Chapter Nineteen

Ace sat in his suite at Cleveland's Ritz Carlton Hotel and read the bound four-color coffee table book. Ace chuckled as he read that Cleveland, formerly known as the "mistake by the lake" was now being self-touted as "The New American City." Ace read with interest the local attractions and focused his attention on Cleveland's Metro Park system – the Emerald Necklace.

As was his custom at each tour stop, Ace planned for a vigorous workout. Though he was months removed from the rigors of daily training, Ace kept his fitness level as close as possible to that of his playing days. Weight training, sensible eating, plenty of sex with a variety of partners (protected of course) and long runs had combined to keep his physique lean and his psyche keen.

Ace laced up his running shoes and got his gear ready to go. Ace bounded from the Ritz's lobby, shared a laugh with the doorman and hopped into a cab for the short ride to the park. Passing Jacobs field, he reminisced about his soccer days and the fun filled days perfecting his craft in Jamaica. Gradually, Ace's mind-set morphed from rock star to soccer star and a smile creased his lips. Ace entered the park and prepared for a vigorous training session. After stretching his lithe body and taut muscles, he began to jog, first slowly and then effortlessly increased his speed. Focusing on the path ahead and his five-minute per mile pace, Ace diverted his eyes and sprinted even faster when he saw Tommy Three Sticks sitting on the park bench.

Left gasping behind was a gap-toothed Englishman.

The security briefing for The Ungrateful scheduled performance at Cleveland's Gund Arena was slightly different than for the previous night's global wrestling event.

Sloan was now overseeing all aspects of not only the investigation, but also coordinating "prevention" efforts.

Present today, in addition to the local security detail and the customary tour security, were over thirty uniformed and undercover police, local FBI agents, representatives from the mayor's office, and members of the tactical planning squads of the equine and canine units.

All concertgoers were to pass through metal detectors. Under normal circumstances, audio and visual recording equipment, weapons, single lens reflex cameras, glasses and cans, cans of spray paint, cans of hair spray, and bootleg merchandise were specifically prohibited from entry into the venue. Tonight, random "pat downs" would occur and specially trained dogs would patrol the arena, focusing on preventing weapons from entering Gund.

The tour pass list was reviewed, and the backstage passes were laminated. Tonight, the tour staff, the local staff, the pass list, security staff and all media, reporters and photographers would be required to augment their credentials with a government issued photo ID.

Becky curled her naked body next to Tommy's and gently ran her fingers through his hair. "Tommy," she inquired lovingly, "ever want to run away from all this madness and kick back and enjoy life like regular people?"

"We are regular people," Tommy answered, "just a little more lucky than the rest. Speaking of lucky," he smiled as he pulled Becky on top, "wanna encore?"

The shrill ring of the telephone startled Tommy. "Doesn't the hotel know what a fucking 'no outside calls' request is?" Tommy asked sarcastically as he picked up the phone. Recognizing the voice on the other end, Tommy slammed the receiver down.

Suddenly, Tommy's interest in Becky was diverted and he lay in deep thought with his mind racing back to his childhood.

Despite her self-promise to concentrate on her career and to ignore all distractions, Morgan couldn't hide from the unfolding developments surrounding her father. Each night, not only were the "The Ungrateful Dead" stories run on television ad nausea, but also now her father's plight was the focus of a none-too-forgiving media. And each morning, the *USA Today* at her hotel door reported the latest, horrific news about her father's trail of money, deception and death.

Morgan's classical musical background was temporarily overpowered by hip-hop as she envisioned herself "walking through the valley of the shadow of death."

Morgan picked up the telephone, "Daddy, it's me."

Paddy O'Keane put down his coffee and tried to comfort Kelly Puccini while she sobbed. Kelly's lips quivered as she looked into Paddy's deep green eyes and struggled to get the words out. "Paddy, my love, I'm still married. And my mother and father, rest their blessed souls, didn't raise me as an adulteress. No matter how I feel about you, I'm a married woman. This has got to end." The rest of Kelly's words were indistinguishable to Paddy, muted by her broken sobs.

Tommy Three Sticks sat nervously on the secluded park bench in Cleveland's Veterans Park. Three Sticks fidgeted his feet and shifted his substantial weight from side to side as he pondered his future. His "business associates" had run out of patience with Three Sticks' inability even to cover his vig on his substantial gambling debts. "Today was the day," Three Sticks thought with the same optimism that led him down the "five team" parlay spiral of economic ruin that placed him in his current predicament.

Three Sticks waited well past the appointed hour and his anticipation gave way to anger as he realized the reality of the juvenile position of begging he was in. The time for pride, however, was well behind him.

Three Sticks was relieved as he turned and faced the familiar face. His relief quickly transitioned to horror as a knife was thrust deep into his massive belly and another thrashed across his throat. Three Sticks' last gasps for breath were silenced by a severed vocal cord and blood gurgling from his exposed carotid artery.

Dr. Chino sat silent and stunned. Nothing he could conjure up could overcome the mounting piles of evidence, the wrath of the deceased's relatives, the ravages of an inquisitively retributive press, and the invectiveness of the FDA agent in charge.

"How could you knowingly formulate diet pills with methamphetamines?" she inquired sardonically. "No deals, no pleas; I'm charging wrongful death, eight counts."

The Gund Arena set-up crew was finishing preparations for tonight's sold-out concert.

Sloan was both pleased with the preparations and excited by the energy and electricity that was pulsating through the venue. Never before had the roadies worked side-by-side with police and FBI agents, who checked everything before and after it was either located, installed, erected, powered, lighted, or modulated. The crew reviewed the production diagram to ensure that the rolling stage was positioned perfectly, the thrusts were correctly aligned with the downstage, and the wings postured just so. The production crew chief realized that the FBI's crew position on the front risers had distorted the placement of both the sound riser and the lighting riser, so the adjustments were made accordingly.

Just as he had at the concerts in Boston, New York, Philly and Washington, John Mercedes labored diligently with the local group of hired hands and scurried to and fro, aligning risers and carrying other various 'front of house' items.

John chuckled silently at the irony of his situation; he was working right next to the authorities he had evaded for so long. Completely anonymously.

Reggie Beasley opened and closed the chamber of his recently purchased "Saturday Night Special." Reggie stroked the shaft, rolled the bullets in his sweat-drenched fingers and looked straight down the barrel.

Reggie tightened the band around his bicep and desperately searched for a vein capable of supporting a puncture from the often-used hypo.

It was "girls' day out" for Angel and Jordan; the Rock and Roll Hall of Fame was the destination. The building was an impressive asset to Cleveland's North Coast harbor. Designed by the world renowned I.M. Pei, the building was intended to "echo the energy of rock and roll." "That it did," thought Angel, as their chauffeured town car pulled into the private back entrance after pausing for Angel and Jordan to check out the 160 foot glass, pyramid-like front of the rock museum. Jordan had made arrangements for them to arrive through the security area to minimize the attention the members of The Ungrateful seemed to find unavoidable these days.

"I promise," said Jordan, "not be a know-it-all and blabber incessantly, but I'd be happy to share my rock and roll experiences and history. So, if you want, I do have a couple of stories about the bands that I'd love to share. Of course, everything is 'hearsay' – so take it all with a grain of salt."

For Angel, being at the Hall of Fame was like being in the home she never really had. For reasons only Angel understood, the bands and rockers were like the family she never had. The halls of Cabrini Green reeked of urine, weed and garbage, but these halls held the sweet smell of success. And family.

Angel meandered slowly, and let her senses succumb to nostalgia prompted by the familiar sights and sounds of yesterday. And as they wandered through the second floor, they took in the exhibits of the Memphis Recording Service, featuring the King, and Respect: The Sound of Soul.

Angel's mind drifted back to Saturday morning's watching *Soul Train* at Cabrini. Clips of the Temptations and Stevie Wonder flashed in her mind's eye. She wondered if the reports that Stevie wasn't really sightless held any truth.

Angel passed the tribute to Ike and Tina and her mind raced forward forty years as she speculated if she would retain her sex appeal like Tina so obviously had.

Angel bowed reverentially before the Aretha Franklin display. There was just something about Aretha that motivated Angel. Maybe it was because her mother abandoned Aretha. Maybe it was because Aretha grew up singing in a church. Whatever it was, Angel felt a particularly strong affinity for Aretha.

And so it went: Angel wandered aimlessly and viewed musical instruments, scores, lyrics, recordings, equipment, and props that gave her a sense of identity and family. And what an extended family Angel was claiming; Ray Charles, Fats Domino, The Coasters, B.B. King, Smokey Robinson, The Supremes, Otis Redding, Etta James, Martha and the Vandellas and, last but not least, Gladys Knight.

Jordan followed silently and watched Angel metaphorically flip through the pages of her family scrapbook.

Angel and Jordan strolled, arm in arm, throughout the exhibit. They visited the incredible Lennon: his Life and Work displays located on multiple floors. Occasionally Jordan would stop and point out some little-known tidbit of information about an enshrinee.

Angel was fascinated as Jordan described the metamorphosis of Aerosmith to absolute sobriety. "A tenuous hold on sobriety it was," said Jordan, "so tenuous that at all their concert events, alcohol was banned from the entire backstage area. No one could drink. In fact, Aerosmith lobbied to make the venues they performed at 'alcohol free zones' during their performances."

Passing the tribute to the Bee Gees, Jordan noted, "It was rumored on the *Dallas* set that The Bee Gees' little brother Andy was drilling Victoria Principal while Bobby and JR were out drilling for oil."

Jordan paused respectfully in front of the Queen display. Angel sensed something, though she wasn't quite sure what. "Queen," said Jordan, "and Freddy Mercury had significant influence on rockers today. Freddy was the first rocker to admit he had AIDS, and he died the next day. Within the industry, Queen has as much respect as any other group."

Jordan chuckled when they passed the tribute to Bruce Springsteen; "Bruce, as many people know, was doing his current wife, who *wasn't* his wife at the time. She was a band member. But ole' Bruce was well connected to television. His wife at the time was an actress on *Sisters*, and *Friends* star Courtney Cox was featured in his *Dancing in the Dark* video."

Jordan explained to Angel that the chances for The Ungrateful to be inducted into the Rock and Roll Hall of Fame this time around were beyond impossible. Potential inductees had to wait twenty-five years from the release of their first album to qualify for the initial nomination to be inducted. Jordan noted wryly, "The Ungrateful's just approaching the starting blocks."

"The Rock and Roll Hall of Fame is governed by a foundation," Jordan continued, "which is composed of rock and roll historians. The foundation selects nominees every year, and then ballots are sent out to over 1,000 experts in the industry – some of who are actually drug-free and lucid – who then vote. The most popular artists on the ballot who get over 50% of the votes are usually inducted."

"Some years it's five, six, seven—just depends on how the votes fall," Jordan mused.

Jokingly, Angel asked Jordan that if there were to be a special "Druggie" wing with the Hall of Fame, who might be inducted. "I'm not certain, but from what I've heard the Grateful Dead would have not only their own wing, but also their own building. Rumor has it that Fleetwood Mac's Stevie Nicks might be enshrined, along with Jimi Hendrix, the Jefferson Airplane and Jim Morrison. But that's just hearsay," Jordan said with a wink.

"For the most creativity employed in a drug induced, mind-altering state," Jordan proclaimed, "I'd have to give the nod to the Eagles' Joe Walsh who, supposedly, glued his hotel room furniture to the ceiling."

"Nicest?" asked Angel.

"Billy Joel, Rod Stewart (despite the stomach pumping rumor), Paul McCartney."

"Quirkiest?" inquired Angel.

"Elvis, Michael Jackson, Little Richard; with special mention to Jerry Lee Lewis for marrying his thirteen-year-old cousin."

"Saddest?" wondered Angel.

"Those who died too early, with so much more to give us," said Jordan, "John Lennon, Sly, Janis, Jimi, Bob Marley, Mama Cass, Roy Orbison, and Otis. So many who died before their time."

"Stupidest?"

"Don't have time to list them all," replied Jordan snickering.

"Biggest egos?"

"The Eagles, the Stones," said Jordan, "but they definitely earned them," she added.

They circled back and returned to the third floor to watch the Inductee and Footage clips in the Multi-media Theater. Angel got goose bumps about thirty seconds into the film, and Jordan's soft: "Jesus" seemed to sum up the reverence both felt at seeing all those unbelievably talented artists on the same screen.

"It's funny how checking this place out reminds you how influential music is," Jordan remarked to Angel. "You know, sometimes because it's my job, I forget that music influences how we dress, how we talk, the movies we watch, politics, religion. You know, music touches us all. It must feel good, Angel, to know that you are touching people with the songs you write and perform. I mean, somewhere out there is a kid who keeps going on because he believes in the music you make. Think about it Angel, just look at how much these artists have meant to you."

"Sometimes it makes me feel an unfair responsibility, though," murmured Angel, "Like with this stuff going down right down. I never asked for people to get hurt. People to die. Man, I just want to sing."

"I know. Hey, screw this melancholy shit, let's hit the gift shop we saw on the first floor; I hear it calling our names – and our dates – the Platinum Brothers."

"You're on."

Jordan and Angel gave the Platinum Brothers quite a workout before they headed to the hotel, with a last respectful look at the House that Rock built.

Becky and Tommy walked out of the kitchen door of the Ritz Carlton. Jumping down from the loading dock, Tommy stood looking upward with arms outstretched waiting for Becky. Demurely, Becky seemingly floated into Tommy's protective arms. Staring lovingly at each other, Becky and Tommy kissed, first tenderly, then passionately. "Tommy," Becky sighed through heavy breath, "we've got to get you to the venue."

The urgency for a timely arrival at Gund temporarily gave way to an overpowering physical magnetism, as Tommy and Becky hurriedly retreated back into the hotel and satisfied each other in the basement supply room. "I love you forever, Tommy," Becky said, as she quivered with waves of aftermath pleasure.

"Controlled chaos" would be an understatement when describing Sloan's press conference. Normally, a FBI press conference is dull, drab, informative, and eminently predictable. By contrast, Sloan was presiding over a conference that was a kaleidoscope of questions posed by both leather-throated and shrill-voiced reporters:

"Do you have a prime suspect?" shouted the journeyman reporter from the *Times*.

"Are all the killings related?" asked the primly dressed petite woman from the AP.

"Are band members suspected?" inquired the beat reporter from the *Plain Dealer*.

"Why did it take so long to link the killings together?" bellowed the mustachioed scribe from *Rolling Stone*.

"Any idea of motive?" queried the diminutive black gentleman from *Entertainment Tonight*.

"Why not cancel the tour?" asked the cigar-chomping reporter from *The National Enquirer*.

"Who's to gain from these killings?" questioned the older woman nobody recognized.

"Indeed," Sloan asked herself, over and over again, "who's to gain from these killings?"

Morgan was pressed for time and she knew it, but somehow the importance of tonight's concert was diminishing along with her visions of stardom and happiness. For the first time she ever remembered, fear crept slowly into her mind and took control of her thoughts. "Dispelling irrational fears should be second nature to someone who has performed in front of tens of thousands," she thought to her disbelieving subconscious. But it wasn't tens of thousands of screaming fans. It was just Morgan and her computer: one ticket? Two tickets? One ticket? Destination: Japan. Morgan's printer spit out a variety of itineraries.

Morgan's mind wandered back to her fourth grade spelling bee championship:

"F U G I T I V E," Morgan mentally spelled out the word that had garnered her the District Championship; somehow, she couldn't muster the courage to repeat the word aloud.

The Ungrateful was unaccustomed to the backstage "superstar" treatment at the previous venues. But tonight, in the bowels of Gund Arena, they were certainly styling. And loving it.

The first indication that they had "arrived" was when the local production staff introduced their "runners". "Just here to take care of whatever business you need."

Next was the introduction to the band's Doctor, "Rock Doc" was how he introduced himself, then the production assistants.

Ace was delighted to learn that they now had an official masseuse. "Salubrious," he thought to himself.

The backstage security was tight. Uniformed policemen patrolled the area. Ace asked Tommy, "How the fuck do they know who belongs and who doesn't? There must be over a hundred working back here – and all in 'show blacks' – the stage manager, electricians, spotlight operators, stagehands, camera cable pagers."

"Easy," Tommy replied, "just keep a look out for anyone not wearing black."

Just then, the catering staff arrived, completely attired in the customary and requisite whites.

"Fuck you," said Tommy as Ace howled.

Jordan scurried backstage and her demeanor reflected the growing angst within her. "Where's the fucking local promoter?" she screeched to no one in particular.

"The mother-fucker sold a fucking sponsorship for the show; it's coming down, and he's going down!" she added emphatically. And finishing with a flourish, she concluded; "What the fuck, it clearly stipulated in the contract rider that there's no branding, banners, signs or other material by the stage any time the audience is in the building. The goddamn stage area is starting to look like NASCAR."

Jordan summoned both security and the stagehands, and her reputation remained intact as the blatant commercialism was removed.

The metro unit of the Cleveland police department responded to the report of a single gunshot. Driving onto the cracked pavement of the motel's parking lot with the black and white's lights twirling, siren silent, the officers played back the dispatchers description: "Single gunshot heard by occupants of the adjacent room."

What was left of Reggie Beasley's brains was splattered on the peeling paint of the walls of the seedy motel. The gun was in Reggie's hand, pointing to where his mouth used to be.

Each patron entering Gund Arena passed through metal detectors, and most were subject to full body pat downs. The security staff confiscated enough paraphernalia to open up a well-stocked head shop.

The concert hall pulsed with excitement, anticipation and fear.

Backstage, The Ungrateful prepared for their unfamiliar role as the headline act.

Angel relaxed, sitting cross-legged on the carpet in a full lotus position.

Ace juggled a soccer ball, trying once again to beat his self-proclaimed world record of consecutive touches.

Tommy went through his customary series of limbering exercises.

And Morgan tapped furiously on her computer.

"You all right, baby?" Angel asked Morgan, "Something's bothering you big time."

"I'm fine, really," replied Morgan, but neither her nor Angel believed the response.

The house lights dimmed, and an eerie silence enveloped the crowd. Suddenly, the arena erupted with a thunderous boom. Before the crowd could move, another eruption of bangs cascaded throughout Gund and echoed loudly with mounting reverberations.

The pyrotechnicians were pleased with their unexpected opening.

A single spotlight shone down on the stage, and billowing fog concealed the identities of the performers.

On perfect cue, four spotlights illuminated the individual members of The Ungrateful, and the cheers from the audience were as deafening as the previous silence.

Morgan's clingy all-white outfit contrasted her darkly complected features and onyx hair. The intense glare of the spotlight shadowed her figure and subtly hinted at the none-too mysteriousness of her feminine charms. As Morgan drew the bow back to her violin, Tommy opened with a chord arrangement that energized the already excited crowd.

Ace laid down a beat that brought the entire audience to their feet, cheering loudly.

Once again, a cavalcade of thunderous booms enveloped the arena.

Angel's vocals were deep and resonating.

For three solid hours, The Ungrateful rocked an increasingly appreciative crowd.

And then the unexpected happened.

The curtain dropped after the last of four encores. The houselights went on.

And every single member of the audience left the building. Alive.

Sloan gathered her staff and conducted a brief post-concert debriefing.

"What went right tonight?"

"What went wrong tonight?"

"What can we do better?"

Sloan's attention to even the tiniest detail, her innumerable computer entries, and her keen mind weren't unraveling the mystery. Just yet. Sloan knew it. Though she was content with the evening's work, she was frustrated by all of the open issues and knew that another all-nighter was in store.

Backstage, emotions ran rampant – delirious happiness, relief, pride, and confidence. The stage hands exchanged high fives, the record label dudes were busy working the telephones, the local promoter was ecstatic, the FBI agents were, uncharacteristically, nonchalant and cavalier, and Jordan felt redeemed and whole.

Ace entertained an entourage of reporters. Morgan had changed into her revealing and customary "post concert" kimono to the delight of many. Angel was ravenous and scarfed the buffet. Tommy and Becky held hands and sipped champagne.

Two uniformed police officers knocked on the dressing room door and entered with an ominous air.

"May we please speak with Mr. Thomas Puccini III?" they enquired solemnly.

Tommy stood up, and Becky hurried to his side.

"May we please speak with you privately?" the Hispanic officer asked respectfully.

"It's OK," Tommy stammered nervously, "she's with me."

Tommy, Becky and the two Cleveland police officers went into the adjoining office and closed the door. The backstage bustle of activity ceased, and a strange silence once again enveloped the arena.

"I am sorry to inform you that your father was murdered today," the officer blurted.

Tommy never heard another word the officer said, as he wailed uncontrollably with his head buried in Becky's shoulder.

Sloan spoke with the detective and her brow furrowed quizzically.

Chapter Twenty

The hotel operator wasn't quite sure what to do. Under normal circumstances, the request to accept the charges for a collect call would be summarily denied. But the operator was insistent that this was an emergency – Mrs. Rosita Mercedes needed to speak immediately with her daughter, Angel.

It was nearly three am, but Angel was still wide-awake in her suite. The combination of the adrenalin rush from tonight's concert and the news of Tommy's dad had left her unable to sleep.

The ringing telephone didn't as much startle her as it annoyed her, yet she answered.

"Mamma, mamma what's wrong?" Angel asked.

"It's Reggie Beasley. He's dead." Rosita said, "His aunt just came over and told me he killed hisself. She said it's all your fault. They be blaming you and that hotshot band of yours, baby."

Ace woke from a short and restless sleep and opened the door of his hotel room. The first thing he saw was the screaming headlines of the *USA Today:* " MORE UNGRATEFUL DEAD."

"That's all we fucking need," he thought to himself.

Jordan cradled the receiver on her shoulder while she scribbled notes furiously. The next tour stop was scheduled to be Chicago, but the tour's future was, in her mind, over.

"I don't care how much fucking money's at stake," Jordan screamed into the phone, "his goddamn father just had his throat sliced wide open. Where's your fucking heart?"

"Both deaths are tragic," she continued. "Reggie's was so fucked up that his death was a matter of when, not how or why. But that's not the issue. Reggie had history with the band. And especially with Angel."

"No, no!" Jordan yelled, "I'll contact the media my fucking self. The mother-fucking vultures can kiss my sweet ass and then all go fuck themselves. The tour's over."

Jordan was so animated and loud that she didn't immediately notice Becky enter the room.

"Hi," said Becky softly, while she and Jordan gently hugged each other.

"Tommy and the band are finishing up with the police questioning and they'd like to talk to you as soon as possible."

"Sure," said Jordan, "How's Tommy holding up?"

"As well as can be expected, considering the circumstances."

Kelly Puccini sobbed softly, as Paddy held her tightly and lightly stroked her hair. "It's all right, honey, let it out, let it all out."

Kelly looked up with eyes as red as her hair used to be, and with a quivering lip said, "It's all my fault, Paddy. I wanted him to go away. It's my fault. It's my fault."

Paddy reassured her gently, saying, "I wanted so desperately for us to be together, but not like this. I'm so sorry. For you. For Tommy. For us."

"Please forgive me, Kelly. If I hadn't come into your life, this never would have happened."

Kelly looked up and said, "Paddy, my life never existed without you. I'm sorry for my husband. I'm sorry for my son. I'm sorry for my God. But you had nothing to do with his murder."

Paddy stared into the distance and pulled Kelly closer.

From a distance, Sloan observed Kelly's and Paddy's exchange but wasn't even remotely sure what was going on.

Stewart Lindsey and the Jamaican Soccer Federation huddled together around the gapped-toothed Englishman.

"You dun nuttin for us yet, mon," Stewart said jabbing a stubby black finger into his hollow chest. "Ana you dun but got one moe chaunce."

"Keep your bloody hands to yourself, or I'll add you to my list," snarled the Englishman. "In a different way, I've got just as much to lose as you if we can't put an end to this music bullox with Ace. But, lord of lords, the boy can fucking fly!"

"Don't worry, be happy!" finished the Englishman mockingly, "Bloody, fucking wankers."

The FDA investigator called the Washington district attorney. Though the "wrongful death" charges were going to be filed in federal court on Monday, she thought it wise to alert her municipal compatriots of the impending charges.

"Dr. Chino?" exclaimed the DA, "his daughter's in the midst of The Ungrateful Dead mess."

"That's affirmative," replied the investigator, "the deaths were methamphetamine related."

"Interesting. Very, very interesting."

"And contact the FBI and Agent Dillard and give 'em the heads up."

Unfortunately, both Sloan and the members of Ungrateful were all-too familiar with each other and with the drill. This time however, she knew the victims, and the questions were both annoying and invasive.

"But not as invasive as the knife that gutted Mr. Puccini," Sloan said sarcastically to herself.

"And where were you yesterday afternoon?" enquired Sloan.

"Running in the park," answered Ace.

"See anything unusual?"

"Mr. Puccini," said Ace. "Alive," he added.

"Tommy," Sloan started, "I'm very sorry about your father. When was the last time you saw him?"

"Ma'am, I've neither seen nor spoken to my father since the beginning of the tour. I don't know if you realized it, but my father was a compulsive gambler and into the 'boys' for some big-time money – over $750,000. I tried to help him out in the past, but it only made things worse. He tried calling several times, really more like all the time, but I never spoke with him. Sometimes Becky did, but she always told him the same thing I used to – that we loved him but weren't going to watch him bet his future away."

Sloan already knew everything that Tommy said, and she was somehow comforted that he spoke the truth.

Tommy never mentioned the last call from Three Sticks, nor the letter the Ritz Carlton concierge gave to him when he checked in.

Huddled in the international departure terminal of Dulles Airport, the elderly and frail Japanese man waited nervously for his row to be called. In both American and Japanese, the gate agent called "all rows for United Flight # 781 to Tokyo. Looking extremely nervous, the elderly gentleman shuffled forward onto the plane.

The alert gate agent noted his demeanor and radioed for help. "We've got a 'golden-ager' with apparent flight induced fear, seat 18A," she said to the lead flight attendant, "be extra nice to him; my grandfather is deathly afraid of flying too."

"Will do, I promise to deliver him safely to the Land of the Rising Sun."

Dr. Chino breathed a deep sigh of relief when the airplane's front door closed and the pilot positioned the Boeing 777 on the runway ready for take-off.

Morgan was extremely agitated and nervous while Sloan ran through both routine questions, and in her opinion, bizarre questions.

"Was Tommy's relationship with his father normal?" Sloan asked.

"Define normal," Morgan stammered.

"Well, how did it compare with the relationship you have with your parents?"

Morgan shifted uncomfortably in her chair, while Sloan noticed her cheeks flushing and her breath quickening.

Morgan's cell phone rang to alert her of a text message. After viewing the message, she smiled widely and relaxed her demeanor completely.

"I'm turning her on," Sloan's male counterpart thought to himself. "My animal magnetism was just too much for little miss rock and roll."

Morgan fluttered her long eyelashes and was almost giddy knowing that her father was airborne and Tokyo bound.

Angel didn't like Sloan and it was apparent. But Angel really hadn't liked any police since her early days in the system.

Her answers were monosyllabic and revealed nothing more than she was concealing something. Sloan made a mental note to follow up with Angel.

Jordan was completely unprepared for the meeting with the band.

Since the beginning of the tour, the dynamics of the band had solidified and the roles of each respective band member had become more or less predictable.

Through a combination of his quick wit, loquaciousness and intelligence, Ace had become, more or less, the band's spokesperson.

Angel's determination and history of overcoming insurmountable odds sometimes seemed dichotomous to her warm and nurturing persona, but if Ace was the brains of the band, she was certainly the heart.

Morgan had always remained supportive, but aloof. However, Morgan was the conciliator when the infrequent disagreements amongst band members arose.

Tommy was an enigma. In the fast-paced and hard charging world of rock and roll, Tommy's incredible talent was the only remnant of commonality he shared with the legions of rock stars who preceded him.

Tommy loved peace and serenity. He loved Becky. He loved music – playing, writing, listening and composing. Everything else to Tommy was a nuisance and a diversion from his few passions. The drugs, the groupies, the parties, the fame, the fortune – really didn't hold much appeal for Tommy.

Instead of Ace or Angel leading the discussion, Tommy spoke with conviction.

"Jordan, we've decided to play Chicago. But not for us, not for you. Not for our record label. We're playing for all the families whose lives we've unintentionally disrupted. No discussion. My dad's funeral is on Wednesday, Reggie's is on Tuesday. We're going to play Friday night. But then it's over. At least for a while."

Morgan added, "We know that Tommy's dad's and Reggie's deaths had nothing to do with us, but it's time. We're going to play Chicago, where it all started for us – then we're all going our own ways."

Ace nodded and simply said, "Bad karma man, totally bad karma."

Angel finished, "Jordan, thanks for everything you've done. It's been real, but Chicago's it for us. Let's go out in a fucking blaze of glory."

Chapter Twenty-one

Becky found herself in the unfamiliar position of mediating between Tommy and his mother. It is one thing to plan a funeral. It's quite another to plan a funeral for a murdered gambler who left a trail of uncollected gambling debts. It's still another to plan for a funeral with a widow and her lover, and her son who was more interested in the funeral of his former manager.

Nonetheless, Becky was determined to help in any way possible and arrange a befitting send-off for the father of the man whose baby was growing inside of her.

Becky contacted Fr. Vincent Morrello at the Puccini's old parish in Chicago, St. Mary's of the Angels. "Father Vince" as he preferred to be called, was a balding and bulging man of the cloth who was well versed in the secular ways and had a keen insight into "traditional" Italian families. Father Morrello assured Becky that he would coordinate all aspects of the service with the funeral home and told Becky to pass along his deepest condolences to the "widow Puccini."

Sloan sat with the FDA investigators and the Washington, DC district attorney in the federal courtroom across the table from the attorneys representing Dr. Chino. Waiting impatiently for him to arrive, the colleagues discussed both the complexity and severity of the impending charges.

At precisely 10:00am the judge arrived. Following a conference in chambers, Dr. Chino was formally charged, in abstenia, with six counts of wrongful death. The warrant for his arrest was immediately issued.

The judge noted the attorney's request to withdraw from the case, but reserved rendering a decision pending the discovery of Dr. Chino.

"You pulled his passport as I instructed?" Sloan asked her assistant, already knowing the answer.

The CPD detective and the FBI agents scanned the coroner's report of the results from the recently completed autopsy on Reginald Caleb Beasley. "Male, age 24. Death consistent with right hand, self-inflicted gunshot to the cranial lobe. Recent injection of methaphetamine evidenced in system. Effects

86

of chronic drug use evident. Additional powder burns and residue indicate deceased recently fired the same gun with his left hand."

"Run ballistics on all gun related victims of The Ungrateful," ordered Sloan.

Alive, Reggie Beasley didn't have much of a family or an entourage.

But dead, Reggie's family, former homies, posse members, gang bangers, dealers, customers, Cabrini Green "boys from the hood," curiosity seekers, and star gazers swelled the First Baptist Church of Chicago well past its capacity.

Reggie arrived in a style quite different from how he left. The all white hearse transported the ornately jeweled all-white casket. The church more resembled a well-stocked florist than a house of God.

Tied to each pew was an arrangement of white Easter Lilies. In front of the altar, surrounding the pulpit, and enveloping the perimeter of the entire church were beautiful and massive amounts of white roses. A single, fragrant white gardenia, and a long stemmed white candle were handed to each mourner upon entry into the First Baptist Church.

Each of the pallbearers wore a simple, yet beautiful, orchid in the lapel of their white tuxedo.

The Reverend Roy Davis solemnly welcomed the assembled multitude and slowly walked to the back of the church where the closed casket rested, topped with a single, shimmer cloth of white silk with gold inlayed embroidery.

As the reverend approached the casket, the lights of the First Baptist Church went dim, and one-by-one, the grievers lit their candles.

The church was illuminated with flickering light, and in the choir loft a single voice said aloud:

"Reggie, this is for you baby, with thanks to Puff."

Angel stood, and with a strong, but quivering voice started:

Seems like yesterday we used to rock the show
I lace the track you lock the flow
So far from hanging on the block of dough
Reggie they got to know that
Life ain't always as they seem to be
Words can't express what you mean to me
And though you're gone

We're still a team
Through your family I'll fulfill your dreams

In the future can't wait to see
If you'll open up the gates for me
Reminisce sometime
The night it took my friend
Try to black it out but it plays again
When it's weird feelin' it's really hard to conceal
Can't imagine all the pain I feel
Give everything to hear half your breath
I know you still livin' your life after death

In perfect harmony, Ace, Tommy and Morgan joined in with the words of Sting's *Every Breath You Take*:

Every step I take
Every move I make
Every single day
Every time I pray
I'll be missing you

Thinking of the day
When you went away
What a life to take
What a bond to break
I'll be missing you

Angel continued solo:

It's kind of hard with you not around
Know you in heaven smilin' down
Watchin' us while we pray for you
Till the day we meet again
In my heart is where I'll keep you friend
Memories give me the strength I need to proceed
Strength I need to believe
My thoughts Reggie I just can't define

Wish I could turn back the hand of time
Bust in the 6
Shop for new cloths and kicks
You and me taking flicks
Making hits stages they receive you on
Still can't believe you're gone
Give anything to hear half your breath
I know you still livin' your life after death

Ace, Tommy and Morgan harmonized;

Every step I take
Every move I make
Every single day
Every time I pray
I'll be missing you

Thinking of the day
When you went away
What a life to take
What a bond to break
I'll be missing you

Sobbing, Angel's words were barely audible to the emotionally charged congregation;

Somebody tell me why
One day morning
When this life is over
I know
I'll see your face

Joining Ace, Tommy, Morgan, Angel, was the Reverend Davis and hundreds of crying mourners;

Every night I pray
Every step I take
Every move I make

Every single day

Every step I take
Every move I make
Every single day
Every time I pray
I'll be missing you

Thinking of the day
When you went away
What a life to take
What a bond to break
I'll be missing you

The Reverend Davis led the funeral procession to the front of the church and spoke with passion, fire and brimstone about the love of Jesus, the eternal fires of hell and the hope of redemption.

In the choir loft the sweet sound of *Amazing Grace* accompanied Angel to the pulpit.

Angel began her eulogy.

"Reggie was my first friend. My first love. My first partner. I had his back. He had mine. The Reggie who died, wasn't the Reggie who lived. Drugs stole his mind. Drugs stole his body. Drugs stole his soul. Drugs stole his heart. Drugs stole his future. If there's any good that can come from Reggie's tragic death, it'll be to save even one brother from Reggie's life of drugs, delusion and despair.

"We be playing our last gig soon, and part of the proceeds are going into the Reggie Fund, to help prevent in the future Reggie's past. Thank you. Be strong. God Bless you."

To the words of *Swing Low, Sweet Chariot*, Reggie's casket was wheeled to the awaiting hearse.

Sloan and the FBI agents stood with the rest of the mourners and exited the church unseen. John Mercedes trailed behind.

Jordan's temporary headquarters for coordinating the Chicago event for The Ungrateful was her suite at the Knickerbocker Hotel. With her laptop, cell phones, fax machine, and Palm Pilot all synchronized, Jordan felt as prepared as she could, given the circumstances, for managing the chaos enveloping the upcoming tour finale. Jordan wasn't at all prepared for what was on the other side of her hotel door when she answered the persistent knocking.

"Hi," Angel said, "Got a minute?"

Jordan didn't really have a minute. "Hell," she thought, "She didn't even have a fucking nanosecond."

The gig was only two days away, and it had been transformed into a media circus, a security nightmare, and the professional opportunity of a lifetime.

The Ungrateful had agreed to simulcast the show across the country on a pay per view basis. "Fuck it," Ace had said, "if we're going out, let's go out stylin."

The Ungrateful's record label had persuaded the band to record the United Center concert for a final "Live" tribute album. And Jordan was responsible for flawlessly pulling it all together.

"Sure," Jordan answered Angel. "Why don't we check out Michigan Avenue Street and window shop while we talk."

"Thanks so much," said Angel, embracing Jordan. "You don't know how much this means to me."

Angel and Jordan walked through the lobby and the uniformed doorman graciously inquired; "A cab for you two lovely young ladies today?"

"No thanks. We'll walk," replied Jordan, as they turned up Walton Street towards the Magnificent Mile.

Angel cradled her arm under Jordan's elbow as they walked past the bustling tourists, loop workers and determined shoppers. Their leisurely demeanor was in sharp contrast to the energy of the passers-by and Jordan's frazzled mind.

"It's just work," Jordan sighed silently as she asked, "Everything all right?"

Angel hesitated at first, and then spoke softly with tears welling in her eyes,

"I know stopping the tour is the right thing to do. But this was my way out. It's my life. You guys are my family. My sense of identity. My being. I'm alive when I'm singing. I'm alive when I'm on stage. And I want to stay alive."

Jordan stared intently into Angel's dark eyes and said, "Girl, go for it. I've been around the scene long enough to know that you've got what it takes to make it alone. Make it alone to the top. And I'll help any way that I can."

Angel felt herself smiling for the first time in way too long, and gently hugged Jordan.

Jordan said softly, "Angel, you can make it, but if I don't get my ass back to work, I'll be flipping burgers."

"Thanks, baby, you're the best," Angel said as she gently squeezed Jordan's arms with both her hands.

Father Vincent Morrello stood in the vestibule of St. Mary's of the Angel's sacristy and pulled the white vestments over his head until they rested symmetrically on his massive frame.

Father Vince glanced into the congregation as he prepared the chalice and cruet for Thomas Puccini III's funeral liturgy; he instructed the two altar boys to light the altar candles and ignite the incense.

Father Vince studied for one last time the note cards he had prepared for his homily and waited as the somber mourners silently filled the well-worn pews.

"In the name of the Father, and of the Son and of the Holy Spirit," Father began his homily, "Brothers and sisters in Jesus, sons and daughters of God, we are here today to celebrate the life of Thomas Puccini III and his passing into a new life with God our Father."

In the front pew, Tommy sat with his mother on his right and Becky on his left. Each woman was dressed entirely in black. Kelly Puccini wore large, dark sunglasses, which concealed both her face and her emotions. Becky sat erectly, holding Tommy's hand tightly. In the pew immediately behind Tommy, sat Angel, Morgan and Ace.

Somewhere in the middle of the church, Paddy O'Keane knelt nervously.

Father Vince continued, "In facing death, we are reminded that God has created each person for eternal life, we affirm and express the union of earth with the Church in heaven in the one great community of saints. Though Thomas is physically separated from us by his death, he remains united with us in the love and spirit of Jesus Christ."

"Bullshit!" Tommy thought silently to himself as Father Vince continued to drone on about what a wonderful person Tommy knew his father wasn't.

"The celebration of the Funeral Liturgy is the source and summit of our Catholic faith," Father Vince extolled. "As an expression of our faith in Jesus Christ, our hope for resurrection for Thomas and the love that God has which will unite us all in love, please extend a wishing of God's peace to those around you."

"Peace of Christ," Paddy said to the gentleman sitting next to him.

"Peace to you," replied John Mercedes.

Not Tommy, his mother nor Becky spoke during the short ride from St. Mary's to the cemetery for the Rite of Committal.

Chapter Twenty-two

In the lobby of the Knickerbocker Hotel, Ace waited patiently for his guests. Two funerals in two days had taxed Ace emotionally and physically. He feared that the funeral for his musical career with The Ungrateful Dead was all but certain.

Always an opportunist, always a realist, Ace was to poised to manipulate circumstances to benefit his chosen ones. Just as Ace had learned to exploit the defensive weaknesses of his opponents on the soccer field, so too could he exploit the weaknesses of his Armani-suited adversaries.

Stewart Lindsey and the Federation entered the well-appointed lobby of the Knickerbocker and were ready for battle. Immediately upon their entry, Ace smiled broadly and came forward with extended hands and warmly embraced Stewart. Both Stewart and the Federation's cadre were surprised and dumbfounded by Ace's friendly demeanor and conciliatory nature.

Ace, Stewart and members of the Federation exchanged pleasantries, and Ace invited them into the private meeting room the Knickerbocker's gracious staff had provided and arranged to Ace's exacting details.

"Have a seat, my good friends," Ace started, "always a pleasure to meet with my own people."

Stewart was both perplexed and nervous. After months of not even being able to speak with Ace, his sudden reversal put Stewart in an extremely uncomfortable position.

"Ace, it's time for you to end this bullshit and get back to the game where you belong."

"Yah, yah, and then you can go on with your little game. I don't think so. Not the way you've got it going down."

"But, but Ace."

On perfect cue, the gap-toothed Englishman entered the room from behind the partition separating the adjoining room.

"I don't think introductions are necessary," said Ace, "but if they are, kindly allow me to introduce my partner. It seems, our limee friend realized that his chances of receiving payment for his much needed orthodontia would be greatly increased if he had associations he could trust."

"I'm not sure what you're up to Stewart," Ace continued, "But it smells like shit and I don't want no part of it."

"Gov," said the gap-toothed Englishman to Stewart, "no bloody bollucks for my partner, or the lottaya are fucked."

Sloan sat in front of a bank of computers in the Chicago field office of the FBI. The screens flickered in the darkness of the office. Sloan represented the best of the best of the new breed of FBI agents. Sloan added two intangibles to the FBI's mix of "new era" attributes – a tireless work ethic and an insatiable curiosity. Bright, articulate, street smart and computer savvy. It were these facets of Sloan's personality that kept her glued to the computer screen at nearly 1:00 am.

Sloan's training in the agency's criminal justice information services division had provided her with invaluable knowledge of the inner-workings of various investigative agencies and her computer proficiency allowed her to access the massive databases stored on hard drives world-wide.

Sloan entered into her whirling computer every conceivable variable and co-joined the analysis with her speculation. As the investigation unfolded, Sloan postulated a number of theories and was certain that she was in the midst of a cesspool. What she wasn't sure of was which of the many unsavory characters was a murderer.

In Washington, DC, Sloan and her team had first begun unraveling the mysteries surrounding Stewart Lindsey and the Soccer Federation. Using information culled from various domestic and international agencies, Sloan was well aware of Stewart's past, and even more keenly aware of Stewart's pressing need for Ace to enter the ranks of professional soccer players. Sloan had retraced Stewart's recent movements and had placed him in Boston, New York, Philly, DC, Cleveland and now Chicago.

Despite all the advances of modern technology and her proficiency with computers, Sloan still preferred to doodle. Maybe it was a throw-back to her formative years, maybe it was the security of absolute privacy unavailable with a computer or maybe because Sloan was determined to keep alive the lost art of making bubble letters – for whatever reason, Sloan's thought process crystallized with pen and paper.

Outside, the dark Chicago night was illuminated brightly by the first stage of a full moon. Sloan glanced at her notebook and then stared intently into the skies and temporarily lost herself in the stars.

"Stars," Sloan wrote in large bubble letters.

Sloan listed the "stars" of the tour and then connected each one with a list of suspects that was shorter by one since Tommy Three Sticks death.

"Paddy O'Keane," Sloan wrote on the tablet as she glanced at her watch and realized that it was nearly 2:00 am. "Perfect," Sloan thought, "it's now morning in England, and the Inspector from Scotland Yard should be in within the next hour or so. Maybe I'll tinkle him on the telly," Sloan chuckled to herself.

From the moment he was released from the Irish prison, Paddy had been under surveillance. The forged passport allowed Paddy to enter the country, but he was never far from the watchful eyes of the international police. It had taken Sloan longer than she would have preferred to coordinate the intelligence from various domestic and international agencies, but once she had, it was obvious that both Kelly Puccini and money were the objects of Paddy's attention. Whether or not Paddy was connected to the murders remained to be determined. What Sloan had determined was that Paddy had been in each of the cities of The Ungrateful's tour.

Sloan picked up the telephone and dialed the 011 code for England.

"Good Morning," Sloan began. The conversation with her counterpart was mostly routine. Professional. Cooperative. However, as unremarkable as the beginning of the discussion was, the end was diametrically opposite. "You mean you've had an undercover agent trailing Paddy and the tour from Boston?" Sloan asked incredulously.

After the call, Sloan resumed her contemplation of the persons involved in this unfolding drama. Sloan's segue to Kelly Puccini resulted from a blurring of doodles. Sloan was a hopeless romantic at heart and an eternal optimist. For numerous personal reasons, Sloan didn't want Kelly involved in this whole sordid affair. "Affair," Sloan said to herself, "how ironic."

But Sloan's professionalism didn't allow for personal feelings interfering with complete objectivity, and Sloan couldn't overlook the fact the Kelly was in each of the touring cities. Sloan couldn't quite understand what potential motive Kelly might have. Money for Paddy? Escape from Tommy Three Sticks? Sloan was perplexed and her doodles became more random.

Just as Reggie Beasley had come up dead, so too did Sloan when she retraced Reggie's steps. Though he was in Boston and briefly detained in police custody in Philly, Reggie's presence in New York couldn't be confirmed. Sloan rewrote his name and underscored it twice. Reggie's motives were as old as time: lust, revenge and money. Each more powerful and poisoning than the other. Sloan pulled out another of her multi colored markers and drew a large circle around Reggie's name.

Dr. Fujimaro Chino's disappearance represented a professional embarrassment for Sloan and further alienated Sloan from her incompetent male subordinates.

Sloan had been, understandably, furious. Communication breakdowns from the most sophisticated crime unit in the world were unexpected. And unforgivable. Sloan had clearly issued the directive to immediately pull Dr. Chino's passport. The fact that Dr. Chino was able to leave the country unimpeded was the lone black mark on Sloan's impressive professional dossier. Sloan double underlined Dr. Chino's name. In black. "Dr. Chino's plane should be landing momentarily in Tokyo," Sloan thought to herself, "at least we can correct our mistakes with cooperating customs officials in Tokyo."

Sloan didn't need to look at her watch. The gentle brightening of the skies alerted Sloan to the fact that she had pulled another all-nighter. "What the heck," Sloan thought, "I did it in college all the time."

Chapter Twenty-three

Paddy O'Keane sat at the table in the smoke filled anteroom of the replica Irish pub. In front of him was gathered an eclectic group of mostly Irish ex-patriots. Paddy started, "Simply stated lads, we're here today to raise money for the cause. For it's money we need to keep our country. While I was in jail, I had time to both think and dream. Every night, the cold and dankness of the prison brigade chilled my body. But I refused to let it chill my soul. And so I prayed. I thought. I dreamed. Almost every night I had the same dream. It was the final of the World Cup. Wembley Stadium. Ireland versus England. Before the game, as a peace offering to the assembled masses, both the Queen and the Pope appeared. The Queen said to the Pope, 'I can make my people excited with just a wave of my hand.' And the Queen waved and the Englishmen clapped and cheered enthusiastically. The Pope replied, 'I can make all of Ireland sing and dance in the street with just a wave of my hand.' And then the Pope slapped the Queen across the face, hard. The dream ended with Ireland kicking England's ass and winning the Cup."

The lads howled uproariously. Paddy continued, "There's really nothing funny about this at all. The Pope's symbolic slap represents how we've been slapped all these many years. It's time for retaliation. It's time for a new tomorrow."

Becky always held Tommy closely in bed. But after making love, Becky held Tommy closer than usual. "Tommy, my love," whispered Becky, "I've got a surprise for you."

"A surprise, what?"

"Tommy, you're going to be a daddy!"

"For real? How?"

"For real! And I don't think I need to go into the ole 'boys have a penis and girls have a vagina routine' Tommy. Birth control is never one hundred percent effective. Are you mad at me?"

"Mad? Never. Surprised? Yeah. Happy? For sure!"

"Tommy, I love you so much! And I've always said that I'd never let anything come between us. But I think our baby is going to be the perfect expression of our love together."

"Becky?"

"Yes, Tommy."

"Will you marry me?"

"Yes, I thought you'd never ask. I love you so much, Tommy. I'm complete when I'm with you."

"Let's not tell the band until after tomorrow's concert. With everyone kinda going separate ways, the wedding might be a good time to bring us all back together one more time."

"Whatever you want, Tommy."

"And, please, don't say anything to my mother."

"I won't, Tommy. I love you."

"I love you too, Becky."

Chapter Twenty-four

The lead flight attendant's voice came clearly over the airplane's speaker system, first in Japanese and then in English. "Ladies and gentlemen, we are approaching Tokyo and we have been cleared for landing. Please ensure that your seatbacks are in their upright position, your tray tables are secured and your seat belts are tightly fastened. The crew will come through the cabin to pick up any unwanted items. We will be on the ground shortly."

Dr. Chino glanced at his text message and inconspicuously entered the rear lavatory of the plane.

The flight attendants doubled checked the cabin. "Everything appears to be in order, except the passenger in 18A isn't in his seat."

"Oh, don't worry, I've seen him move around quite a bit during the flight."

"Yeah, one of the advantages of flying on these big birds is you can usually move around and at least get some exercise."

"Ladies and Gentlemen, United Flight #781 has landed safely in Tokyo, where the local time is 8:13 am. On behalf of the captain and crew, I'd like to thank you for choosing United. Please remain in your seats with your seatbelts fastened until we have arrived at the gate and the captain has turned off the seat belt light. Remember to use caution when retrieving your items from the overhead compartments as items stowed may have shifted during the flight. Thanks again for choosing United and have a wonderful day."

A frail, elderly-looking lady exited from the lavatory at the plane's rear and joined the cue of deplaning passengers passing though Japanese customs.

Jordan paced nervously in her well-appointed suite on the top floor of the Knickerbocker Hotel. Jordan chuckled as she remembered the old vaudeville routine of the spinning plates, and pictured herself running back and forth attending to the multiplicity of items that would crash and break without her simultaneous attention.

The decision to simulcast and offer the concert on pay-per-view had been an easy one. The logistics of coordinating the production were impossible. Under normal circumstances, just promoting the pay-per-view would entail weeks of effort and a legion of staffers and interns. But these decidedly weren't normal circumstances. In this instance, Jordan had the ironic benefit of an intensive media scrutiny resulting in headlines across the country and publicity money couldn't buy. Early field reports indicated that across the country, radio stations and club owners everywhere were planning "Dead" parties with large screen video monitors, drink specials and costume prizes.

For a moment, Jordan allowed herself the luxury of reminiscing back to her early days in the business when she was a local promoter and Buffett was playing to wildly costumed and enthusiastic "Parrot-heads." "I wonder if the feeding frenzy surrounding those concerts could even approach the intensity of what we're going to experience?" Jordan thought.

Initially, when The Ungrateful had announced the Chicago gig would be their last, Jordan had cancelled the balance of the tour and contacted the respective venues. However, the outpouring of support had been so overwhelmingly strong, the concert was now going to be simulcast in the tour's original remaining cities. Kansas City, Dallas. Phoenix. Las Vegas. Los Angeles. San Francisco.

Jordan had heard two rumors, one of which delighted her and one which saddened her greatly. Jordan had expected devastating financial losses resulting from the cancellation of the balance of the tour. However, just the opposite was occurring. Demand was so strong for the simulcasts – from Kansas City all the way to San Francisco - that the abbreviated concert tour was going to be a financial windfall, "Shit," Jordan said aloud, "all that revenue without any of those expenses."

The reminder of the deaths littering the trail of past concerts tempered Jordan's elation at the financial prospects. "Fucking macabre motherfuckers," Jordan shouted aloud to no one, as she recounted reports of bookmakers establishing an "over and under line" on the number of deaths at The Ungrateful's final concert.

Jordan resumed working at a frantic pace, careful never to sacrifice efficiency for expediency. Jordan thrived on the energy and excitement of work, and her adrenalin overload was sufficient to carry her through the multiplicity of tasks she had rightfully earned a reputation for flawlessly handling – the record label, the local promoters, artist management reps, security.

The telephone call from FBI Special Agent Sloan Dillard interrupted Jordan's work and troubled her greatly.

Chapter Twenty-five

John Mercedes picked up the telephone, and for the countless time, dialed the number. Just like before, John hung up the phone before the first ring registered. But unlike previous times, John redialed the number and waited impatiently and nervously for her voice.

"Hello...hello...hello...who is this?"

"Hi, Angel."

"Who is this?"

"Angel, it's me, John. John Mercedes. I'm your father."

"I ain't got no father. Never had. Never will."

"Angel, listen. Please. I'd like to meet. And talk."

"Listen, I don't know what kind of sick asshole you are. I never had a father. And I don't have one now." Angel slammed the receiver down as tears welled up in her almond eyes.

The telephone rang again and Angel said to herself, "Be strong girl, nobody got your back but you. You got this far by yourself. You'll go where you want by yourself."

"Hello."

"Angel, please don't hang up. I just want to talk. I'm your father."

"Listen, asshole, like I said before, I ain't got no father. If I did, my father wouldn't have let me grow up in Cabrini Green. He wouldn't have left my mama and me by ourselves. He wouldn't have allowed drugs to be sold in the hallway by our door. He would've been there so I didn't have to steal to eat. He would've been there so I didn't go to juvie. He would've been there so I could have a birthday party. He would've taken me to see Santa. He would've been there to love me. He would've been there when I needed him. And I don't need some gold digging, crazy mother fucker like you to be calling now."

The possible irony of the motherfucker reference wasn't lost on Angel as she again slammed down the receiver. Now the tears not only welled – but the streamed down her olive brown cheeks. Angel curled up in the fetal position and sobbed uncontrollably.

"Death don't erase debts. Not the size of Three Sticks's. Get the fucking money. From his wife. From his kid. From the fucking tooth fairy. I don't give a fucking rat's ass from where. Just get me my fucking money."

"Paddy me-boy, isn't it 'bout time you tapped ole Kelly for something other than a booty call?"

"Whaddya mean?"

"Face it Paddy, Kelly's got access to more green than St. Patrick himself, rest his blessed soul. Her ole man ran both liquor and numbers for the mob. He also came from old family money. The Puccini family's been solid mob in Chicago since before Capone.

"And now that the old bastard got his throat slit, the insurance money's got to be rolling in soon. And her son's raking it in big time. Face it Paddy, your lightning rod's found a double pot of gold."

"Or triple." Paddy laughed as they toasted their good fortune.

The security detail at Chicago's United Center was reminiscent of small-scale military maneuvers. The major difference was that military maneuvers usually had an identifiable and recognizable enemy to focus on.

FBI Special Agent Sloan Dillard was overseeing the preparations and was ultimately responsible for preventing the unthinkable from happening to the unsuspecting by an unknown.

In addition to the customary precautions, Sloan had mobilized the FBI's Critical Incident Response Group for The Ungrateful's last concert. Sloan, in cooperation with the tour's security chief and the local Chicago police, agreed that all concertgoers would pass through metal detectors. All carry-ins would be prohibited, including purses. The Chicago police force's canine patrol would work the perimeter of the United Center. Surrounding the stage, facing the crowd would be a ring of uniformed Chicago policemen. "And remember," Sloan concluded, "ear plugs for the police barricade around the stage – it's going to be loud." As Sloan returned to her computer, she thought to herself, "If the killer attempts anything at the concert, he's either extremely brave or extremely stupid."

Over the last few days, Sloan had left virtually no stone unturned as she coordinated the investigation and searched for clues to the killer's identity. There were 11,400 active FBI special agents, but Sloan never felt more alone or excluded from that fraternity as she pored over reports from the National Crime Information Center's Index of Criminal Justice information. The name

Stewart Lindsey flashed on her cross-reference query; and Sloan scrolled down eagerly.

Chapter Twenty-six

Kelly Puccini answered the telephone and was startled to hear the ominous sounding voice in the receiver, "Mrs. Puccini, my name is FBI Special Agent Sloan Dillard, and I need to speak with you about your husband's business affairs. And your affair."

Stewart Lindsey's activities were being closely monitored on both sides of the Atlantic. For some time, it was apparent to the authorities that Stewart had been smuggling cocaine for the Columbian cartel. The soccer association was an excellent alibi and diversion for Stewart's unwitting mules. As the head of the Federation, Stewart had complete access to both the players and their gear. For some time, shipments of cocaine accompanied the unsuspecting players on their travels.

The authorities knew that they could have Stewart at anytime they wanted, but what they really wanted was his source. And just as Ace eluded defenders, so too had Stewart's suppliers eluded the collaborating forces of Scotland Yard and The FBI's drug smuggling investigation.

"Good afternoon, I'd like to speak with Morgan Chino."

"This…this is Morgan Chino."

"Morgan, it's Special Agent Dillard. I'd like to meet with you again."

"For, er, for what?"

"I'd like to meet with you to discuss your father's unlawful disappearance from the United States."

"I'm not…"

"Ms. Chino, I would also like to discuss your possible involvement in your father's affairs and any role you may have played in his apparent flight from justice."

"I… I… can meet, whenever, but we've got our final concert on Saturday night."

"Fine Ms. Chino, let's plan on meeting on Sunday afternoon at two o'clock."

"Whatever."

FBI Special Agent Sloan Dillard bolted upright in her bed. "I can't believe I've overlooked it for so long," Sloan sighed incredulously. Sloan quickly picked up the telephone and knowing she would get her office voicemail left the following message; "Agent Dillard, I can't believe what an total nincompoop you are. Each of the murders has most likely been captured on videotape. Boston was recorded. New York was live on MTV and VH1. Philly was recorded. Washington was an HBO Special. I'd seriously recommend that you subpoena all tapes and engage the FBI's video analysts to review. And Agent Sloan, please don't let this happen again. By the way, you rock, girl."

Sloan smiled sleepily and pulled the down comforter over her head and drifted away.

Chapter Twenty-seven

"The last god damn thing I need is another meeting with some fucking bitch from the FBI!" Jordan yelled to no one as she hung up the phone. "Who gave her the right? And now, of all fucking times."

"I'm in the lobby and I'll be in your room shortly to meet," echoed in Jordan's ears as she scurried to half-ass clean up her suite littered with reports, papers, plans and contracts.

Jordan's ranting and feeble efforts to establish an atmosphere of professionalism and control were interrupted by the single rap on the door of her suite.

"FBI Special Agent Sloan Dillard."

Jordan walked toward the door and mockingly thought to herself, "I wonder exactly what 'Snoop Dog' wants from me now."

Jordan's thought process and nickname for Special Agent Dillard was significantly altered when she opened the door and was greeted by a strikingly attractive woman who exuded professionalism and confidence.

"Ms. Taylor, FBI Special Agent Sloan Dillard. It's nice to see you again. I hope I'm not interrupting too much."

"Jordan, please."

"Thank you for agreeing to see me on such short notice, but time isn't really a friend to any of us now."

"Tell me about it! I'm up to my fucking, er... excuse me, my frigging eyeballs in hungry alligators and it's feeding time."

"So are we both, Jordan. Now the sooner we can get started, the sooner we can get back to fending off the ravished beasts."

"Fine."

"Jordan, I understand that each of the concerts on the tour have been recorded. How many cameras have been used?"

"Ammanuel Ezure, please."

"This is Ace."

"Good afternoon, Mr. Azure. I'm FBI Special Agent Sloan Dillard and I would like to speak to you."

"Ace… and you're already speaking to me."

"Mr. Ezure, I just finished another meeting in the hotel. I'm now in the lobby and would like to speak with you, immediately."

"Chill, I'll be down."

Sloan sat in the overstuffed armchair facing the elevator and waited impatiently. Ace exited from a crowded elevator, and Sloan observed an exchange that left Ace laughing and another man smiling. For some reason, Sloan noticed the prominent space between the smiling man's front teeth.

Sloan stood and confidently walked toward Ace and extended her hand.

"Mr. Ezure, thank you for meeting with me on such short notice."

"It's Ace, baby, and I'll meet you whenever you want. You packing heat?"

"Mr. Ezure, I've arranged a private room where we can meet for a brief discussion."

"A private room? I'm not that easy baby. No flowers?"

"Mr. Ezure, the gentleman in the blue sport coat and gray pants sitting over there is my associate and he will be accompanying us."

"Man a three-way. This new FBI is really something!"

"This way please, Mr. Ezure."

Sloan led the way down the corridor, and Ace followed, mesmerized by the gentle sway of her body that the quick pace just couldn't conceal.

"Mr. Ezure…"

"Please it's Ace, baby."

"Fine, it's Ace, but no more 'baby.'"

"Whatever."

"Okay Ace, describe your relationship with Stewart Lindsey."

"Ain't no relationship. The mother fucker, er….excuse me, the lying rat bastard, cock-sucking, mother fucker, owns my soccer contract."

"Are you aware that Mr. Lindsey has been the focus of an ongoing investigation and is known to be smuggling drugs?"

"You're shitting me."

"What is not known is who is supplying Mr. Lindsey."

"Wow."

"Ace, who was the gentleman you got off the elevator with?"

"You mean 'goalpost'?"

"Goalpost?"

"You ever seen that dude's teeth?"

Chapter Twenty-eight

Miguel Zabala looked out from his balcony and surveyed the city below him and the mountaintops in the distance. Miguel smiled as he observed the bustle of the native *Caraquenos* as they scurried amongst the ornate Spanish colonial style architecture. Miguel appreciated the sanctity; serenity and anonymity Caracas provided him. For Miguel, the city's cosmopolitan nature, modern high-rises and skyscrapers contrasted with the underground assembly operations and pavement cracked landing strips and was welcome relief from the rigors of orchestrating and operating an international cocaine smuggling operation. "Mules and Maseratis," Miguel often said as he contemplated the dichotomy between his various lifestyles.

From his penthouse apartment, Miguel could easily see the El Avila National Park, and he enjoyed watching as the people played basketball, tennis, bicycling and dominoes. To his right, Miguel looked down at El Parque Este, the central park of Caracas, and could barely make out what he knew was a spirited games of *bolas criollas*.

But Miguel's favorite pastime, baseball, was also the quasi-national religion of Venezuela. In fact, if many native Venezuelan men told the truth, baseball was *the* religion of the men, while Catholicism was relegated to the women and children.

One day soon, Miguel knew, he would own the Caracas Leones. And Miguel would take his place proudly aside George Steinbrenner as a captain of industry, a visionary businessman, and the owner of his country's most prized, respected and storied professional sports franchise.

Miguel walked back into the room where his lieutenants and under lords awaited. "Muchacos, our friend Stewart becomes more of a problem everyday. He is past due and my tolerance has ended. And my friend in America, John Mercedes, informs me that Stewart's being tailed."

Chapter Twenty-nine

It was a short cab ride from the Knickerbocker Hotel to the United Center, but Jordan needed the change of scenery and welcomed the opportunity to be temporarily free of the investigation and back preparing for tomorrow's concert. "Too many fucking distractions," Jordan thought as the cab inched forward on Michigan Avenue.

The snail's pace of the cab's progress normally would have infuriated Jordan. Any wasted moment was a setback, and Jordan considered an aggregation of such moments a defeat. But today, the diversion was welcome and Jordan watched the businessmen scurry like ants and the shoppers go in and out of the retailers along the Magnificent Mile.

The cab's lack of progress was stalled even further by a red light and Jordan glanced out of her window towards the congregation of people in front of Water Tower Place. Jordan squinted as she thought she recognized a face and attempted to bring it closer into focus. As the man and his companion walked toward Jordan, his face became increasingly familiar, but Jordan couldn't close the association.

The light turned green and the cab inched forward as the man approached Michigan Avenue and signaled for a cab. Jordan's mind raced and she remembered where she had seen the face. "He's a dead ringer for one of the set-up crew for the concerts," Jordan thought, "but no roadie wears designer suits."

John Mercedes' Rolex sparkled in the bright Chicago sunlight as his cab pulled to the curb. John entered first, and the gap-toothed Englishman followed.

"Hi Becky, it's Angel, girl. How's it all going?"

"Oh hi Angel, everything's great."

"Can you put Tommy on the phone?"

"Oh, sorry, Angel, he's just getting out of the shower. Can I take a message?"

"Yeah, sure. Tell Tommy the band's meeting at 2:00 to talk over tomorrow night's gig and rap about what happens to all us afterwards."

"2:00, sure. We'll see you there."

"Ah, Becky, sorry girl, but this meeting's just for the band. You understand we've been through a lot together, and the journey's ending. We just need to be by ourselves for a while. Don't worry girl. I won't let Tommy out of my sight. I've got his back for you."

"OK. 2:00, I'll tell him."

The receptionist buzzed Sloan, interrupting her trance-like focus on the screen. "Excuse me, Sloan, I'm sorry to interrupt, but your appointment is here."

"Please tell Mrs. Puccini I'll be a few moments," Sloan said as her eyes again riveted on the screen. Sloan called in her associate excitedly, "Look at this!"

"What?"

"Right here. The lab boys are breaking down videos of each of the concerts. We're starting at Boston. Right from the beginning. Here. Zoom. Right there. Stop. Recognize him?"

"Well I'll be god-dammed. Isn't that the guy we saw getting off the elevator with Ace this morning?"

"You bet your ass. Whoops. You bet it is. That's 'goalpost.'"

"Good afternoon, Mrs. Puccini. I'm FBI Special Agent Sloan Dillard, and this is my associate. Thank you for coming down to meet with us this afternoon. We'd like to ask you some questions. But, first, please accept our condolences on your loss."

"Thank you very much. I appreciate it. It's been very difficult."

"Mrs. Puccini."

"Kelly, please."

"OK, Kelly. Were you aware of any financial difficulties your husband may have been experiencing?"

"Late husband."

"Yes, I'm sorry, were you aware of any financial difficulties your late husband may have been experiencing?"

"Mr. Puccini and I had been married in name only for quite some time. Really, the whole marriage had been a farce. Except for the beginning. So he never really talked to me. You know, like a husband talked to a wife. Like two people who really loved each other would talk. But some things you just know. And Tommy talked to me. Tommy told me his dad was in trouble.

That he helped him out when he could. But it was getting too much. That he was done. Tommy said no more money. Ever. And Becky called and asked, no one told me to keep him away from Tommy. That he was interfering with his life."

"Besides family, Kelly, were you aware of any of your husband's business associates?"

"Late husband."

"Again, I'm sorry, Kelly. Your late husband's business associates."

"Well, usually all his calls went to his cell phone. But at the end, he was getting calls at home. At all hours of the night and day."

"Kelly, did you recognize who was calling your late husband?"

"Well, sometimes, caller id picked them up. Sometimes it was 'out of area.' But most of the voices I could tell were 'family' – you know, like Italian."

"Most of the voices?"

"Yeah, I remember two calls, one from an Englishman and the other sounded Spanish."

"Are you sure?"

"Ma'am, coming from where I did, I'd never fail to recognize English slime. The Spanish I'm not too sure about, though."

"Kelly, tell me about your relationship with Paddy O'Keane."

"Relationship?"

"Yes, Kelly, relationship. Please let's not play games and make this more difficult for everyone. I know your background. I know your maiden name. Paddy has been under observance throughout his incarceration. The surveillance intensified after his release. So your actions and interactions with Mr. O'Keane have been observed."

"An 'undercover' investigation?"

"One might say that, Kelly, but tell us what you know."

Chapter Thirty

One-by-one, laconically, Ace, Angel, Morgan and Tommy walked into the room.

"Dude, I feel like Sean Penn in *Dead Man Walking*," said Ace as he closed the door behind him.

"Least Sean had Madonna once," said Tommy, "the only thing you've ever had is your hand."

"Fuck you."

"Right back at you dude."

Angel waited until they were all settled in and started, uncomfortably.

"A while ago, we all got together to start something really special. And special it was. Tomorrow it's all gonna end. Least for a while. I just wanna thank you all. For everything. You guys are the family I never really had. I love you all."

"Even Tommy's sorry-hairy white ass?"

"Even Tommy's ass. Ace, how you know whether it's hairy or smooth? You been holding on me? You better leave Tommy's ass alone, or Becky'll have your sorry black ass in a sling so tight your balls will pop."

"Hey, hey, come on now."

"We all made a lotta money so far, and I've got a thought."

"Bet it's lonely."

"It is, but anyway, there's been some real bad shit happening on this tour, And maybe it's related in some twisted-fuck way to us. Whaddya think if we establish some sort of fund for the families of people who've become known as 'The Ungrateful Dead?' You know, kinda like a benefit."

"Angel, I think that's a great idea, I'm in."

"You better ask Becky first or she'll skin your hairy ass."

"Whatever."

"I'm in too, all the way. And how about a benefit for my dad's legal fund while we're at it?"

"Hey whaddya hear about that?"

"Not much, I'm scheduled to meet with the investigator from the FBI on Sunday."

"That's three of us, how 'bout you, Ace?"

"Ah, yes my friend. Remember my old man? He'd get up some time before noon. Lie on the beach. And then when he felt like it, he'd sell some shit to the tourists. Then he'd kick back and relax. Smoke some weed. Party. Start all over the next day. One day, he approached a rich tourist who said to him, "I'm an extremely successful businessman, and I can help you. Instead of just selling a little, why not work early in the morning, all afternoon and into the evening? Then you can sell a lot and with the profits you can hire others to sell for you. With their profits you can make your own trinkets, cut out the middleman and enjoy even greater profits from manufacturing and distribution. With those profits you can leave Jamaica, move to New York and run an ever-expanding enterprise."

"And do what then?" my dad asked.

"Eventually, you'll be able to sell your company for many dollars and retire." "And then what?"

"You'll be able to afford to relax on a tropical beach and sleep till noon."

"Fuck it, it's just money. Let's make some good out of this shit."

"Okay, we all agree. Thanks. Any idea of what's next for you?"

Morgan returned, exhausted, and unlocked the door. Entering her well-appointed suite, Morgan flung her purse on the bed and noticed the blinking red light of the hotel telephone. Morgan wanted to ignore it – hell she wanted to ignore the entire world.

"Good afternoon, Ms. Chino. How may I be of service?"

"I just returned to my room and saw the light blinking on my telephone."

"One moment please, Ms. Chino…Ms. Chino a priority Federal Express package has arrived for you. Shall I have the bellman bring it up?"

"No thanks, I'll get it myself. Where shall I ask?"

"The front desk will be more than happy to accommodate you."

"Thanks."

"Thank you very much, Ms. Chino. And have a wonderful day."

Morgan tussled her hair and studied herself in the mirror. Morgan noticed her eyes didn't twinkle as brightly, and her smile – the few times she managed to smile – wasn't as bright as before. "At least I have something to show for all this misery," she thought to herself.

Morgan exited the elevator and didn't notice the gentleman nattily attired in a blue blazer and gray slacks sitting in the over-stuffed armchair.

"Good afternoon, how may I be of service?"

"Um, yes. I just returned to my room and the light was blinking and the operator told me I had a Federal Express package waiting."

"Certainly, your name and room number?"

"Morgan Chino. 1413."

"One moment please, Ms. Chino. I will be right back."

"If you will please sign here."

Morgan's signature was erratic and her heart raced as she read the 'from' line.

"Thank you very much, Ms. Chino, and have a wonderful afternoon."

Morgan's hands trembled as she fumbled with the door lock clumsily. Finally, opening the door, Morgan locked it securely behind her, then bolted the door and attached the chain.

Morgan closed the drapes and sat down. She nervously opened the package and read: "More…Danger….Miguel Zabala….Sorry. Be careful. Love, Dad"

Morgan trembled with uncertainty as her mind raced. "More" and "Danger" were two of their songs Angel had penned, but Morgan had never heard of Miguel Zabala.

The gentleman in the blue blazer and gray slacks approached the front desk and spoke in hushed tones to the front desk manager, who went into the back room and appeared a short time later with the package delivery log.

Chapter Thirty-one

Sloan hustled back to her office for a long-overdue conference call. Sloan's even-tempered demeanor had been extremely challenged by the revelation that Scotland Yard had dispatched an undercover emissary to observe Paddy O'Keane. Professional courtesy would have dictated that she had been informed at the onset of the investigation.

"But we had no idea that an investigation was underway," the British Inspector sighed in a slightly condescending tone Sloan found greatly irritating.

"Let's move beyond this; bring us up to speed on what you know," Sloan said.

"OK, but it's a lot."

"Fine, go ahead."

"Paddy O'Keane worked extremely hard while incarcerated to keep alive the dwindling fire for the IRA. Quite simply, Paddy became trapped in a time warp. Much like the Japanese soldier who emerged from a jungle in 1990 and who has believed that World War II has been going on all this time, so too does Paddy work for a memory that isn't connected to the reality of today."

"So what's he doing here, and why are you observing him?"

"Paddy's effort to raise money for the 'cause' is a smokescreen and diversion that only Paddy's unaware of. In actuality, his efforts are helping the European cartel expand the international distribution efforts of Miguel Zabala."

"Miguel Zabala?"

Miguel Zabala represented a totally new breed of drug dealer.

Miguel was educated in the United States, graduating from Northwestern University's Kellogg School of Management. Earning dual degrees in Business Administration and International Economics, Miguel returned to his native Venezuela determined to develop a twenty-first century business model and apply it to Venezuela's natural resources.

Miguel set up his corporation and staffed key positions with well-educated, forward thinking business associates. Miguel's sophistication and attention to detail were reflected in the mission statement of "Uno," the holding corporation for his massive and ever-expanding empire, "to generate profit through the development and distribution of recreation resources."

Miguel was a keen believer in the basic tenants of business and marketing that the packaged goods marketers he studied in college employed; market analysis, business opportunity development, market segmentation, key opinion leader development, paid sampling, product line expansion, affiliate marketing, international expansion, branding, business logistics and cost sharing.

Miguel's sophistication was evidenced in every facet of his business model, and he prided himself on his marketing savvy.

Miguel proudly launched his empire from a suite atop the Gran Melia Caracas, for Miguel believed that image was a critical component of any firm's success. And while the native Caraquenos dined on golfiatos and empanadas, Miguel feasted on international cuisines and delicacies to reflect and enhance his growing reputation as a global financier.

Caracas, Venezuela is where Miguel managed his wealth, but San Cristobal, Venezuela is where his wealth originated. For deep in the Venezuelan countryside, well hidden from the proud Spanish mansions dotting the countryside, Miguel's drug cachacos neatly packaged a wide variety of drugs and readied them for shipment to an ever-expanding base of international distribution points.

Chapter Thirty-two

Stewart Lindsey was panicked, and for good reason. Stewart's association with Miguel Zabala had been, in the beginning, a windfall. Miguel provided Stewart with an unlimited supply of "recreation resources." Stewart, in return, offered Miguel access and a cost effective delivery option to an international client base.

Stewart however, had ideas even bigger than Miguel's, at least for a while. It was Stewart's decision to divert payments from Miguel that precipitated his increasingly ominous predicament and accelerated his need for Ace to return to the soccer pitch, thus freeing up Stewarts' portion of Ace's $48,000,000 transfer fee. Which, according to the way Stewart structured the contract, was a handsome $47,750,000.

FBI Special Agent Sloan Dillard sat in her office with the lights out and stared at the skyline illuminated by the lights of Chicago's skyscrapers. Sloan absently doodled and began to reconstruct thoughts, feelings, facts, insights, suppositions, and intuitions on her pastel note pad:

Known for certain – six dead
Motive – unknown, most likely money
Prime suspects – Stewart, Paddy, Dr. Chino
Unlikely suspects – The Ungrateful Dead, The CDs, Kelly, Becky, Jordan
Deceased suspects – Reggie Beasley, Thomas Puccini III
Question – Did Three Sticks slit his own throat?
Question – Is one killer responsible for all murders?
Question – Who is the gap-toothed Englishman?
Question – Who is John Mercedes?
Question – Does Miguel Zabala have anything to do with the murders?
Observation – Ace has got a great ass!

Sloan chuckled at the last entry, but hey, she was entitled to a little levity for tonight was going to be another late one. First Sloan needed to process the necessary paperwork to subpoena Kelly Puccini's telephone records. Next was the laborious process of viewing the tapes and videos from New York, Philly, DC and Cleveland. Then the double and triple checking of security precautions for tomorrow evening's concert. Sloan knew, that by the time she left the office, tomorrow night would have already evolved into tonight.

"It's really not 'The Last Supper,'" Jordan said to Angel, "but we've got to get together and preview tomorrow night's concert, and I thought dinner might be nice."

"Yeah, it's cool. I'll get 'em all together."

"7:30, my suite?"

"7:30."

Jordan contacted the Knickerbocker's catering department and made the arrangements. Fortunately, her suite was large enough to comfortably accommodate their few, selected guests.

Angel arrived first and gave Jordan a warm hug that lingered. Next came Tommy and Becky. Ace followed with a morose looking Morgan.

"Why the sad face, baby?" asked Angel as she hugged Morgan, "It had to come to an end eventually."

"Oh, it's just everything all coming down at once."

Jordan poured wine for everyone, but Becky politely declined as Ace ravaged through the mini-fridge for a Red Stripe.

"Not there, buddy. Look on the counter, I had catering bring up your stripes."

"*Gracias.*"

"*De nada.* And now I'd like to propose a toast. To a group of musicians who are as great as their band's existence was short. Thank you for allowing me to be a part of your greatness and to touch the dream."

"And here's a small memento of my appreciation," said Jordan as she handed Tommy, Ace, Angel and Morgan an ornately wrapped package from Tiffany's. "Go ahead, open it."

Ace raced with Tommy to see who could open his first, while Angel and Morgan slowly undid the wrapping. Ace won, and displayed a large gold coin. On each side of the coin "The Ungrateful" was etched on the top, with the word "DANGER" on one side and "MORE" engraved on the other.

Morgan didn't share the other's appreciation for the gifts, and surprisingly wished it were already Sunday afternoon at 2 PM.

"Angel, how did you choose the titles of the songs?"

Chapter Thirty-three

Unfortunately, the events were such a common occurrence that they had become routine. The Chicago police entered the blood splattered room at Cabrini Green, and saw the lifeless body of a man with a pistol in his hand pointing to where his head used to be.

"If he had any, what's on the walls are what's left of the little brains he had."

"Careful, don't touch anything, homicide will be here shortly. Check for drugs, his arm was banded like he was ready to shoot up."

"Any ID?"

"Jamaican. Lindsey, Stewart."

"Witnesses?"

"Yeah, one."

"Thank you very much for coming forward. Did you see anything out of the ordinary?"

"Yeah man, I did."

"What?"

"A white dude. At Cabrini. At night. If that's not unusual, nothing is."

"Doing what?"

"Anybody's guess. Maybe looking for some dental insurance. There are choppers, and then there are choppers. But this dude's smile was something else."

Sloan's pager beeped, and she immediately knew from the tone that an emergency was at hand. "One of the beautiful things about modern technology is the freedom it provides for being in control of interruptions," Sloan thought to herself. "But this isn't going to be an interruption." Sloan dialed the number as adrenalin started pulsing through her body and her mind raced.

"Chicago Police Department. Homicide."

"Yes, good evening, this is FBI Special Agent Sloan Dillard."

"Oh, yeah, the captain thought you might like to know."

"Know what?"

"One of your suspects in the Ungrateful mess joined the ever-growing list of victims."

"Victims?"

"Yeah, his brains are splattered on the walls of a Cabrini tenement. Arm banded. Shot full of meth. Gunshot through the mouth."

"Name?"

"Lindsey, Stewart."

"Thank you very much."

Sloan ended the telephone call and immediately placed a call to headquarters.

"Good evening, this is special Agent Sloan Dillard, please connect me with ballistic support."

"Ballistics."

"Hi, Dillard again. Can you run a match on the deaths of Reginald Beasley and Stewart Lindsey? Stat."

"You'll know as soon as we do."

"Thanks."

Chapter Thirty-four

"Good evening, Mr. Zabala. I am sorry to inform you that Stewart Lindsey died tonight."

"Sorry?"

"Yeah, sorry the mother fucker didn't die much sooner, before all this interest in our operations developed."

"Relax, my friend. Business is simply a matter of minimizing risks and maximizing rewards. Our acceptable risk level is now once again at a tolerable range."

After the band opened their mementos, they quickly dispersed and Jordan was alone in her suite. The enormity of tomorrow night's grand finale weighed heavily on Jordan's mind. She introspectively recounted her performance since the beginning of the tour and was, actually, quite pleased with herself.

"This is to all those whom thought a woman couldn't pull it off," she said mockingly as she raised a glass of chardonnay and toasted herself.

The ring of the telephone interrupted Jordan's self-congratulatory mood.

"God damn it, anyway," Jordan said aloud as she walked to the telephone.

"Hello, Jordan Taylor."

"Jordan, we've got problems."

"Oh?"

"Big, big, problems."

"Go."

"There have been bomb threats called into the arenas at some of the pay-per-view locations. I don't have all the information, but I'm certain of Kansas City and Dallas, I haven't heard anything from Phoenix, Las Vegas, Los Angeles or San Francisco. Yet."

"That's because the fucking wackos in those cities are a couple of hours behind the crazies in the Midwest." .

"Funny, real funny."

"Listen, don't panic. I didn't think I would ever admit it, but I'm grateful now that I've got a contact in the FBI. Hold tight until I contact her. Okay?"

"OK, but be quick, the press is bound to be on the trail any minute, and

122

when this gets out all hell will break loose."

"Good evening, Sloan Dillard."

"Sloan, it's Jordan, Jordan Taylor."

"Oh hello Jordan, whatever could prompt you to contact me at this hour of the evening?"

"Sorry to disturb you, but I just got a call from one of my staffers. She told me that bomb threats have been called into the venues in Kansas City and Dallas simulcasting tomorrow night's concert."

"Word travels quickly in rock circles."

"You already knew?"

"Jordan, we've had all the arenas under virtual lockdown since the finale was announced. One of the advantages of working for an organization with over 11,000 co-workers in cities throughout America is that you can take preventative measures. We've been on high alert. All the arenas are secure and are being patrolled by the agency, by the respective police forces and by canine units. We've been lucky, there hasn't been anything booked at these locations and they're whistle clean. I've already scheduled a press conference for tomorrow at 9:00 to alleviate these fears. I'm not saying that something can't happen tomorrow, but if it does, it will because security will be breached tomorrow, not before. And I'm confidant that won't happen either. Not on my watch."

"How did you know that these bomb threats might occur?"

"Crazy times bring out the worst in people. And these are definitely crazy times."

"But you thought far enough in advance to premeditate the security?"

"Murder is premeditated. Security is pre-planned."

"Speaking of murder, any suspects?"

"One thing we're not short of is suspects. I've never been involved in an investigation that has more motives. Greed. Jealousy. Desperation. And money, money, money. More motives, more suspects. Including you."

"Me?"

"Jordan, until this thing is all sorted out, everyone is a suspect."

"And just think, I was starting to actually like you."

"Just respect me."

"Ok."

"And one other thing. Tomorrow. Be careful. And good.., er, break a leg."

"Thanks, and right back at you."
"Goodnight."
"Goodnight."

Chapter Thirty-five

Becky walked arm-in-arm with Tommy down the street towards the United Center. "This isn't really where you'd want to be walking at night," Tommy said.

"Tommy, anywhere with you is where I want to be. Daytime. Afternoon. Nighttime. Anytime. Anyplace. I love you, Tommy. Always. Please be careful tonight."

"Never worry, Becky, I've got two to take care of now, so I'll be doubly careful," Tommy said gently patting Becky's stomach.

"Thanks, baby."

"Baby! Thanks."

Becky kissed Tommy goodbye at the rear security entrance of the United Center. Though the concert was more than six hours away, the perimeter of the United Center was already a flurry of activity. Three different radio stations were doing live remotes. A rather large armada of trucks featuring antennas, transmitters, receivers, monitors, thick cables, generators, conductors, electronic scanners and circuit breakers were carefully parked in a manner that belied their random appearance.

The merchandise vendors, both authorized and gypsies alike were everywhere. Ticket scalpers, buyers and sellers patrolled the surrounding streets on bicycles and roller blades in search of commercial partners. Gawkers were everywhere and a free-spirited young lady held a large sign on a placard offering, "Loose joints for $3.00, breast flashes for $2.00." A gregarious passer-by inquired when she would be offering the "buy one, get one free special." The friendly exchanges eventually changed when a man offered "two bits to see your fucking tiny two small tits," and then the enterprising young lady told him to "go back to fucking England and find a dentist."

Indeed, to Becky, it appeared that the circus was in town. But only for one more night. Ever.

Inside the United Center, Tommy was subjected to the most invasive security check ever, under the watchful eye of Sloan Dillard and a cadre of agents, police and security. Ace entered just as Tommy was cleared and waited

125

in the security queue.

"Excuse me, Sloan, can you come here and give me a hand?"

"Emergency?"

"No, procedure."

"Just a moment, I want to ensure that the pass list security screen is correct."

Sloan watched intently as Ace was searched and allowed herself a small smile for her indulgence. "Still has got a fine ass," she thought to herself.

The Ungrateful's dressing room resembled a microscopic view of amoeba on a petri dish. People everywhere. Make-up. Wardrobe. Producers. Sound Techs. Light men. Security. More security. Jordan. Hangers on. Moving about. Bumping into each other.

And Ace, Angel, Tommy and Morgan.

The band huddled in a corner and reviewed everything for the night's performance. Not only were they extremely talented musicians, but they also exhibited a maniacal attention to detail.

Angel reviewed the sets and the play list, "We're opening with 'More' and closing with 'Danger,' and in between we'll kick more ass than ever."

"Yo!"

"Right on!"

"Can we not play 'Danger'?" Morgan asked both hopefully and sarcastically.

Chapter Thirty-six

"Not on my watch," Sloan said to herself. "Not on my watch, especially tonight!"

The crowd had swelled outside of the United Center, eagerly awaiting the opening of the doors. The chaos was somewhat controlled and a festive, playful nature enveloped the masses. Inside, Sloan patrolled the vestibule of the venue and calmly, professionally and firmly voiced various instructions through her two-way radio.

Chicago's finest were out in force, both inside and outside of the building. Mounted policemen rode lazily, but alertly throughout the crowd. Both inside and out, canine teams tugged on their leashes and sniffed everywhere. Unfortunately for their harried handlers, the pervasive and distinctly aromatic residue of marijuana set off delirious yelps, but it was explosives, not weed that was the concern this evening.

Inside, two undercover drug detectives were passing the time with a couple of Sloan's FBI agents playing "alphabetical names for weed."

Acapulco Gold.
Banji
Cannabis
Doobage
Erb
Fu
Ganja
Hooch
Illinois Green
Juantia
Kanya
Lumbo
Mariweegee
Nickle
Oregano
Panama Gold
Queen Anne's Lace

Reefer
Shit
Two-toke
Wacky Tabbacky
Yerba
Zib

"There's no fucking term 'zib'!"
"Sure there is, can't help it if you feds are isolated from the streets."
Just then the radio crackled with Sloan's voice, "Everything all right?"
"Sure is, just coordinating procedures and tactics with our gracious hosts."
"Ahem, two things. First, always make sure your radio is not transmitting when you're playing games while on duty. And secondly, I hate to admit it, but 'zib' is a term. They could've gone with 'Zacatecas Purple,' 'zeltoid,' or 'zol,' but Chicago's finest win with 'zib.' Now get back to work, or you'll be playing unemployment bingo next."
The agents doubled checked to ensure their two-way was temporarily out of operation.
"Asshole."
"Bitch."
"Cunt."
"Dillard."

All four broke out into uproarious laughter.

Entry into the United Center promised to be laboriously slow. In addition to passing, single file, through metal detectors, random concertgoers were patted down. Anything that could remotely be considered a weapon was being confiscated, file clippers, scissors, tweezers and even roach clips.
Despite the ominous, oppressive and sometimes invasive security precautions, the mood of the crowd was generally pleasant and cooperative.
"We don't want anyone to become members of 'The Ungrateful Dead,'" said the policeman overseeing the front gates.
Slowly, one-by one, each of the seats of Chicago's United Center was occupied by an enthusiastic, and possibly somewhat apprehensive, Ungrateful fan.
Jordan coordinated last-minute details with the various producers and technical support staff and was pleased that all seemed to be in order.

Sloan received confirmation calls that all was in order from, sequentially, Kansas City, Dallas, Phoenix, Las Vegas, Los Angeles and San Francisco.

The house announcer instructed the audience that no video, audio or pictorial recording of tonight's concert was permitted.

Backstage, Ace, Angel, Tommy, and Morgan gathered for one last time and hugged each other.

"Let's rock and roll!"

Spotlights panned the audience, and electricity shot through the crowd as the curtain rose to a thunderous applause.

"Not on my watch!" Sloan repeated to herself.

Chapter Thirty-seven

The flight from Tokyo had been uneventful. Despite being airborne for most of the last forty hours, Dr. Chino leisurely emerged from the plane and calmly made his way to the customs station at O'Hare, secure that the customs officials would neither know him as Dr. Chino nor recognize him. Not that it really mattered. What mattered was that everyone thought that he was in Tokyo. What really mattered was that Dr. Chino had some unfinished business to attend to. Dr. Chino glanced at his watch. "With any luck," he thought, "I should be able to clear customs and get to the United Center for the second half of the concert. Ain't life grand?"

Becky glanced at the clock on the hotel nightstand and saw that it was nearly 8:00 PM. The flickering of the message light caught Becky's attention and piqued her interest. She punched the appropriate phone button and heard the recorded introduction, "Meridian Message service, you have three messages. Message # 1, recorded today at 4:45 pm... 'Hi Beck, it's Jake. Josh and I were heading back to Oregon, but we thought we'd stop in Chicago and catch the concert. Hope to hook up with you later. Love.'...Message #2, recorded today at 5:02 pm... 'Hi Tommy, it's Mom. I just wanted to wish you good luck tonight. And please, be careful. I love you. Bye.'... Message #3, recorded today at 5:35 pm. 'Hi Tommy, it's Kelly. Tonight. Maybe?'"

The flow of boiling blood rushed into Becky's cheeks, flushing them with a crimson tinge. Becky threw the phone on the bed as the recording resumed, "There are no further messages. To save this message, press 1, to delete it, press 2." By the time the recording reached, "to hear this message again, press 3," Becky was already on her way to the United Center.

The glare of the spotlight temporarily blinded Angel, but the roar of the crowd energized her. "Hello Chicago!" she shouted enthusiastically. For the following split second, Angel was pissed at herself. "Lame ass greeting," she thought, "Trite and the greeting used by every sorry-ass rock band. Ever."

Angel's introspection was interrupted by Tommy's shout-out of, "Hello Windy City!"

And Morgan's, "Hello, World!"

And Ace's ironic, "Hello... and goodbye." By the time Ace got to, "I don't know why you say hello, I say goodbye," the crowd was standing and cheering louder than any post-gig ovation the band had ever witnessed.

The chords started to gently reverberate, the crowd's noise retreated into a din of excitement and Angel said, "Tonight is for you. Enjoy. And thanks for the ride."

As the band cranked up the opening of *More*, the crowd's noise returned to its previously deafening decibel level. The spotlights swirled and focused on Morgan and she reveled in the mingling adrenalin. For the first time in way too long, Morgan remembered just how much fun it was to be performing. "Give 'em what they want, girl," Morgan said to herself, and she slyly, demurely and ever so sexily stroked the bow of her violin. And as she drew back the bow, Morgan was faintly aware of her breasts tingling and nipples tightening beneath her silky white halter-top.

Tommy focused intently on his guitar strings as if they were suddenly going to either disappear or mysteriously change. Tommy had never felt more charged or more ready. Tonight, of all nights, was going to be his night. And Tommy was confident that this was going to be the performance of his life. But it was the performance after the gig Tommy was concerned with.

Ace sat erectly and proudly behind his drums. Already, sweat glistened from his shirtless body and the lights illuminated his glistening, muscled frame. Gently tapping the skins, Ace laid a beat down that was Morgan's cue. As she coaxed the first beautiful notes from her violin, the spotlight focused on Angel and the crowd's cheers cascaded as the opening stanza of *More* reverberated throughout the United Center.

Before the final notes of *More* echoed through the arena, all 20,000 fans knew they were witnessing something truly special. Over 100,000 other fans watching on pay-per-view in concert halls across the United States shared those sentiments.

FBI special agent Sloan Dillard nervously paced in the security center. Watching intently the numerous television screens displaying the feeds from cameras strategically located throughout the United Center, Sloan fought the losing battle of not getting caught up in the excitement and emotion sweeping the entire complex.

For a brief moment, Sloan's thoughts subconsciously drifted back to her first live concert when she saw the Bangles. Sloan snapped back to reality as she realized her head was moving from screen to screen with a strange gyration similar to the Bangles' movements accompanying their hit song *Walk Like an Egyptian*. She reminded herself she was in a new millennium and not back in the mid-eighties.

Sloan watched the stage door screen intently as she noticed what appeared to be a brief commotion at the pass list entrance. Though the screen was somewhat grainy, Sloan recognized Becky as she impatiently endured the mandatory pre-entry pat-down and security check.

Jordan had witnessed thousands of live performances before. From her early days as an intern on, Jordan had been, first and foremost, a fan. She loved music. She especially loved live music. Any kind. The energy was captivating and, for Jordan, almost addictive. Never, ever could Jordan remember a performance that even closely matched tonight's energy and excitement. Despite a myriad of responsibilities – coordinating the live feeds, supervising the backstage entourage, monitoring the merch people, barking instruction into her two-way, Jordan found herself caught up in the performance. Maybe it was the music. Maybe it was the energy. Maybe it was the looming finality. Maybe it was her close personal feelings for the band – especially Angel. Maybe it was her professional vindication. Whatever it was, it was powerful. And Jordan vowed not to succumb to the emotional forces that powerfully tugged at her and were causing her "balls of brass" to seemingly and appreciably soften.

John Mercedes had been to many concerts before, but never one like this. John caught himself smiling when he glanced over at his companion feebly and unsuccessfully attempting to whistle through generously spaced teeth.

Kelly Puccini was standing along with the other 20,000 wildly cheering enthusiasts. But Kelly wasn't clapping. That was impossible because her hand tightly clenched Paddy's.

It's certainly an unpopular word with the general public, but "profiling" was an acceptable, and sometimes necessary practice in the security industry. Though Sloan had not given any indication of profiling characteristics, the front gate security force was attuned to trusting their instincts when conducting the pre-entrance checks.

And nothing was suspected when a middle-aged Japanese gentleman entered the United Center well past the rise of the opening curtain. Dr. Chino proceeded, unimpeded, through the security screen and into the arena. Any effects of jet lag were immediately blasted away as the sound, energy and movement of the crowd enveloped him. Dr. Chino moved as close as he could to the stage, and the sight of Morgan made his heart quicken. When the majority of the thousands of men in the audience saw beauty, sensuality and sexuality in Morgan, Dr. Chino only saw innocence. And a trace of vulnerability. It was that vulnerability that Dr. Chino was concerned with.

For three solid hours The Ungrateful mesmerized the audience. Each song filled with more energy and passion than the previous. After the third curtain call, the band fired up the familiar opening of *Danger* and the crowd was near delirious with excitement, anticipation and appreciation.

"They're making Springsteen look like a short hitter!" Jordan heard over the crackling of her two-way.

Sloan double and then triple checked to ensure that all of her forces were mobilized. "They're just about done. Cross check and all call." Sloan chuckled silently as her flight attendant imitation went unappreciated and unnoticed to all but herself. "Ah the curse of superior intellect and creativity," she mused self-indulgently.

The ending was unscripted. Unanticipated. And unimaginable. Angel came back out for an unscheduled curtain call. To her side appeared Tommy. Then Ace. Then Morgan. The crowd was wild with excitement. And the security threatened not only to bend, but also to break as 20,000 fans pressed forward to the stage.

"Fuck," Sloan thought, before she could remind herself that she didn't swear. "Secure the stage. Secure the stage!" she barked into the walkie-talkie. "Jordan, Jordan. Come in. Jordan. What the hell's going on?"

"Relax, your guess is as good as mine, but rest assured, it's all good," Jordan replied. "And watch your language. We're on an open frequency and you might just disturb these virgin ears."

"My aching ass!" Sloan thought to herself.

Angel stood center stage, flanked by the rest. Holding hands, without speaking a word, their a capella voices silenced the crowd and resonated in the ears and souls of the fans as the sang John Lennon's *Imagine*:

Imagine there's no heaven
It's easy if you try
No hell below us
Above us only sky
Imagine all the people
Living for today

Imagine there's no countries
It isn't hard to do
Nothing to kill or die for
And no religion too
Imagine all the people
Living life in peace

You may say that we're dreamers
But we're not the only ones
I hope someday you'll join us
And the world will be one

Imagine no possessions
I wonder if you can
No need for greed or hunger
A brotherhood of man
Imagine all the people
Sharing all the world

You may say that we're dreamers
But we're not the only ones
I hope someday you'll join us
And the world will live as one.

On stage, the band embraced. Walking backward, slowly, they waved goodbye to an emotional crowd. The curtain dropped ceremoniously, one last time. As the house lights came on, the parting peace and serenity was shattered by the sounds of two gunshots, screaming and then all out mayhem.

Chapter Thirty-eight

The din of the crowd's frantic, panicked screams made the urgent voices coming from Sloan's walkie-talkie inaudible. The only sounds she could really understand were the self-mocking, haunting and tortuous "Not on my watch!" refrain that her mind incessantly replayed.

"Secure all exits, secure all exits!" Sloan ordered. But it was too late.

In preparation of the concert's end, all doors had been opened in hopes of facilitating the orderly egress of nearly 20,000 fans.

The security staff was helpless to stem the flow of humanity, that, if impeded had the real potential to result in a human stampede.

Sloan was left with no other option than to immediately rescind her order and watch helplessly as a mass murderer faded anonymously away.

The shrill wailing of sirens pierced the Chicago night and gave Sloan some semblance of comfort that law and order still existed.

In front of the now empty stage, EMTs worked feverishly on two young ladies, each fighting a valiant, but futile battle with the clutches of death. Blood was everywhere, resulting from two separate but expertly placed gunshots, each leaving the victims with only a hope for a quick death. And death did come quickly. The EMTs draped the victims, readied them for the body bags and the morgue, while the homicide detectives began their painstaking search for clues.

Backstage, Angel and Morgan embraced each other and sobbed uncontrollably. Tommy stared, trance-like into the distance and Ace paced nervously.

Jordan wasn't quite sure what the appropriate action was in a situation like this; she only knew that some action was required. Jordan quietly asked that everyone leave, with the exception of the band. As the door closed, the five remaining people looked hopelessly at each other with distant eyes searching for reasons that didn't exist.

For the first time in only God knew how long, Jordan knelt down, bowed her head and prayed out loud. Jordan didn't know how to pray even silently, but somehow the words came straight from her soul and touched the hearts of the band. "God, please take care of those who were shot tonight. Please love their families and comfort them. And please God, Help. Help us all."

Five people stood in a circle, embraced tightly and sobbed. Angel wiped away the tears streaming from her eyes and said simply; "I'm so sorry. I love you all so much. I'm going to miss each and every one of you, but I'm never gonna miss this scene. I love you. Thank you. Goodbye."

Angel walked through the door and headed to her limo for the short ride back to the hotel.

Tommy, Ace and Morgan watched her walk away and realized that Angel had said everything that needed to be said. Without a further word, The Ungrateful was no more.

Jordan prayed once more, this time silently.

Jordan's silence was interrupted by Sloan's voice, "Excuse me, but I need your help. Now." The command was firm, but not overbearing, and considering the circumstance, appropriate.

"Anything you need."

"I need the video tapes of tonight's concert. All cameras. All angles. The simulcast may be the only clue we've got to work with."

Jordan relayed the instructions as Sloan made arrangements for the video techs from the agency to begin the review process.

Chapter Thirty-nine

Dr. Chino stood motionless and unnoticed behind the United Center and smiled with relief as Morgan emerged from the building. Only now, and for the first time in days, could Dr. Chino allow himself the pleasure of sleep. "And what a pleasure it will be," Dr. Chino thought.

Tommy opened the door of the hotel room and Becky rushed to greet him. Hugging him tightly, Becky sobbed, "Tommy, I'm so glad your safe. With me. I saw it on the news. It's so terrible."
"I want to go," Tommy said.
"Where?"
"Home."
"When?"
"Now."
Kelly Puccini was startled when she answered the loud rapping on the door of her house to find Tommy and Becky on her front porch at 3:15 am. Tommy was even more startled to see Paddy O'Keane lumber down the stairs in his boxers.

John Mercedes sat in the dark room with the blue haze of cigarette smoke circling his head. John spoke quietly and unemotionally into the telephone, "Two gunshots, two deaths, instantaneously." In the background, the gapped toothed Englishman ferociously tapped on his keyboard.

It had been quite some time since Morgan had slept in her apartment in Evanston, and it sure felt good to be home. Not only that, it just felt good. Ace's body rhythmically moved in unison with hers, and the fear, emotion and sadness of the last few days gave way to waves of passionate pleasure. Both Morgan and Ace desperately needed not to be alone tonight. They needed someone to hold. To love and be loved. The intense physical pleasure was a much appreciated side benefit to a more basic human need.

"Remember how this all started?" Morgan asked Ace.

"Soldier Field. Score once, and the fans give me a standing 'O.' Score two more times and now it's you with the big 'O', only you're not standing."

Ace replied laughing heartedly. "God this feels good," Ace proclaimed.

"The sex?"

"No baby, the laughter," said Ace as he lovingly stroked Morgan's hair and gently kissed her on the cheek.

The lobby of the Knickerbocker Hotel was a sea of human madness. Reporters were everywhere, reporters from newspapers, magazines, tabloids, local television stations, cable news outlets and the national networks. The normal cadre of The Ungrateful groupies swelled with each moment, and the gawkers and curiosity seekers added to the overflow crowd. Hotel security and local police collaborated to cordon off an area and, at least, the departing guests could check out and go about their normal business. Not that there was anything normal about today.

Sloan distinctly remembered her departing instructions to each member of the band, crew and entourage, "...and nobody leaves town without receiving my express written permission."

Unfortunately for Sloan, the band wasn't instructed to stay at the hotel, and now she added the mystery of their local whereabouts to her growing list of perplexities.

Sloan had arranged a 9:00 am press conference and scheduled it for a ballroom in the Knickerbocker.

When she entered the room, the bright television lights and the eruption of photographers and flashes temporarily blinded her.

Sloan proceeded directly to the podium with a dispatch that belied her shaken confidence. Sloan slowly sipped water, cleared her throat and turned on the microphone.

"Ladies and gentlemen, I am FBI Special Agent Sloan Dillard and I am the agent in charge and responsible for coordinating the activities of collaborating law enforcement organizations – both domestically and abroad – as we seek to identify and apprehend the individual or individuals responsible for the recent deaths associated with The Ungrateful concerts.

"First and foremost, we would like to express our deepest condolences to the families and loved ones of the victims. Our prayers are with them, and we wish them God's love and strength.

"Secondly, I want to assure you that the FBI and local enforcement agencies are doing everything in their power to assure the public safety. We are convinced that these abhorrent actions are directly related to The Ungrateful tour, and there is no reason for the general public to be concerned for their personal welfare. I cannot stress the preceding statement strongly enough. There is no danger to the general public.

"Thirdly, I urge any of last night's concert-goers who saw anything even remotely out of the ordinary to immediately contact authorities." The irony of the 'even remotely out of the ordinary' remark wasn't lost on Sloan as she considered last evening totally surreal. "We have established a hotline to immediately access the investigators. The number is 1-888-369-4410. Once again, the number is 1-888-369-4410. We urge anyone in attendance last evening to think carefully and recollect. Last night, two innocent young women were murdered in cold blood and there were more than 20,000 potential witnesses. If you saw anything, please come forward. You have a civic duty and a duty to humanity." Sloan cringed when those words emerged as she thought she was sounding preachy and slightly condescending.

"And finally," Sloan concluded, "Last night's concert was recorded by sixteen different cameras. Because of the interest in The Ungrateful and the simulcast, cameras were interspersed throughout the United Center. The tapes from these cameras are being analyzed as we speak by FBI video technicians. I am extremely confident that we will emerge from this process with not only strong leads but with conclusive and indisputable visual evidence that will lead to the eventual conviction of the assailant.

"Thank you very much, because of the sensitive nature of the investigation, I will not be entertaining any questions. Thank you for you attention, support and understanding."

Sloan left the podium with the same slight confident swagger with which she entered, only this time she wasn't faking it. Reporters feebly shouted questions at Sloan, knowing in advance the futility of their efforts.

Chapter Forty

Miguel Zabala watched the satellite coverage of the press conference with rapt attention. Miguel was simultaneously keenly disappointed and greatly relieved that Sloan did not mention suspects or even allude to a short list. "Not an all-bad piece of fine American ass," Miguel thought to himself as he watched Sloan control the crowd. "But remember 'business first, pleasure always,'" Miguel reminded himself as he recited his unwritten, personal mission statement.

The recent murders had made things uncommonly complicated for Miguel and the attendant attention was the antithesis of his business anonymity model. Though death sometimes accompanied the trafficking of drugs, Miguel prided himself on his visionary approach to commerce, and murder and mayhem were vestiges of an archaic and barbaric past and certain to ratchet up the pressure another notch or two.

But Miguel was confident that he could handle the pressure. Hell, Miguel was confident that he could handle anything. And now, his confidence would only be enhanced as he snorted the finely granulated white powder and experienced a rush of euphoric pleasure.

Miguel thoroughly analyzed all aspects of the situation and concluded that the most efficient solution would require his personal intervention. Though it was not his usual custom to become personally involved, Miguel realized that the true measure of an executive's mettle was his ability to positively impact outcomes under difficult circumstances. And these were undoubtedly difficult circumstances.

Miguel prepared to immediately leave for Chicago.

Despite being proclaimed as "one of the world's most beautiful women" and the pervasive notoriety The Ungrateful was experiencing, Angel walked, unnoticed, down the ever-busy State Street. Wearing a black Nike baseball cap with her hair pulled back into a ponytail and threaded through the back, dark sunglasses, jeans, running shoes and an oversized Gap hooded sweatshirt, Angel was innocuous and seemingly invisible to the busy passers-by.

Ducking into Starbucks, Angel patiently waited in line as the ever friendly and efficient staff quickly moved from one caffeine fix to the next.

"Venti coffee, please."

"Room for cream?"

"Yes, please."

Angel faded into the background and waited patiently for Jordan to arrive. The only hint of Angel's status was the $20 bill in the tip jar, but, of course, nobody knew who the generous benefactor was.

Jordan arrived and proceeded to the counter and sighed, "Life is simply too short to tolerate bad coffee. How about a grande double mocha? Please."

Jordan wrapped the sleeve around the cup and clutched it as she saw Angel and smiled brightly.

"Hi there! How goes it?"

"As well as can be expected. And you?"

"Same."

"What's up?"

"Jordan, the band made a decision recently, only last night we never got to talk. You see, the problem is that only three of us are in on this and we don't want to alienate anyone."

"Go on, and relax."

"Jordan, neither Ace, Morgan nor I want the money from the tour. We want to donate it to the families of the victims. I made a little before. It's enough to tide me over until I go solo. Ace has got his soccer contract, and Morgan's got more modeling gigs lined up than there are pervs who downloaded her. We want to do this. Only thing is, we don't want anyone to know. And we don't want to hurt Tommy. It's just that Tommy's in a much different position. You know, with Becky. And his mom. And there's still guys calling him about his dad. See, once this all blows over, Ace and Morgan and I can get back in the cash real quick. But Tommy, Tommy's got all sorts of other issues to deal with.

"So can you help us Jordan? Help us help those who got killed because of us. But don't let anyone know it's us. And don't let anyone know Tommy's not part of it. Please don't make Tommy feel any worse than he already does."

"You're so special, Angel. You know you can count on me. I'll get it done. And Angel. Thank you. Thank you so much."

"For what?"

"For just being you."

"Jordan, one other thing."

"Go on."

"I slept over at my new old man's last night."

From past experiences, Jordan knew that, when she felt the time was right, Angel would fill her in on the necessary details. Jordan also knew that pressing for more information would be fruitless so she simply asked, "Was it all right?"

"Yeah, definitely."

Chapter Forty-one

Sloan sat in the mini theater, surrounded by video technicians, investigators and other agents. Sloan had participated in these sessions before, but this time, she was absolutely amazed. Maybe it was because of her involvement in the proceedings, maybe it was because of the technical advances the computer allowed, maybe it was the surprising discoveries, and maybe it was just the specter of last evening's events. Half-filled Styrofoam cups littered the room that would normally have challenged Sloan's fustidiousness and were joined by littered fast food wrappers. As the techs manipulated the images on the screen, zooming and constantly enlarging the image, Sloan watched in amazement.

Sloan certainly didn't consider herself a prude. Though she was monitoring screens the previous night, she was continuously shocked at what had escaped her watchful eyes. Since the cameras had been rolling since the opening of the doors, Sloan was viewing much of the raw footage for the first time. Conservatively, Sloan estimated that there were at least 50 women who flashed their breasts, and attributed the capture of those images to a resourceful cameraman. "Definitely a cameraman," Sloan thought. Though the image was grainy, the consensus amongst the viewers was that the two people wildly gyrating in the midst of the dancing were, in fact, copulating. "And the concert was just starting," someone wondered aloud if an encore performance occurred.

A different camera angle reviewed the entry of the fans. "Stop, freeze it right there!" Sloan ordered. "Now go in as close as you can. Enlarge. Enlarge. There. Right there. That's Mickey Delaney, the lead singer of The CDs. Wonder why he wasn't on the pass list? And coming all by himself."

The camera continued to show the faces of thousands of anonymous strangers while Sloan's mind raced with various postulations. Most involving Mickey Delaney.

The group continued to view the footage from various lobby cameras when Sloan again blurted, "Hold it there. Zoom. Zoom again. Freeze." The images of Jake and Josh Rose filled the screen and again Sloan's mind raced back to her spreadsheet and their presence at most of the tour's previous venues.

"The boys from narcotics would have a field day with these tapes," Sloan observed, as the images of numerous drug transactions were replayed on the screen. "Never knew all this could be happening" as the camera panned in on two people of indeterminable sex passionately kissing and groping.

Towards the front of the stage, the camera focused on a young woman who wearing a colorful cloth fabric loosely wrapped around her body, alternated kissing the man to her right and the woman on her left. "Quite a scene," someone observed and then added, "I'm so out-of-touch with what's happening today. Hell, I don't even know if that's a 'sarong' or a 'sari' she's wearing."

"I think it's a sarong," blurted Sloan, "But if I'm so wrong, I'm so sorry." The ensemble was amazed at Sloan's rare attempt at humor and laughed appreciably. Sloan was quite impressed with her spontaneous cleverness and welcomed the momentary relief from the intense pressure.

The painstaking review of each of the tape from each of the cameras continued. The front lobby security feed proved to be both the most enlightening and the most confusing. One by one, suspects on Sloan's original short list were confirmed to be in attendance: Paddy O'Keane, Kelly Puccini, and John Mercedes. Sloan made a mental list of the original suspects not confirmed: "The senior Mr. Puccini, Stewart Lindsey and Reggie Beasley all have legitimate alibis," noted Sloan sarcastically. "We know that the band was in attendance, so only Dr. Chino and Becky haven't been verified by the front entrance cameras. But if Becky came, she would have come through the rear pass list entrance." No sooner had Sloan finished the sentence when she shouted, "Freeze it." The camera panned in on a middle-aged gentleman. "Well I'll be god-damned." Sloan enthusiastically exclaimed, temporarily forgetting again that she didn't curse, "But lookee here. If that isn't our good friend Dr. Chino."

Intuitively, Sloan found the attendance of the Rose boys the most problematic, the attendance of Mickey Delaney the most troubling and the image of Dr. Chino the most unnerving. But Sloan had been thoroughly trained to augment her intuition with hard facts, and the laborious discovery process continued.

Chapter Forty-two

Morgan opened her eyes and gradually saw the bright sunlight streaming into her bedroom. She was surprised by the sun's warmth and even more surprised when she realized that her head was resting on Ace's chest and her naked body wrapped protectively in his powerful arms.

Tommy awoke in his bedroom and looked across the room at the matching twin bed and saw Becky still sound asleep with her mouth agape. Tommy was annoyed by the sun's light and infuriated when he heard Paddy's voice in the adjoining master bedroom. "I can't believe my mother's fucking shacking up," Tommy thought and he struggled to return to sleep's peace. But sleep wouldn't come back to Tommy and he couldn't erase the weird images of his mother that tormented his thoughts.

John Mercedes awoke to the sound of the tapping on the keyboard. Though the sun was completely blocked by the hotel's heavy drapes, the green light of the computer screen illuminated the room. "You'd think after all these years, they'd at least pay for separate rooms," John thought to himself as he wiped the sleep from his eyes and prepared for what promised to be an event filled day.

"Morning," John murmured.

"Top of the morning to you, governor."

From the adjoining suite, John heard stirring and said loudly, "Morning dear."

"Morning Dad," Angel replied, as the gap-toothed Englishman spewed coffee all over his monitor.

For approximately the hundredth time, Angel carefully removed the letter that mysteriously appeared a short time ago and changed her life forever – both her past and her future. Though, rationally, Angel knew that it was impossible to alter history, the letter had significantly changed her past, empirically, at least – and promised Angel a different, and better, world of tomorrows. With eyes moist in anticipation of another happy filtering of her early years, Angel read, again:

Dear Angel,

Twenty-two years ago, I was a young lieutenant in England's Royal Air Force. As part of a United Nation's sponsored seminar for various NATO nations, I traveled to New York. While I was there, I met, and fell in love, with a beautiful woman with wavy, jet black hair, fire in her eyes and a smile that could illuminate the darkest skies. On my last night in New York, we celebrated our relationship, pledged our undying faithfulness and – you can guess the rest.

Upon my return to England, I made plans to arrange her visit to the United Kingdom and begin the rest of our lives together. But all of my letters were returned – unopened, my calls never answered. For whatever the reason, she shut me out of her life forever.

Four months ago, I arrived in the United States as part of an international assignment. As a part of my job, it was necessary for me to check on the backgrounds of the members of the CDs and The Ungrateful. There was something mysterious and unexplained in your history and I immersed myself in filling in the blanks of your childhood. Though you have no idea what I do professionally, let's just say that I have access to some sophisticated resources unavailable to the average person – and tests that I surreptitiously ran have confirmed that we share DNA and that I am your biological father.

I've been around since the beginning of the tour – first to follow someone, and something, else – and lately to watch over you, to protect you, and hopefully, meet you and begin to know you.

It would be trite for me to apologize – but I'm so sorry for all that you've been through and all that you (and we) missed.

You have every right to tear this letter up and never see or speak to me – and I'll respect your wishes. It's just that now that I know that I'm your father, I'd like to be your dad too, and also your friend.

Whatever you decide, I'm so very proud of you.

Be strong. Be happy. Be safe. And please, be forgiving.

Love,

John Mercedes (Dad)

Chapter Forty-three

It was nearing 7:30 in the morning and Sloan and her crew had reconvened after some much-needed sleep. They had been consistently putting in eighteen hours days and had watched the tapes for almost seven consecutive hours yesterday. "If nothing else," Sloan thought, "I'm getting to be quite an expert on what to expect at rock concerts." The video technicians had spliced the tapes from all of the different cameras, and sequentially looped them together to view the final moments before the previous evening's pandemonium broke loose.

Sloan played back in her mind's eye the sequences which unfolded preceding the shooting: the playing of *Danger*, the applause, the encores, the band appearing back on stage, the singing of *Imagine*, the curtain dropping, the house lights rising, the sounds of gunfire shattering the serenity, the screams and then more screams.

Watching all of this unfold on video was eerily surreal for Sloan until the ending of *Imagine* was played back in super-slow motion. Sloan watched as the video technician froze the frames, which provided the first confirmed glimpse of the killer.

Directly in front of the stage where masses of fans had gathered, swayed, danced, and boogied, a hand could be clearly seen pointing a gun at the head of one of the unsuspecting victims – a hand belonging to a person wearing a New York Yankees baseball cap backwards.

Despite the best efforts of the techs, this was the only shot identifying the killer.

"The curtain dropped, the house lights came up, and that was supposedly it, so most of the cameramen called it off for the night. After the gunshots, nearly everyone was running for cover, so the automatic security feeds are all that we have to go on, and there's a couple of seconds when they're down as they refocus and adjust to the lights," explained the tech.

"A backwards New York Yankees hat? You're telling me that with sixteen cameras and 20,000 fans that's the only hard evidence we have? A fucking backwards Yankees cap!" Sloan said incredulously, forgetting again that she didn't use that type of language.

Chapter Forty-four

Jordan awoke in her suite in the Knickerbocker Hotel and immediately went to work. For Jordan, the work was a catharsis and allowed her to immerse her Type A personality in tasks that temporarily obliterated the events surrounding The Ungrateful "Back in the saddle again," Jordan thought to herself as she reviewed the accumulation of over seventy-five e-mails flagged either "urgent" or "high importance."

Jordan's perspective had changed appreciably over the last few days, and what was urgent on Wednesday seemed innocuous and unimportant today.

Jordan's first e-mail correspondence was to the tour's accountant requesting a copy of the financial statements from each of the respective performances. Jordan followed that e-mail up with a query to the chief financial officer at headquarters. Jordan knew that finance results of each of the performance would have to be verified prior to any disbursement of funds. Though partial disbursements could be made before an audit of the books was completed, Jordan was interested in a final resolution as quickly as possible.

Jordan's experience led her to believe that the entire financial review process should be relatively uncomplicated, and since the dollars were to be distributed evenly amongst the performers, a unanimous assent of the band prior to distribution was a virtual certainty.

Having set the financial ball rolling, Jordan's next order of business was to verify with each of the simulcasting venues their gross receipts.

John Mercedes nodded uncomfortably and grimaced as he listened to the demanding voice on the other end of the telephone. On the extension in the adjoining room, the gap-toothed Englishman listened intently.

John's protestation's of, "It's too soon, It's too fucking soon," fell upon deaf ears and he heard the words he dreaded, "Please contact the American authorities and fully disclose your activities and findings."

"But, but,"

"But nothing, do as you're instructed and all will work out."

John slammed the phone down, momentarily cleared his head, and dialed the phone.

"Good morning, FBI Special Agent Sloan Dillard."

"Good morning, Agent Dillard. This is Scotland Yard Investigator John Mercedes. My partner and I have been undercover following the activities surrounding The Ungrateful tour and we would like to meet with you to discuss our investigation and what we have uncovered."

Sloan was taken aback and more than miffed. More than chagrined. She was fucking pissed off.

Temporarily casting aside her impenetrable shield of professionalism, Sloan blurted, "You have the audacity to tell me that you have been following this murderer in a professional capacity, and you are just now coming forward? Your inactions may have directly contributed to the deaths of innocent victims. I don't know how you sleep at night or look yourself in the mirror."

Sloan was temporarily embarrassed for her lack of professionalism, but the outburst felt damn good.

"Inspector Mercedes," Sloan continued, "Normally I would apologize for my lack of professionalism, but your egregious lack of decorum, consideration and cooperation is unforgivable. Especially in light of the continuing murders."

"I can certainly understand and empathize with your feelings, Agent Dillard, but I am confident that after we meet you will understand why we did what we did."

"I am not certain that I'll ever understand what you did, Inspector Mercedes, but I will attempt to put my personal feelings of contempt behind until this case is solved. I will meet you today at 12:30 PM in the Chicago office."

"See you then."

"Right."

John Mercedes boldly extended a hand while saying, "It is my pleasure to meet you, Agent Dillard."

Sloan was temporarily intrigued by his deep-set brown eyes, dark tan and jet-black hair, thinking, "This guy looks more like Pierce Bronson, than Pierce himself – if it weren't for his delightfully wicked hint of Antonio Banderas." Sloan caught herself and refocused on her professional disdain, but the electricity, though not pulsating, was slightly surging through her body.

"Agent Dillard,"

"Sloan, please."

"Sloan, I'd like to formally introduce my partner, Inspector Kevin Pace."

"Nice to meet you, Mr. Spacey," Sloan replied.

"Pace, not Spacey, Pace."

"I'm quite sorry, Mr. Pace," Sloan muttered, slightly cursing the pneumonic memory trick that forced her to focus on the prodigious gap between Mr. Pace's teeth and think 'Kevin Spacey.'

"Shall we commence?" John Mercedes inquired.

"Shall we commence?" Sloan thought to herself. "He's quite the pompous ass."

"Yes, let's begin," Sloan said as she led them down the hall to the conference room.

The field office of the Chicago division of the Federal Bureau of Investigation is not quite as luxuriously appointed as the Bureau's Washington headquarters. Instead of reclining leather chairs surrounding a glass covered deep cherry-wood table, Sloan, John and Kevin sat in brightly colored, plastic molded chairs and strategically positioned themselves around a cheaply laminated, unsteady table.

John cleared his throat and started, "First of all, please accept my apologies for any difficulties this may have caused you. But I assure you, there is nothing that we know, saw or did in any way that could have contributed to the tragedy that unfolded. The truth be known, it will indeed be a tragedy if our efforts over the last years are wasted and the reign of terror of Miguel Zabala continues.

"For quite some time, we have known that Miguel Zabala is the head of a global drug cartel. Based in Caracas, Venezuela, Miguel's empire reaches all corners of the globe."

Sloan thought to herself, silently, "The globe doesn't have corners." Politely, Sloan didn't interrupt, and John continued.

"Miguel considers himself a modern business man, a conglomerate if you will. The effects of his of vast empire are many, and his strategic vision is worldwide dominance of the vice industry. In Europe, Miguel is involved in drugs, gambling, liquor, and is funding Irish insurgents as a precursor to his full-fledged entry into the Emerald Island. In the Far East, Miguel's operations are focused on the distribution of drugs and pornography. I doubt, Sloan, that you regularly surf the net for Japanese porn, but if you were so inclined, you would touch one of the many tentacles of Miguel Zabala.

"In South America, Miguel is the drug business. He has totally integrated the drug supply chain and runs the operation based upon the underlying business principles of the modern American corporation – employee empowerment, strategic orientation, tactical implementation, bottom line focus, team building, equity enhancement, continuous improvement, total quality management – he's even rumored to be implementing something called 'Six Sigma.'

"And once again, Sloan, I doubt if you partake, but if you ever utilized the services of a prostitute in South America, you would unwittingly be adding to the corporate coffers of Miguel Zabala."

"Thanks, for the info, John, but I don't think *that* will be the deterrent." Sloan chuckled.

"And in the United States, Miguel's empire is burgeoning. Of course there is the drug trafficking, but also gambling, liquor wholesaling, pornography – kind of an international smorgasbord of sin and corruption.

"It's almost eerie how this came together, and how none of it has come together yet, either.

"Scotland Yard has been monitoring the activities of Paddy O'Keane since the day the iron bars slammed behind him. Paddy has been instrumental in keeping alive the network of insurgents who perpetuate a battle, which rightfully should have died many years ago. Upon Paddy's release, Inspector Pace was assigned to monitor his activities. We have reason to believe that Miguel Zabala is laundering money through Irish insurgents."

While he continued to talk, Sloan found herself in the uncomfortable position of becoming mesmerized, both personally and professionally, by the man she found loathsomely deceitful not too long ago. There was just something about John – maybe it was his Bond-like international aura, maybe it was the ease from which he had extracted himself from the vice-like grip of Sloan's disdain, maybe it was his increasingly obvious professional expertise – whatever it was, it had connected with Sloan in a way she hadn't even remotely considered possible.

John continued, "While Inspector Pace was monitoring Paddy, I myself was working other aspects of Miguel's investigation. For some time, we have known that Stewart Lindsey was a mule for Miguel. We just couldn't prove it conclusively. Stewart led us to Ace. Though we could have arrived at the same place from a variety of different directions, because we knew that Miguel was the connecting link for the methamphetamines that Dr. Chino was utilizing in his diet pills. We also believe that Miguel was behind the mob that Thomas Puccini was unfortunately indebted to.

"So, Sloan, we were pursuing the same suspects you were investigating, only from a different angle. It is unfortunate, but because of Ace, Tommy and Morgan, Miguel Zabala definitely had a vested interest in The Ungrateful. And as you may or may not know, I am the biological father of Angel. At least I think I am."

Sloan stared intently at John Mercedes and tried to sort everything out. The task for even Sloan's keen mind was complicated by the intricately woven tapestry of overlapping relationships.

And Sloan, try as she might, couldn't quite figure out John Mercedes. Hell, she couldn't even begin. Sloan thought of Winston Churchill's famous quote of "an enigma wrapped in a riddle inside a mystery," and the similarities to John Mercedes.

Sloan had only known him for less than an hour, yet she was intrigued. He was brash, he was sensitive. He was overbearing, he was considerate. He was good looking – no he was stunningly handsome. He was nearly fifteen years older than Sloan. And it was becoming increasingly apparent to Sloan that he was the consummate professional with an unwavering commitment to excellence. Kind of like herself.

Sloan's pensive thoughts were interrupted when her administrative assistant buzzed in to the conference room on the speakerphone.

"Excuse me, Sloan, there is a call for you on line two."

"Please inform the caller that I am in a meeting and will return the call shortly."

"I already did. He insists on speaking with you immediately."

"Do you know who it is?"

"Yes. Dr. Fujimaro Chino."

"Tell Dr. Chino I will be right with him."

FBI Special Agent Sloan Dillard, and Scotland Yard Inspectors John Mercedes and Kevin Pace exchanged quizzical glances, and Sloan alerted the techs in the adjacent room that she wanted a trace on the call.

"Do you want us to leave?" John inquired."

"No, it's well past the time when we should have been collaborating. Let's work together from now on. OK?"

"Agreed," John replied, partly because he wanted to – partly because he had been ordered to earlier in the day – and partly because Sloan Dillard had gently awakened something within him that had been slumbering deeply for many, many years.

Dr. Chino waited patiently and knew that the FBI was feverishly working behind the scenes to trace his call. It mattered not to him. What mattered was

Morgan Chino. And Miguel Zabala. And vindication. And revenge.

"Good afternoon, this is FBI Special Agent Sloan Dillard."

"Agent Dillard, this is Dr. Fujimaro Chino. I realize that there is presently a warrant out for my arrest. I am calling to tell you that I intend to cooperate fully with the authorities and will shortly surrender myself. However, it is important that any efforts on your behalf to arrest me be delayed for a short while."

"Why?"

"Agent Dillard, for some time I had imperceptible traces of methamphetamines included in my miracle diet formula. I purchased those ingredients from an agent for Miguel Zabala. I am certain that the recent deaths attributed to my formula were the result of additional lethal substance that Zabala, without my knowledge, incorporated into the formula."

Sloan listened intently as the tech broke in excitedly.

"We've got his location, should we send a black and white to pick him up?"

"No, not yet."

Dr. Chino continued, "Though I'm not certain, I have reasons to believe that the killings were a message to me from Miguel not to cooperate. Anyway, Miguel Zabala is arriving in Chicago shortly and I'm scheduled to meet him tomorrow."

Once again, Sloan was interrupted when her administrative assistant passed a note.

Sloan read the note, and passed it to John Mercedes. The note read:

"Sloan, your 2:00 appointment has arrived and is in the lobby. What shall I tell Morgan Chino?"

Sloan remembered speaking with Morgan a couple of days earlier and scheduling the appointment for today. However, the stunning events of the last few hours had left Sloan slightly mentally disheveled, and the meeting with Morgan had temporarily escaped her usually photographic memory.

Sloan covered the speaker and looked at Inspectors Mercedes and Pace asking, "What do you think?"

"Dr. Chino's telling the truth, from what I've heard so far. For the past couple of years, I've been working undercover and trying to infiltrate Zabala's organization. It's been a difficult process, but I've been directly communicating with him. I'm set to meet with him this evening. Moving in on Chino now would spook Zavalla and jeopardize tonight's meeting."

"What did you want to accomplish this evening?" asked Sloan, somewhat pleased that John Mercedes was now offering information and contributing proactively.

"Just to make contact, put a face with a name, see how far I can take this."

Sloan picked up the telephone, "Dr. Chino, thanks for contacting me, I will contact the appropriate authorities. I expect you in this office at 8:00am sharp. In the meantime, please hold, there is someone who you should speak with."

"Hello."

"Daddy, oh Daddy, it's you."

Chapter Forty-five

In a way, Sloan was thankful that Kevin Pace was accompanying John Mercedes and her as they adjourned for lunch. Kevin would provide the necessary layer of insulation between Sloan's increasingly uncomfortable, but warmly intriguing, thoughts about John Mercedes. Curiously, John Mercedes thoughts were approximately identical to Sloan's. Kevin meanwhile was blissfully ignorant of the undercurrent of tension and busily conversing with Scotland Yard headquarters.

Kevin returned to the conversation with an incredulous and bewildered look on his face and, inadvertently, sprayed saliva on Sloan through the gap in his teeth as he proclaimed, "They want us to arrest him tonight."

"What? Are they fucking crazy?" John Mercedes excitedly responded.

"Settle down, Johnny. Here's their thought process. And thinking through it, it doesn't seem to be that bad of an idea.

"Scotland Yard, The Washington Bureau of the FBI and various other international agencies have been shadowing Miguel for many years. There's little that we can actually hang on him, though he's suspected to be involved in more vice than the Devil himself."

"John, when headquarters instructed you this morning to cooperate with Agent Sloan, they had already thought through the plan. The FBI or Scotland Yard won't handle the arrest. It will be local. The Chicago Police on some charge. We know he'll be out in less than twenty-four hours. But it will be a message. We'll have photos. And prints. And we might just scare him into doing something that will be self-incriminating."

"I don't like it. I don't like it one god damned bit."

"Neither do I," added Sloan, "but I don't think they're either soliciting our opinions or tallying our votes."

"But what about my undercover work?" John wondered.

"Headquarters assures me that all will eventually work out for you and me. But not for Miguel." Pace concluded.

Miguel Zabala entered the lobby of Chicago's Four Seasons Hotel and approached the front desk clerk. The ever professional demeanor of the Four Season's staff was somewhat challenged by Miguel's "entourage."

"Good afternoon," Miguel said in perfect English. "The Zabala party has arrived. And oh, what a party it will be."

Accompanying Miguel were two stunningly beautiful Latino lovelies, each of whom personified the essence of Venezuelan beauty – dark eyes, caramel-colored skin, high cheek bones, velvety black, wavy hair – and their transparent tops and plunging necklines visually confirmed that their beauty and sensuality extended well below their necks.

"I have booked two adjacent suites," Miguel said with a smile creasing his lips, "One for me, and one for my sisters."

"Certainly, sir," the clerk stammered.

Less than thirty minutes later, a knock on the door of Miguel's suite was answered by one of his sisters.

The young waiter stopped pouring from the magnum of chilled champagne when the Chicago Police entered the master suite. Their first observance was the other "sister" passionately kissing the extremely well dressed man. Rising in surprise, his Rolex watched glittered as he shook the wrinkles from his Armani suit. Watching in the background were Scotland Yard Investigator Kevin Pace and FBI Special Agent Sloan Dillard.

"Chicago Police. You are under arrest."

"For what?"

"Uh, conspiracy to commit prostitution."

"You've got to be fucking kidding me. I've done nothing."

"You have the right to remain silent. Anything you say can, and will, be used against you in a court of law. You have the right to an attorney present now and during any future questioning. If you cannot afford an attorney, one will be appointed for you free of charge if you will. Any questions?"

"Yeah, can you go fuck yourself?"

Roughly, the cuffs were tightened.

"Excuse me, please."

FBI Special Agent Sloan Dillard and Scotland Yard Investigator Kevin Pace stepped aside as the young Hispanic waiter wheeled the cart down the hall.

Miguel Zabala smiled at one sister and winked at the other as he pushed the cart by the unsuspecting law enforcement officers and disappeared into the awaiting service elevator.

Chapter Forty-six

Jordan waited patiently for the return call from the chief financial officer. Jordan always appreciated talking with the folks from accounting, she found their drab, lifeless, boring world a welcome diversion from the wild and unpredictable world of rock and roll.

Jordan had mentally calculated the tour's gross receipts to date and estimated that The Ungrateful's portion of the aggregate was approximately $4,000,000.

"Not bad," Jordan thought, "a cool million bucks per person."

Jordan knew what was happening with the three million dollars or so from Angel, Ace and Morgan, but she speculated just how Tommy's portion was going to be divided between Becky, Kelly, Tommy Three Stick's debts and God only knew what else. Jordan felt genuinely proud of the entire band, and thoroughly sorry for the unwitting and undeserved mess that Tommy was in.

Jordan answered the telephone in her "professional" voice.

"Jordan Taylor."

Jordan instantly somewhat recognized the voice on the other end, but instead of the CFO's customary laconic droning, he was animated and agitated.

"Jordan! Jordan! For Christ's sake, Jordan. I've never seen anything like this before. I've been in this business for over twenty years, and I thought I'd seen it all. Until today that is. I can't fucking believe it. Can you, Jordan? Can you fucking believe it?"

"Hey, slow down. Slow way down. Take a deep breath. Relax. Why don't you back up and tell me the whole story. From the beginning. And then I'll tell you whether or not I fucking believe it."

Jordan had a premonition, though, that she wasn't going to fucking believe it.

"Prior to any tour, we customarily set up custodial accounts for each artist. That way, money earned from the beginning of the tour can immediately be deposited in an interest bearing account. As you know, Jordan, sometimes the money involved is rather significant, and the accrued interest on what could amount to millions of dollars is meaningful, especially in these tax brackets.

"The accounting process is purely 'cookbook' – straight formulaic. I reviewed the establishment of the accounts – everything was handled in the appropriate manner – firewalls were established and usual security precautions were activated.

"The interval deposits were made after each tour event, after the requisite money was forwarded to our friends at the Internal Revenue Service.

"Jordan, everything was in order. Deposits were made after each event – Boston, New York, Philly, D.C., Cleveland, and Chicago. But there's no money in any of the accounts. Angel - $0.00. Ammanuel Azure - $0.00. Morgan Chino - $0.00. Tommy Puccini - $0.00.

"For Christ sakes, Jordan, there's over $5,000,000 missing. We tried to find it. It moved from our bank in Los Angeles to an off-shore account in the Bahamas, and then to some rinky-dink, store-front bank somewhere in bumblefuck Venezuela."

"You're right. I don't fucking believe it."

Sloan and John Mercedes were commiserating when her cell phone rang,

"Sorry to bother you Sloan, but didn't you tell me that you started in the accounting entry program with the FBI?"

"Yes, why?"

"We need to meet."

Chapter Forty-seven

Tommy Puccini sat in his bedroom and strummed his guitar – just like he had done countless times before – only never before did his melodic tunes accompanying the wretched grunts of morning sickness, and the even sicker sound of his mother's Irish lover in the adjacent bedroom.

"Just how the fuck did I ever get myself into this mess?" Tommy thought as his fingers glided effortlessly across the strings of his twelve-string acoustical guitar.

The ring of the telephone interrupted Tommy's self-absorbed pity-fest,

"Oh, hello Kelly, can you hang on one sec, there's another call coming in? Hello."

"Paddy O'Keane, please," said the voice that Tommy certainly didn't recognize but had a faint hint of a South American accent.

"Just a minute."

"Hey, Kelly, we're going to have to talk later, OK?"

Tommy clicked back but the line was dead. Then the telephone rang again.

"Good Morning, Paddy O'Keane, please."

"May I tell him who's calling?"

The line went dead, but the heavy English brogue left no doubt as to the second mystery caller's nationality.

Tommy checked on Becky who emerged from the bathroom looking pale and frail. Tommy gently tucked her back into bed and went downstairs.

Tommy flicked on Sports Center and as the previous evening's scores flashed on the screen, Tommy recounted the miserable state of Chicago professional athletic teams.

The Bulls were just plain awful ever since Michael Jordan, Scottie Pippen and the others went their separate ways. The Cubs, well, what could be said about the hapless Cubs that had not been chronicled an infinite number of times before? The Sox? The Chicago White Sox were nothing more than an afterthought to Tommy – ever since their infamous "Disco Demolition Day." And the Bears? Tommy took a delightful, perverse pleasure in the woes of the Chicago Bears. And why? Because Tommy was a life-long fan of the finest organization in the entirety of professional sports – The Green Bay

Packers.

Tommy remembered back to the grief he continually endured growing up as one of the only Packer fans in the entire State of Illinois. He remembered gleefully – and like it was yesterday – when his Mom and Dad had been summoned to the principal's office, at St. Mary's of the Angels.

Miss Dornbach, Tommy's sixth grade homeroom teacher asked who in her class were Bears fans, and the entire class, with the exception of Tommy enthusiastically waved their outstretched arms.

"Tommy?"

"I'm a Packer fan."

"Packers?"

"Why?"

"'Cause my dad is."

'That's not a good reason. If your dad was a moron, and your mother an idiot, what would that make you?"

"A Bears fan."

Tommy thought his reply was extremely funny. Unfortunately for him, neither Miss Dornbach nor Sr. Arturo, the principal of St. Mary's of the Angels, shared an appreciation for his witticism. To the delight of his classmates and St. Mary's custodial staff, Tommy's punishment consisted of a solid week of after-school blackboard cleaning.

For Tommy, the punishment was more of a visit to paradise, for Tommy's reverence for Miss Dornbach's beauty was greater than Beaver Cleaver's for Miss Landers'.

A short time later, Becky joined Tommy in the family room. Tommy watched intently as Becky leaned over to kiss him good morning, grateful that she had thoroughly brushed and gargled after her previous bout with morning sickness, and noticed a slight bulge in her stomach – the first visible signs of her pregnancy.

"Becky, you're…you're showing!" Tommy exclaimed.

"I'm showing how fat and ugly I've become."

"No Becky, you're showing signs of our love. You're showing how beautiful you are. You're showing how much fun this baby will be. Our baby."

"Oh, Tommy! I love you so much. Do you think the baby will change us? You're the most important thing in the world. I'm so protective of our relationship. I was afraid that as I got big, you'd stop finding me attractive. I could never take that Tommy. I love you so much."

Patting her stomach, Tommy simply said, "I love you too, Becky. And I love our baby."

Suddenly for Tommy Puccini, life was again good.

Chapter Forty-eight

Sloan Dillard was surprised when she returned to her office and was met in the lobby by a young woman delivering flowers.

"A delivery for Sloan Dillard."

Sloan was grateful that she intercepted the flowers before any of her staff had the opportunity to witness what would be the fodder for endless rounds of gossip.

Sloan generously tipped the appreciative delivery girl $20 and retreated behind the closed doors of her office.

Sloan lingered over the beautiful fragrance, and her fingers somewhat nervously fumbled as she opened the card,

"Sorry about your bust – John."

Agitated and irritated, Sloan adjusted her brazier and wondered what about her breasts would warrant such an overt, mean-spirited comment from someone she hardly knew.

Sloan cheeks were flushed with an intense crimson color as she embarrassedly realized that the "bust" John was referring to was the bungled attempted arrest of Miguel Zabala.

Sloan gingerly unwrapped the paper and found a simple, but beautiful bouquet of pink tulips interspersed between multicolored roses. The effect was eloquently simple, and Sloan's mind rushed into places she never knew existed.

Sloan allowed herself scant moments to daydream, then went about the laborious task of sorting out everything that was happening.

Sloan was experiencing a cavalcade of unfamiliar emotions, and she was unaccustomed to not being in control – and that lack of control was probably the most unsettling.

First there were the troubling uncertainties surrounding The Ungrateful investigation, then the completely different set of dynamics introduced by Miguel Zabala, and all of this was infinitely compounded by what shouldn't be happening between her and John Mercedes. Sloan made one of her infamous "bubble letter" to do lists:

Contact the FDA and have them re-run the mass-spectrometer tests to check for additional ingredients in Dr. Chino's formulation.

Crosscheck ballistics for Ungrateful deaths with those of Reggie Beasley and Stewart Lindsey.

Schedule interview with Mickey Delaney

Review the tapes of all previous concerts and double-check for presence of backwards New York Yankees baseball cap.

Interview Josh and Jake Rose

Determine how Miguel Zabala was alerted to our supposedly "surprise" visit.

Visit Victoria's Secret and splurge – just in case.

Sloan's pensive list making was interrupted when her administrative assistant informed her that Jordan Taylor was waiting in the vestibule.

Sloan welcomed Jordan into her office and offered her a seat and a beverage. Jordan politely asked for water, but wasted no time at all in completely informing Sloan of everything she knew surrounding the disappearance of over $5,000,000 dollars of The Ungrateful's money. Jordan detailed her CFO's investigation and the trail of the money from Los Angeles to the Bahamas to Venezuela to only God knows.

Sloan listened intently and scribbled notes, neatly but feverishly. Sloan spent the first two years of her agency training ferreting out similar information and adrenalin pulsed through her body in anticipation of the pleasure of forensic accounting.

Jordan's replay of the CFO's activities provided enough of a jumpstart for Sloan to circumvent many of the laborious tasks associated with such an investigation.

"This is going to take a while, but you're welcome to stay," Sloan said to Jordan as she began to coordinate the simultaneous querying of the vast FBI computer network.

Jordan watched in amazement as Sloan methodically tapped commands into her keyboard.

Less than seventy minutes later, Sloan sighed a contented "Ahem."

"The money was ultimately wired to two separate banks, two separate accounts.

$3,000,000 was forwarded to The Central Bank of Ireland. Though I cannot disclose the account's owner, I am hopeful that we can recover the money. The other $2,000,000 was wired to a bank in London. Once again, I am not at liberty to disclose the name of the person who controls the account."

Sloan's eyebrows furrowed as the name "Kevin Pace" flashed on the screen, Bank of London, Account # 5ZCl127-548.

Sloan made a mental note to cross the question of how Miguel Zabala was alerted to the supposedly surprise visit at the Four Seasons off her bubble letter list.

Jordan's incessant questions remained unanswered, and though she wasn't satisfied with Sloan's response of, "I'm sorry, the information is confidential due to its association with an ongoing investigation." She understood.

Sloan, though, couldn't quite understand either the existence or the significance of "Mrs. Paddy O'Keane" having joint ownership of an Irish bank account now flush with over $3,000,000.

"And won't Kelly Puccini be surprised also?" Sloan thought to herself.

Chapter Forty-nine

It took Jordan longer to contact each of the band members and arranging a group meeting that was convenient for all to attend than she had anticipated. Even so, from Jordan's personal perspective, the meeting was way too soon. Hell, if she could postpone it forever she would. But professionally, Jordan readied herself for the challenge of telling the band members that the money they had worked so hard for had disappeared – at least temporarily – she hoped.

Jordan's suite at the Knickerbocker had, once again, been designated as the meeting place. Jordan's thoughts harkened back to her childhood when she had a secret clubhouse and her friends would gather to play. But this was going to be difficult work.

Ace and Morgan were the first to arrive, arm-in-arm. Jordan had carefully planned and measured her greeting demeanor to ensure that she conveyed the proper mood – deliberate, serious but not overly somber.

Jordan's preparation was obliterated when Ace's thousand-watt smile illuminated the room and he playfully flirted with Jordan and good naturedly intimated that he could deliver Jordan to the same lofty level of sexual ecstasy that Morgan was now regularly enjoying.

Jordan temporarily lost herself trying to recall the distant memory of her last fulfilling sexual rendezvous, and she was slightly jealous of Morgan's treasure.

Angel knocked softly on the hotel door and greeted Jordan with a warm embrace; exchanged high fives with Ace and a lingering hug with Morgan. Tommy shuffled in a short time later and hugged everyone. To Jordan, it was obvious that the lingering effects from the trauma they had witnessed significantly impacted Ace, Morgan, Tommy and Angel.

Jordan offered beverages and uncomfortably waited to begin. There was an uneasy air of apprehension hovering in the air, and Jordan wanted to start and end as quickly as possible.

"Just when you think the worst is over and things couldn't possibly get any worse," she started, "another unpleasant surprise."

"Yesterday, a detailed audit of the tour's finances was completed and we began preparations to release the funds from each of your custodial accounts. Despite assurances from both the tour accounts and our chief financial officer that the most stringent security measures possible were in place, I learned that all of the money from each of your accounts had been embezzled. The FBI is involved in a full-scale investigation and has followed the money from Los Angeles to the Bahamas to Venezuela. The authorities are uncertain at this time if the money is somehow related to the murders. The only thing certain, at this time, is that there is no money left in your accounts. The chief financial officer is investigating the options with the FDIC, but I'm not certain where that's going to come out. In any event the missing money is well beyond the $100,000 per account FDIC insurance limit.

"I realize that each of you have different financial needs, and my company is in a position to authorize short term loans to cover any immediate cash requirements that you may have."

"It is what it is," was all that Ace said.

"At least nobody's getting killed," added Angel as Morgan nodded in agreement.

"Fuck," Tommy muttered dejectedly.

"I'm certain that the FBI will be in contact with each of you shortly," Jordan concluded, "the investigation is being handled by – I think you know her – Agent Dillard."

"She the one with the fine ass?" Ace asked as they all headed out the door.

Chapter Fifty

Sloan Dillard greeted John Mercedes as he entered her office. Standing, she nervously extended her slightly sweaty hand and watched appreciably as John's mysterious eyes appeared to pierce right through her.

"Hello John, I'm afraid we're going to have to move our meeting to another location. The office is going to be swept for bugs shortly. You know, after the Four Season's incident, one can never be too careful."

"You know, after being undercover all this time, it's weird to be out. Kinda nice though. Maybe I'll have to properly thank Mr. Pace the next time I'm fortunate enough to bump into him."

Miguel Zabala listened to the conversation, hoping against hope that Kevin Pace's hiding place for the bug wouldn't be discovered. But Miguel was thoroughly familiar with the sophisticated equipment that would be utilized by the FBI and knew that his little secret would be no longer.

Sloan motioned for John and they left the office as the techs arrived.

"Shouldn't take long, Ms. Dillard; we've got a pretty good idea of what we'll find."

Sloan and John left her office and headed outside towards the adjacent courtyard.

"Well, I'm confused," started John.

"I'm so glad that you are too," said Sloan, immediately regretting her words since she could tell by the quizzical look on John's face that he was confused by the investigation and not the whirlwind of emotions whizzing through Sloan's brain.

Graciously, John didn't let on, simply smiling to himself and continuing,

"If Kevin Pace was working both for Scotland Yard and for Miguel Zabala, we have to assume that everything we know, Miguel knows."

"That isn't overly daunting, because we only really know for a fact that a number of people are dead, and Miguel's running an international operation of vice," Sloan interjected sarcastically.

"Sloan, I'd like to step back from the investigation for a moment and discuss where we are."

Sloan's soaring heart was grounded when her pager buzzed alerting her to some significant discovery by the techs.

"Can we talk later?" Sloan asked somewhat dejectedly, hoping that John would once again summon the courage to begin the perilous journey across the professional bridge that prevented them from discovering what she hoped was the inevitable.

The techs smiled proudly as Sloan and John entered the office,

"Whoever planted this was quite clever and very professional. We'll send it to Washington for the lab boys to evaluate further, but the device is as sophisticated as I've ever seen."

"Where did you find it?"

"That's the ingenious part. We found the device imbedded in a comb. There is probably $25,000 worth of high tech listening devices planted in a $1.00 comb. We'll know more when the lab results are issued. The comb was neatly placed under colored magic markers in Sloan's top left desk drawer. The only thing that tipped us off was that the bug left a slight gap in the comb's teeth."

John Mercedes couldn't help himself from smiling at the ironic British humor exhibited by his former partner turned traitor.

Chapter Fifty-one

The telephone rang, and Becky shouted downstairs to Tommy, "I'll get it."

"OK."

"Hello."

"May I please speak with Tommy?"

"Can I tell Tommy who's calling?"

"Ahem...ah...yes, this is Kelly."

"Will Tommy know what the call is about?"

"Yes, it's a personal matter."

"I'm sorry; Tommy's unavailable, and listen, you psycho bitch, never call this fucking number again!" Becky screeched as she slammed down the receiver and sobbed silently.

"Who was it, honey?"

"Just a telemarketer."

"Psycho bitch?" Kelly chuckled to herself, for Kelly's close friend often called her "Sybil" in honor of her distinctive personalities, which she aptly had named:

Scarlet: The Martyr who whines incessantly about how hard she works and how unappreciated she is.

MC (named after Marylyn Chambers): The dirty little tramp who has very little moral conscious when it comes to anything sexual.

Glen: Do not cross this woman unless you enjoy the scent of boiling bunnies.

Courtney: Rocker chick. Cares only about partying and rocking. Once joined two strippers on stage and removed her own shirt and bra.

Martha: Devoted homemaker and mommy.

Ellen: Prefers the company of women to men... and not just for shopping.

Eve: Mysterious. Elusive. Deeply evil at heart.

Sissy: White trash who wears plunging necklines, clothes a size too tight and a too short skirt.

But today, today Kelly was just Kelly the wedding coordinator.

Becky looked carefully at herself in the mirror, and her depression intensified. In the place of the youthful, shapely and vibrant woman who had captured the heart of Tommy Puccini and fallen madly, hopelessly, passionately and dangerously in love with him was a bleary-eyed, slightly bloated and increasingly rotund mother-to-be. Becky felt physically ill as the stranger peered back from the mirror at her, and her disappointment intensified when she realized that the nausea creeping into her throat wasn't morning sickness but physical repulsion.

Becky's eyes reddened further as she strained to muffle the sounds of throwing up. After brushing her teeth, she spent an extraordinarily long time applying make-up, and readying herself for another day with Tommy.

Coming downstairs, she was surprised to see Tommy in the kitchen. For some reason, the surprise of seeing him in blue jeans, a T-shirt and a crisply starched white apron immediately lifted her spirits and temporarily erased the haunting sounds of Kelly's voice from her memory.

"Bon jour, Madame, this way, *s'il vous plaît."*

Becky was amazed as Tommy led her into the dining room and saw the table beautifully set for two. In the center of the table were twelve of the most beautifully vibrant red roses Becky had ever seen, tastefully arranged with greens and baby's breath. On either side of the floral centerpiece were silver candlesticks, ablaze with dancing red lights. Adjacent to the candles were two long-stemmed, fluted champagne glasses.

The bright morning sun filled the room, and the combination of the dancing sunlight, the flickering candles and the surprise made Becky slightly light-headed. Tommy gently took her by the hand, kissed her softly on her cheeks and pulled the chair back.

"Brunch will be served presently, Madame. But first, may I toast your beauty, my undying love for you and our new family."

Becky's eyes swelled with enormous tears, and she stammered, "Oh Tommy, you're so wonderful, but I can't...drink...You know....the baby."

"Then let's just toast," said Tommy as he raised his glass, and Becky did the same.

With one hand holding their champagne glasses and the other holding each other's, Tommy and Becky raised their glasses. Tommy's was overflowing with effervescing bubbles, while Becky's slightly clattered. Becky put her glass down and looked inside to discover the most brilliantly large diamond ring she had ever seen.

"Oh Tommy," were the only words she could muster as she was overcome with yet another wave of emotion.

Tommy spoke softly, "We've been through so much already, and we'll be through so much together in the future. But it's the future I want to talk about now. Becky, I'd like to get married. On Saturday. Of this week. You see, the band's all going their separate ways soon, and I'd like them to be with us. I've done some checking. I spoke with Josh and Jake, and they both will come. I talked with Father Morrello, and he promised to take care of us. I'd rather not get married at St. Mary's of the Angels, but considering the circumstances, it's the best we can hope for on such short notice. What do you think? Can we do it? This Saturday?"

"Oh Tommy, yes – but there's so much to do – the dress, the flowers."

"I'm already working on it. I've hired a wedding coordinator who's going to help you."

The knock on the door interrupted Tommy, and Becky could hear hushed whispers in the hallway.

Tommy entered the room, accompanied by a stylish, middle-aged woman.

"Becky, I'd like you to meet Kelly. She's been helping me with the wedding plans, and she's here to take you shopping for a dress."

Tommy waited until Becky and Kelly headed out of the door to go shopping. He dialed the familiar number and said, "Everything was perfect. I can never thank you enough."

Chapter Fifty-two

Sloan chuckled as John called his superiors and informed them that the office had been combed for bugs and was certified to be clean. Sloan watched and listened with growing admiration of John's professionalism as he unemotionally gave a detailed, factual account of Kevin Pace's known and suspected activities.

Sloan knew that her slow motion fall for John was accelerating at a dangerous pace, but the combination of his over-the-top good looks, unforced sensuality, professionalism, delightfully wicked sense of humor and genuine warmth combined to significantly compromise the usually detached and reserved Sloan Dillard.

As John continued with the trans-Atlantic call, Sloan answered the blinking local line. Sloan listened intently as the dispatch sergeant for the Chicago police department recounted the recently reported crime scene.

"Have homicide secure the area. Nobody enters until I arrive with my team. Got that? Nobody." Sloan barked in a harsh tone that irritated her as she listened to herself.

Interrupting John, Sloan said, "Excuse me, but I think you'd like to know this now – the Chicago Police just found Kevin Pace. His brains are scattered on the wall behind him. But the police discovered a suicide note – at least they think it's a suicide note."

Before Sloan had finished the sentence, John had ended his overseas call and the two of them were racing down the hall. In the excitement, neither realized that they were holding hands.

Sloan ducked under the yellow tape proclaiming "Crime scene, do not enter," and passed the uniformed police officers guarding the room, with John following closely behind.

The various authorities from the Chicago Police Department had respected Sloan's request and left the original scene undisturbed.

The back of Kevin's head was splattered against the wall and trickles of dried blood trailed down the wall. In Kevin's right hand was the gun, and below his left hand was a piece of paper.

Carefully, Sloan picked up the paper with tweezers and read the words, which meant nothing to her now, but hopefully, when deciphered, would unlock the overlapping mysteries.

Sloan read the note aloud, "A-C-E."

John Mercedes brow furrowed intently, and a small smile creased the corners of his lips.

"Kevin Pace may be more clever in death than he was in life. For sure, he is more loyal. Let's go."

"Where?"

"To my hotel suite."

"But – John – John."

"Relax."

Once again, Sloan's face flushed as she realized that she and John were on completely different planes.

John knew that within his hotel room were the answers to many different questions.

John and Sloan emerged from the room, ducked under the yellow tape and quickly headed down the hall. This time, both of them realized that they were holding hands.

Chapter Fifty-three

Jordan called Angel and was surprised to find that Ace and Morgan were with her.

"Hey, you guys got a couple of minutes? I'd love to get together and go over some loose ends."

"Yeah, but no place high powered. We're laying low and not up for any crowd scenes."

"How about Flapjaws?"

"Flapjaws?"

"Yeah, kind of a Chicago tradition. Not so famous as Billy Goats, and much less touristy, it's a friendly place with a warm ambiance and great food. Not far at all from your hotel. Just down the road."

Jordan was somewhat surprised when she entered and saw a rectangular bar being expertly worked by a perky blonde with an engaging smile and eyes as big as the moon. Jordan's vow of anonymity was smashed to smithereens when the blonde bartender extended her hand and warmly said, "Welcome to Flapjaws, my name is Haley. What's yours?"

"Er…Jordan."

"Pleasure to meet you Jordan. Welcome to Flapjaws. Hey everyone. Say 'hi' to Jordan."

Jordan was amazed as this eclectic group of apparent strangers greeted her with the same warmth as Haley had.

Just then the door opened, and an elderly couple entered, followed by a yuppie couple. Each received the same friendly greeting, and within minutes the entire group was immersed in a collection of fragmented conversations.

Jordan took advantage of the diversion caused by the new entrants and gracefully disappeared into a back booth. She soon was joined by Angel. Ace and Morgan followed shortly, holding hands with eyes that smiled warmly and a passion that burned brightly.

"Hey, thanks for coming. I've got some news and I thought it'd be better if we did this in person."

Ace stood up, and grabbed Jordan and kissed her passionately on the lips, saying, "Oh thank you Jordan, you've found our money. You're so special."

Angel and Morgan laughed appreciably as Jordan's cheeks flushed with color.

"No, I'm afraid not," Jordan replied as the color slowly drained from her face, but the sensation of the kiss was emblazoned in her mind as she tightly crossed, then re-crossed her legs.

"Tommy gets married on Saturday."

"To who?" asked Angel facetiously.

"To whom!" Morgan gently corrected her.

"Hey, hey, easy now. Is that any way for the bridesmaids to talk?"

"Say what?"

"Yeah, Tommy's arranging this, and he's asked me to ask you two to be the bridesmaids. He knows it's not real conventional, but there's really nothing conventional about the wedding. This Saturday. Day after tomorrow. St. Mary's of the Angels. Two o'clock.

"And oh, Ace, as Tommy's best man, he is expecting you to throw a kick-ass bachelor party."

Chapter Fifty-four

John opened the door to his hotel suite, and Sloan was surprised to find an uncommonly neat, tidy room. John led her directly into the bedroom and suggested that she sit on the bed. John went directly to the desk and turned on Kevin's computer. Sloan got up and nervously paced while John waited for the computer to boot.

The door to the room of the adjacent suite was slightly ajar, and Sloan's heart sank quickly when she saw scattered about, clothing and toiletries that obviously belonged to another woman.

Sloan steeled herself and prodded her professional demeanor to prevail against the devastating premonition that what could have been never would be.

John's subdued cursing interrupted Sloan's abject thoughts.

"What's wrong?"

"It's the password. He's changed it. I can't get in. The security's so tight with these that we'll have to send it back to Scotland Yard. That's our only hope."

"Why not try some obvious ones?" asked Sloan, not really believing that they could guess the deceased Kevin Pace's password, but hoping that the extra time and diversion would allow her to collect her thoughts and regain her composure.

John started typing, "Ace," "ACE," "A.C.E.," "ace," "Kevin Pace 1," "Paceman," "Pacman," each entry was followed quickly with "INVALID PASSWORD."

John excused himself to answer a knock on the door, and Sloan overheard John happily exchange greetings with a female visitor.

Sloan pretended to be diligently attempting to break the encrypted password, but was actually daydreaming as she mindlessly typed the password "GOALPOST."

John startled her when he entered and said, "Sloan, I believe you've already met, but I'd like to introduce my daughter and suitemate, Angel."

Angel, who had never been greeted with a warmer smile, the warmth of which she didn't quite understand, extended her hand saying, "Nice to see you again, Agent Dillard."

John looked on in amazement as the computer screen flashed, "WELCOME."

Sloan returned to the computer feeling duel surges of power. The fact that the woman sharing John's suite was both his daughter and Angel was a double stroke of luck, more importantly for Sloan, though, was the information to be gleaned from Kevin Pace's computer.

Sloan's hopes that her computer proficiency would enable her to easily decipher Kevin's clues were dashed when she opened the computer and typed "FIND: ALL FILES." Sloan continued following the progressive prompts:

Name & Location, Date, Advanced Search:
Named:
Containing Text:
Look In:
Include Subfolders:
Browse:
Find Now:

With each different prompt, Sloan typed in variations of "A.C.E." and the computer's response was always the same:

"12,152 (files) found – 0 Matches"

Sloan settled in for what promised to be a long and laborious session in front of Kevin Pace's laptop.

John sensed her determination and realized his greatest current value to the investigation was to stay out of Sloan's way and to be as supportive as possible.

John excused himself by saying, "I've got a couple of errands to run. Will you two be okay alone for a little while?"

Without looking up from the screen, Sloan muttered "Mmhm," and Angel said, "Just get out of here, Dad, I'm sure we'll be fine."

John's heart soared as he closed the door behind him and realized that Angel had called him "Dad."

Sloan's attention was riveted on the computer screen and she affixed another modem to allow herself access to the Bureau's vast network. But she knew that it would be know how, determination and instinct that would unlock the riddle that Kevin Pace so graciously left behind.

"He's fallen hard for you, you know." At first, the words and the meaning escaped Sloan's comprehension. Angel continued, "I can tell – he's warm for your form."

Sloan smiled graciously and simply replied, "Angel, thanks for the observation, but there's a pressing priority right now. The killer's still out there."

Angel nodded appreciably and said, "Hey, let me know if I can help at all. Until then, I'll be in the other room, Mom."

Sloan could hear Angel's distinctively delightful laughter fading into the walls of the adjacent suite as she refocused her attention on the screen.

Sloan continued on with search queries, with each one reaching the same unsuccessful destination as the previous one. After having exhausted every possible variation of "ACE" that Sloan could conjure, she sat dejectedly and stared absent-mindedly at the screen.

Sloan replayed everything that she had learned to date, and then, forced by habit, opened the hotel desk drawer, took out a piece of stationary and started writing in large bubble letters "ACE" and then "Ammanuel Ezure." Sloan jumped up and ran excitedly into the adjacent room,

"Sorry to barge in, but, by any chance, do you know Ace's middle name?"

"Doesn't have one."

"Damn it. Oh, excuse me, darn it."

Angel smiled, adding, "Ace didn't have a middle name, he always joked that his parents were so poor when he was born they couldn't even afford a middle name. So they just gave him a letter. Ace's middle name is 'C.'"

Before the words were out of Angel's mouth, Sloan was back at the desk and had typed in "Ammanuel C. Ezure."

Sloan was so intently focused on the screen in front of her that she didn't realize that Angel was behind her with her hands on her shoulders. The computer whizzed as Angel let out a shriek of delight and Angel and Sloan hugged victoriously.

John Mercedes entered the room and looked on incredulously as two very special people were celebrating different discoveries.

John's arms were bundled with white bags and containers of take-out Chinese which he set on the table saying, "Thought you'd need some nutrition for all the work ahead."

It was somewhere between the won ton soup, the chicken sub gum chop suey and the szechuan shrimp that Sloan's smile subsided. Only slightly, though.

Over the next six hours, Sloan unraveled an international trail of vice, corruption, drugs, and money.

Due in large part to Kevin Pace's meticulous record keeping and computer proficiency, Sloan was able to recreate enough evidence to at least persuade a judge to issue an arrest warrant for Miguel Zabala.

Significant work remained, however, to first arrest Miguel and then to convict him. Fortunately for Sloan, both Fujimaro Chino and Paddy O'Keane would have sufficient motivation to cooperate with the prosecution for Miguel.

Unfortunately for Sloan, there was nothing in Kevin's vast cyberspace vaults that even remotely connected Miguel to a single murder. Much less seven.

Sloan glanced at her watch and realized it was nearly 3:00 AM. Sloan looked over at John who was peacefully sleeping, fully clothed atop his covers. Even in slumber, there was something powerfully sensual about John Mercedes, and Sloan was determined to unlock that mystery. Not tonight, however.

Chapter Fifty-five

St. Mary's of the Angels was resplendent in beauty. Even Kelly, the consummate perfectionist, was delighted. Every third pew was adorned with a simple bouquet of white sweetheart roses, elegantly tied with a satin bow. In between the bouquet pews was a single candle, shining brightly and illuminating the pathway from the church vestibule to the altar.

In the front of the church were five classical musicians – playing the harp, flute, cello, violin and trumpet – clad completely in black, softly mixing the timeless melodic sounds.

Father Vincent Morello stood, facing the congregation of three, and looked to the back of the church.

As the quintet struck the opening chords of Beethoven's *Ode to Joy*, Ace and Tommy, wearing simple black tuxedos, joined the side of Father Morello and anxiously waited for the procession to begin.

Angel and Morgan wore eloquently simple, baby blue, off-the-shoulder dresses that slowly fell to mid-leg. Appropriately, the dresses were cut conservatively, but even so, the fabric couldn't entirely conceal the beauty, shapes and femininity lying beneath. Ace stirred in appreciation and marveled as the lights of the candles shimmered off the single strand of pearls around the maids of honors' necks.

As Morgan and Angel slowly walked to the altar, the quintet accompanied their procession with *Jesu, Joy of Man's Desire*. Next, Becky slowly began the ceremonial walk down the aisle, with the sweet, traditional sounds of Mendelssohn's *Wedding March* filling the nearly empty church with the familiar sound of anticipation. On Becky's left was her brother Josh, on her right was Jake.

Becky's bouquet was simple, but beautiful. Fresh cut, seasonal flowers were interspersed with a kaleidoscope of colorful mini roses and tied with a pink bow. Becky's hair was in an "undo" and a simple veil highlighted her beauty. As she slowly stepped forward, her hands and bouquet dropped slightly and came to rest atop her ever-growing stomach.

Tommy smiled in wonderment, appreciation and love as Becky approached the altar. Josh and Jake delivered Becky to the waiting arm of Tommy, and the Rose brothers returned to joined Kelly Puccini, Paddy O'Keane and Jordan Taylor in the vast, empty church.

Father Morello, at the express request of Tommy, kept the ceremony mercifully short. The reading from Corinthians reminded Tommy and Becky just what love is, and Tommy couldn't help chuckling aloud about the gospel passage invoking Becky, with the words, "Wives, obey your husbands." Ace smiled at the irony.

A short time later, Father Vincent Morello turned to the congregation saying, "The Mass has ended, go in peace to love and serve the Lord. I now present you with Mr. and Mrs. Thomas Puccini."

Tommy and Becky walked gracefully down the aisle, though Becky didn't remember her feet ever touching the ground.

Chapter Fifty-six

Sloan knew that the chances of Miguel Zabala surrendering were non-existent. John Mercedes knew that Kevin Pace had blown his cover, and told Sloan "his chances of lulling Miguel into a false sense of security approximated the Cubs chances of winning a World Series."

And somehow, that's how Sloan's plan was originated.

In the previous eight hours, Sloan had thoroughly digested everything that Kevin Pace had detailed about Miguel Zabala. Sloan augmented that information with random bits of intelligence she had gathered, and overlaid that information with insightful questions to John Mercedes.

Slowly, Sloan transitioned her razor-sharp FBI mind to the mind of a Venezuelan national, boldly eluding authorities in the United States.

Sloan chuckled at her good fortune as she scanned the sports section of the *Chicago Tribune* – and desperately hoped that her instinct was on target. If not, she was again subject to ridicule and humiliation. "Fuck 'em," she thought, specifically choosing her words with deliberation and care.

Sloan gathered her team together in a Chicago Police Department conference room.

"This afternoon at 1:00 PM, the Chicago Cubs are playing the Atlanta Braves at Wrigley Field. The Atlanta Braves feature a star-studded line-up, including All-Start first baseman Andres Galarraga. Andres Galarraga is as close to a Venezuelan national hero as there is. We know of Miguel's affection for baseball, and though we have no proof, we suspect that he may be in attendance. We have purchased seats throughout Wrigley and will have our people in the press box and in the lofts across Waverly. Fortunately for us, and unfortunately for Miguel if he is in attendance, many people at baseball games are looking through binoculars, so our spotters shouldn't be obvious. We'll have a couple of undercovers dressed as vendors, so peanuts may be on the house. Again, I stress that we have no confirmed evidence to suggest that Miguel Zabala will be in attendance, so, at the least, we should see a good game."

Sloan continued, "We have made arrangements for Leslie Nielsen to umpire behind home plate." Sloan waited with a well-timed pregnant pause, and earned a well-deserved round of muffled chuckles and soft laughter for her Lieutenant Frank Drebin *Naked Gun* humor.

"We'll coordinate all communications through me. My home base will be in the broadcast booth, but I'll be moving through the stadium at various times. Oh, and excuse me for not introducing him earlier. On my left is Inspector John Mercedes from Scotland Yard. John has been following the trail of Miguel Zabala for quite some time. John will be working under me today." Sloan delighted herself with the deliberate double entendre. "Any questions? Good."

The afternoon sun drenched the Wrigley crowd. Though most rational Cub fans had long ago resigned themselves to accept the inevitable futility that the storied franchise had long embodied, a select delusional few still hopelessly clung to the irrational belief and impossible notion that they might one day live to see a post-season Cub's victory. In fact, so remote was that chance that some pundits speculated that the reason the Cubs didn't have a website was because "they couldn't string three 'w's together" in June, much less in September or October when it really mattered.

Thirty-five thousand people in any situation present difficult surveillance circumstances. Thirty-five thousand people standing, cheering, moving to the concession stands, going to the restrooms, doing the "wave," and scrambling for foul balls presented a maximum challenge to Sloan's organizational abilities and patience.

Sloan had sectioned off the stadium and assigned a small grid to each of the numerous spotters. The job of each spotter was to observe all people and report any suspicious resemblances immediately to Sloan.

She had expected the process to be laborious, but as the late afternoon's shadows started to descend upon Wrigley, Sloan's optimism began to fade. The only thing remotely interesting that caught Sloan's attention was the sight of Josh Rose, wearing a New York Yankees cap – backwards.

Sammy Sosa's monstrous home run in the bottom of the sixth inning energized the crowd, the Cubs and the investigation team.

In the top of the seventh, with the Cubs trailing 5-2, the fans began to buzz in anticipation of the seventh inning stretch. Ever since the death of the legendary Harry Caray, the Cubs had invited various dignitaries to lead the crowd's singing of *Take Me Out To The Ball Game* and the identity of the performer was always a closely guarded secret and subject to intense fan speculation – almost as intense as guessing the actual attendance or the winner of the ubiquitous sausage race. A diverse group of performers, politicians, actors, musicians and athletes like Mel Gibson, Dick Clark, Governor Jesse Ventura, Donald Trump, Rockers Billy Corgan and Eddie Vedder, Mike Ditka and Jay Leno had serenaded the Wrigley crowd as a tribute to Harry Caray.

The top of the seventh ended with Sammy making a routine catch of a fly ball off the bat of Andres Galarraga. The fans' eyes turned to the press box, and the public address announcer said, "Ladies and gentlemen, I direct your attention to the center field bleachers."

Standing with microphones, Ace, Tommy, Angel and Morgan belted out what was most likely the most wildly applauded version of *Take Me Out To The Ball Game* in the history of organized baseball. Long after the song had ended, the fans still stood cheering.

Sloan continued to scan the crowd with her high-powered binoculars, and her attention was drawn to an unlikely threesome sitting in the midst of the left field bleacher bums. "Sitting, while everyone else is standing. Unusual," Sloan thought to herself. More unusual was the attire.

Sloan adjusted the glasses and focused in. Unmistakably, Miguel Zabala, attired in an Andres Galarraga jersey and accompanied by his two "sisters" from the hotel, sat in the left field bleachers in Wrigley Field, calmly sipping a 16-ounce beer and eating a hot dog.

"Suspect identified. Suspect identified. Left Field Bleachers. Third row. Move cautiously. Let's bring him in."

Sloan rushed from the press box and scurried to the left field bleacher area. In the runway, John Mercedes, squeezed her arm softly, winked and said, "You're the best."

The rest of the agents mobilized, the police were in back up position and a small army of disguised concessionaire hawkers, vendors and ushers assembled.

On Sloan's cue, the left field bleachers were infiltrated with undercover agents. Miguel Zabala's only resistance to his arrest was a plea to "let me finish my fucking beer."

The Cubs lost 5-2.

Chapter Fifty-seven

The news of Sloan's creatively conceived, boldly implemented and flawlessly executed arrest of Miguel Zabala spread like wildfire throughout the law enforcement and intelligence community.

For the first time in quite a while, Sloan felt professionally fulfilled. And somewhat exonerated for the debacle surrounding The Ungrateful's farewell concert at the United Center.

Sloan reached her office early Monday morning with an extensive "to do" list that was already growing exponentially. Miguel Zabala's arraignment was scheduled for 9:00 on Tuesday morning, and Sloan's evidence would be instrumental in persuading the Federal Judge in United States District Court that Miguel Zabala would most likely flee the country if he were released on bail.

As part of the Zabala situation, Sloan needed to coordinate thoughts and activities with John Mercedes regarding Paddy O'Keane. Paddy had suddenly become a valuable component, and his testimony would be critical toward the eventual conviction of Miguel Zabala. So too with Dr. Fujimaro Chino.

Sloan thought it ironic that two fugitives from justice would be utilized to prevent a third from becoming one. Even Alanis Morrisette couldn't write a verse like that.

Sloan had previously scheduled a Monday morning meeting with the FBI video technicians to review the progress, or lack thereof, in developing any further information or leads from the numerous hours of footage from the various concerts. So far, the only significant revelation was the blurry image of a backward New York Yankees baseball cap.

Also on the agenda for the day was a conference call with John Mercedes and Scotland Yard for updates on the international aspects of the investigation and the search for any clues regarding the mysterious disappearance and trail of The Ungrateful's money.

Sloan booted her computer and was overwhelmed by the number of congratulatory e-mails she had already received – the chief of the bureau, Scotland Yard, the head of BATFA, Chicago Police Department's Chief of Police, and a cadre of fellow FBI agents, including Sloan's former nemeses

185

– Special Agent "No one" and Special Agent "One on One."

But the most gratifying e-mail was from John Mercedes and said simply, "To celebrate, let's have a special dinner. Warmest regards." Sloan knew that the salutation of "warmest regards" was chosen carefully – not too forward, not too professional, just right. To Sloan, everything about John Mercedes appeared to be "just right."

Chapter Fifty-eight

Jordan Taylor sat forlornly in her suite in the Knickerbocker Hotel. In front of Jordan were three large suitcases and a variety of laptops, cell phones and the new age communication devices that needed to be packed away neatly and readied for shipment back to Los Angeles.

For Jordan the past six weeks had been tumultuous, indeed. They had also been the most exhilarating, emotionally challenging and professionally rewarding of her career. Jordan smiled as she recounted the success of the tour – from both a financial and executional standpoint. Everything under Jordan's direction had been handled flawlessly, and her reputation as a brass balls entertainment executive had undoubtedly been augmented.

But to Jordan, the professional aspect mattered not. From a personal perspective, the tour had been a complete and unmitigated disaster. Six murders. Two apparent suicides. And a small group of people who Jordan really cared about was shortly going to scatter across the country – no across the world.

Jordan's melancholy was enhanced as she stared at the empty suitcases and the bulging drawers and closets filled with appropriately professional attire. Jordan desperately wanted to postpone the daunting task of neatly packing away what seemed to be not only her entire wardrobe, but also what may have just been the best part of her life. Just as she wanted to somehow prolong, extend and develop everything that what was good about the last six weeks.

And so, Jordan did what any rational, hard charging, brass balls mover and shaker would do under similar circumstances – she urgently procrastinated. First, Jordan busied herself with a myriad of meaningless phone calls to the home office. Then she reviewed a large pile of written correspondence. The accumulated e-mail presented both the greatest challenge and a much-welcomed sense of accomplishment as she replied, deleted and forwarded. Finally, Jordan reviewed the unsolicited photos that stringers and freelancers had sent in hopes of someday becoming real "paparazzi."

Jordan had previously segregated the photographs by venue; so, beginning in Boston, Jordan replayed the entire tour, one venue at a time.

The different photographers each had a distinctive style, and Jordan wondered if their various, respective sexual orientations were revealed in their pictures. Jordan expected that, because of Morgan's burgeoning presence in cyberspace, her photos would dominate, at least in terms of numbers. And Jordan's expectations were fulfilled – there were more close-up breast shots of Morgan than imaginable, each one directly appealing to the prurient interests of an ever-growing and appreciative throng of adolescent males.

For reasons Jordan understood entirely, there wasn't a bad photo of Angel in the entire collection. From Boston, to New York, to Philly, to DC, to Cleveland to Chicago – Angel was stunningly beautiful in any imaginable setting, and the cameras had captured and memorialized her perfectly.

The photographs of Ace and Tommy, though not nearly as numerous, were just as revealing. Ace's physical prowess was evident in each picture and Tommy's passion and intensity were captured.

The photographs of the crowds triggered Jordan's memory, and she recalled with amazement the unprecedented energy and electricity that charged the fans of The Ungrateful. Jordan skimmed over a couple of pictures of women flashing their breasts and was certain that the enterprising photographer had already posted these on the internet and was hawking them to various porn purveyors.

Jordan continued to be amazed by a number of things that she saw caught on film by the cameras, but one particular image from Boston troubled her greatly. She instantly studied the crowd shots from subsequent dates and became increasingly uncomfortable. There, unmistakably, in the audience was Becky Rose, now Becky Puccini.

Jordan knew, as did everyone from the band, that Becky didn't attend the concerts. Tommy's and her routine was the subject of many behind the scenes laughs and gentle ridicules – walking hand-in-hand, kissing gently, the outdated "break-a-leg."

This was definitely unusual, and Sloan had ordered Jordan to contact her immediately if she came across anything "suspicious and unusual." "Fuck," Jordan thought, "I can't be accusing, or even casting suspicion, on Becky – or anyone else. She may be a little protective and over the top, but she's like family."

Jordan returned the photographs to their respective files and immediately began to pack in earnest. Though her flight wasn't scheduled to leave O'Hare for Los Angeles for nearly five more hours, Jordan contacted the concierge and requested that a limousine be available to transport her to the airport within thirty minutes.

Chapter Fifty-nine

Ace returned, drenched in sweat, to Morgan's apartment. Final arrangements were pending for Ace to join the venerable Manchester United. Though Ace prided himself in keeping in peak physical shape, there was a world of difference between impressing gullible groupies and determined defenders with his prowess. Ace knew that his prolonged absence from the soccer field would be obvious to all the first time he stepped on the field; he was determined to minimize any embarrassment and shorten the learning curve as much as possible.

So, since the beginning of the tour, Ace worked out religiously and intensely. Curiously, like the rest of The Ungrateful, Ace was as far removed from the dope-smoking, hard drinking, women chasing rockers as one could be. Well, at least the dope smoking and hard drinking part. And his recent, regular dalliances with Morgan had propelled him far away from the women chasing moniker as well.

Ace knew that even if he arrived in England in phenomenal physical condition, he still wouldn't be even close to "match fit." So, to compensate, he worked even harder. With less than eight weeks remaining until the start of the English Premiership, time was not Ace's ally. But overcoming phenomenal odds was second nature to Ace, and but another challenge to overcome.

Ace emerged from the shower, with droplets of water glistening and contrasting with his midnight black skin. Morgan looked on appreciably as Ace toweled off his rippled abdomen and well-defined back. Something powerful in Morgan stirred, and she moved seductively closer to Ace and breathed warmly on his neck. Ace's commitment to his training regimen was unwavering, and he resisted the overwhelming impulses and Morgan's sensuality for almost two whole minutes until they found themselves in the usual throes of sexual ecstasy.

Ace held Morgan tightly, saying, "I'm gonna really miss this, miss you, baby. Wanna join me in England? We make quite a team, you know."

Morgan kissed Ace gently on the cheek and said, "You've got your rainbow to chase, Ace, and I've got mine. We were fortunate to share this part of our lives together. But it's time for both of us to move on. You're off to England. You're going to be a bigger soccer star than you are a music star. Especially because you've got that most single important attribute of all great soccer players – a single name – Ace, Pele, Maradonna. You'll be great, Ace. And you'll always be a part of me. Whenever I think of you, I will smile. I'm off to New York in a couple of days. You know, that 'super model' thing. I'll never forget you Ace. Never forget you and that magic wand of yours."

Ace and Morgan lay silently, holding hands. Feeling alive. And grateful.

Chapter Sixty

Sloan realized that she had less than twenty-four hours to help construct an airtight case to prevent, at least temporarily, Miguel Zabala from being released and disappearing forever.

The pressures of the unsolved murders from The Ungrateful Tour were mounting, but the recent arrest had provided Sloan with, at least, a temporary reprieve from the intense focus of the press and public. Reluctantly, Sloan instructed her administrative assistant to postpone all of the day's previously scheduled meetings.

Sloan was scheduled to meet in downtown Chicago with the United States Prosecuting Attorney at 11:00 AM. Prior to that meeting, Sloan had arranged a conference call with the lead investigator from The Federal Drug Administration's criminal division. Anecdotally, Sloan was beginning to believe that Dr. Fujimaro Chino was guilty beyond any reasonable degree of doubt of being hopelessly naïve, and undoubtedly guilty of violating the FDA's truth in labeling statutes. Sloan's instincts about Dr. Chino were supported both by the limited evidence known to her and by John Mercedes' more extensive investigation which corroborated her findings. Sloan was hopeful that the Administration authorities were sympathetic to at least entertaining discussion about a plea for leniency with Dr. Chino in exchange for his testimony against Miguel Zabala.

Chapter Sixty-one

Sloan Dillard entered the Everett McKinley Dirksen Building in downtown Chicago, and immediately her worst fears were realized – the arraignment of Miguel Zabala was going to be accompanied by a media circus.

A mob of photographers, reporters, camera men and various other media types had filled the lobby of the building and surrounded Sloan in an attempt to get some sort of interview or statement.

Sloan's standard, "No comment" was greeted by a rejoinder of pleas, questions and speculation. Sloan proceeded, with some difficulty, through the throng in hopes of gaining quick access to the elevators, and the peace awaiting her behind their closed doors. Those hopes were dashed when Sloan realized she was going to be subjected to the extremely thorough security measures implemented for an alleged international criminal of Miguel Zabala's stature.

The federal marshals conducting the security checks were professional, courteous and painstakingly careful. As the line slowly moved forward, Sloan was thankful for their conscientiousness, as the enormity of the implications of Miguel's arrest, impending trial and – hopefully – his ultimate conviction weighed heavily on her mind.

The elevator ascended quickly to the twenty-third floor of the United States District Court. Sloan slowly entered the same, venerable, oak-paneled courtroom in which, over thirty years ago the "Chicago Seven" were tried for conspiracy.

Sloan had a keen recollection of the Chicago Seven because, as a part of her FBI studies, she had written an extensively researched dissertation concluding that, "the Chicago Seven Conspiracy Trial was a monumental, phantom-like event with massive potential implications and negligible consequences."

Whatever it actually was, the 1970 trial of seven radicals accused of conspiring to incite a riot at the 1968 Democratic National Convention was, unarguably, one of the most unusual courtroom spectacles in the history of American jurisprudence. Sloan recalled the antics of Yippie founders Abbie Hoffman and Jerry Rubin and how the irrational behavior of United States

Federal Judge Julius Hoffman and the illegal bugging of the offices of the Chicago Seven's defense attorneys by the Federal Bureau of Investigation eventually led to the convictions ultimately being overturned on appeal in Circuit Court.

Since Miguel Zabala's arrest, Sloan had worked virtually around the clock to coordinate and cajole various governmental agencies. Returning to her office immediately following the incarceration of Miguel, Sloan initiated dual, and delicate, negotiations to properly incentivise Dr. Fujimaro Chino and Paddy O'Keane to testify against Miguel Zabala.

The deal brokering concerning Dr. Chino was complex beyond Sloan's comprehension – not the desired end result – the process.

The FDA had accomplished their primary objective, to insure public safety, by previously effectively shutting down the entire operation of Dr. Chino's American Pharmacal Company. The FDA, through its earlier investigations, realized that Dr. Chino was most probably an unwitting front for Miguel Zabala's nefarious plans, and the FDA was most anxious to lend assistance to dismantling Miguel's American drug operations.

Sloan's initial FBI training had provided her with the rudimentary basics of government inter-agency cooperation, but the reality and complexity of Dr. Chino's situation gave her a first-hand look into the difference between theory and practice. In one way or another, Dr. Chino's immunity talks involved agencies as divergent as the Department of Justice's United States Drug Intelligence Center, Drug Enforcement Administration and the Department of State's Bureau for International Law Enforcement Affairs and the Office of International Criminal Justice. And Sloan was able to reach a satisfactory compromise with all. On a Sunday evening.

In exchange for his testimony that Miguel Zabala was the source of supply for the methamphetamines found in his weight loss product, Dr. Chino was granted immunity from prosecution – for the drug-related charges. Sloan was careful to insist that any immunity did not extend to any eventual charges that might arise from the investigation surrounding the Ungrateful murders. Dr. Chino had signed the notarized confirmation statement and agreed to testify, truthfully and honestly, at all future judicial procedures regarding Miguel Zabala.

Sloan was concerned that the haste surrounding Dr. Chino's arrangements may have, unintentionally, left some less-than-tidy loose ends. However, John Mercedes had confirmed the veracity of Dr. Chino's ignorance – and though ignorance isn't forgivable – Sloan considered it vastly preferable to the intentional crimes perpetrated across the globe by Miguel Zabala. "The greater good for the greater number," she rationalized.

Paddy O'Keane's situation was infinitely simpler than Dr. Chino's, but complex nonetheless. Technically, Sloan and her associates at the Immigration and Naturalization Service were powerless to sanction Paddy O'Keane in any way. His passport was in order; he was well within his allowable time visiting the United States, and Paddy had been a model tourist – complying with all appropriate United States laws, rules and regulations. It was apparent to Sloan that Paddy would quickly see through a bluff and realize that any idle threat posed by INS would pale in comparison to the very real danger that betraying Miguel Zabala would represent to Paddy and the cause.

Sloan's revelation of her knowledge of the existence of both Mrs. Paddy O'Keane and her secret Irish bank account changed Paddy's perspective. Immediately. For, though the existence of Mrs. Paddy O'Keane was immaterial, the bank account was the first step in laundering money. Any investigation into its history would unravel a trail of damaging information to Paddy's cohorts in particular, for the entire cause in general and for the invaluable counter-intelligence into the activities of Scotland Yard. "An undercover operation" as Paddy and his wife humorously referred to it. Paddy signed the affidavit agreeing to testify against Miguel Zabala, thinking, "The greater good for the greater number."

Sloan was confident that her collaboration with the various government agencies and the prosecuting attorney, along with the attendant preparation, professionalism and presentation would precipitate circumspect courtroom behavior. Sloan was hopeful that the combination would be successful in convincing the presiding Federal Judge that: (1) the expected motion by the defense to dismiss charges be denied, (2) there was sufficient evidence to formally charge Miguel Zabala in Federal Court, (3) Miguel Zabala, with no family, known business or ties to the community represented a clear risk for flight and that bail should be denied, and (4) that any attempt to extradite Miguel to his native Venezuela be vigorously resisted.

Sloan realized that they were opposing a formidable legal mind and reputation. Miguel Zabala had the foresight and fortune to engage noted New York criminal attorney, Alvin Jeffrey Silver as the lead defense counsel.

Silver was once a child prodigy from a working class Bronx family who parlayed incisive wit, opportunistic instincts and an indefatigable work ethic into an immensely successful criminal law practice with an impressive string of victories from coast to coast.

Silver was reputed to have the most astutely keen legal mind in the United States. Combined with his stunningly handsome face, chiseled frame and passionate oratory skills, Silver was a one-man legal dream team with the disarming ability to befriend both impressionable juries and reticent judges alike. The result was an oppressive, intimidating record of victories amongst even the most challenging of circumstances.

And these circumstances did, indeed, promise to be most challenging.

Sloan was less than enthusiastic with the Presiding Federal Magistrate. The Honorable Samantha Johnson was a middle aged, African-American, Federal Judge with a reputation for judicial brilliance, accompanied by an explosive temper, an intolerance for incompetence and liberal advocation of victim's rights.

At precisely 9:30 AM, the bailiff announced in a loud, gravelly voice, "Hear Ye, Hear Ye, Hear Ye, United States District Court, Northern District of Illinois is now in session, The Honorable Samantha Johnson presiding. All Rise."

Without glancing at either the prosecuting or the defense tables, Judge Johnson struck her gavel resoundingly and stated; "The United States vs. Miguel Zabala."

Sloan was anticipating that Miguel Zabala, dressed in an orange jump suit with hands cuffed behind him and legs tethered with loudly clanking chains, would be led into court, surrounded by Federal marshals. Instead, Sloan's attention was drawn to the defense table where Attorney Alvin Jeffrey Silver was listening intently to a solitary, solemn Federal marshal.

Silver rose dramatically, stating, "The defense moves to have all charges against Miguel Zabala dropped immediately."

Greatly annoyed that her courtroom decorum was being upstaged, Judge Johnson first admonished Silver for his untimely motion, but inquired, "On what grounds do you so move?"

"On the grounds that Miguel Zabala is dead. He asphyxiated on his aspiration."

"Say what?" asked Judge Johnson – incredulous at the information and stunned at her unprofessional response.

"He choked on his vomit."

Sloan realized that Miguel Zabala may have taken the secrets of the deaths of Kevin Pace, Stewart Lindsey, Reggie Beasley and the six murder victims to his grave with him.

But maybe not.

Chapter Sixty-two

FBI Special Agent Sloan Dillard stood erectly at the British Airlines departure gate at O'Hare airport. John Mercedes' flight from Chicago to London's Heathrow Airport was scheduled to depart in less than one hour. Sloan's flight back to Washington, D.C. was leaving shortly after that, but in a different concourse – leaving precious little times for a goodbye that was way too preliminary. Sloan had less than fifteen minutes to comprehend and condense a life-long absence of true love into a meaningful, rationale goodbye that conveyed her appreciation for the past and her hope for the future.

Sloan watched through eyes that were, against strict commands to the contrary, slowly filling with tears. John Mercedes had procured his seat assignment from the gate agent, confirming a departure that Sloan dreaded – for what was, and for what might have become.

John walked slowly towards Sloan, looking more statuesque and handsome than ever. For reasons Sloan understood only too well, she now felt a creeping resentment of dashingly good looks, his cool demeanor, piercing eyes and chiseled physique.

John loosely embraced Sloan, and simply said, "Thanks, it's been real. Let's stay in touch. OK?" With a soft kiss to her cheek, John spun quickly and slowly disappeared into the tunnel leading to the 747.

Sloan watched incredulously as the goodbye she had dreaded, feared, scripted and rehearsed evaporated. If not for surprise and anger, Sloan would have broken down completely, but the shock of John's departure quickly transitioned her hurt to an unaccustomed emotional disengagement. Sloan turned without looking back and headed for United Flight 1722 to Washington's Dulles International Airport.

Sloan was mildly surprised when the United gate agent informed her that she had been upgraded to first class. She entered the plane and was somewhat confused by the dozen long stem red roses occupying her assigned seat 1A. The attached card read:

Dear Sloan:

I'm so sorry; I'm terrible at goodbyes. And at expressing my feelings. But I'll try, because you deserve it.

I'm afraid. For so many years, I've only relied on myself. I've only been 'me.' But now I can see an 'us' and that thought, as pleasant as it is, is threatening. And now Angel has come into my life.

The time apart will allow me to sort things out. And to figure myself out. I already know that I love you. I need some time to make sure that I don't hurt you.

Love,
John

Chapter Sixty-three

Tommy and Becky's honeymoon consisted of an afternoon at the Cub's game, followed by an evening of luxurious pampering at Chicago's Four Season's Hotel. Tommy ironically mused about the absence of passionate sex, but Becky's pregnancy, now nearing the end of the second trimester, somehow limited the acrobatic creativity of their earlier sessions.

Unknown to Becky, both the wedding ceremony and the hotel had been funded through the generosity of Jordan, who had graciously agreed to front the necessary funds for cash-strapped Tommy.

Becky was more than a little surprised when Tommy informed her that they were going to return to his childhood home for a short while "until things turn around." Though Becky had envisioned a bright white painted colonial house with forest green shutters, a wrap-around porch, and an expansive well-manicured lawn, all surrounded by a white picket fence on a tree lined street, Tommy's mother's house was preferable to hotels teeming with groupies and temptation. "Whatever you want Tommy, just as long as I am with you."

Tommy and Becky descended to the lobby to check out and head back to their new home.

"You gonna try and lift me over the threshold?" Becky asked playfully as the clerk informed Tommy that the bill had already been taken care of and there was someone to meet him in the hotel restaurant.

Tommy and Becky, walked, hand-in-hand, into the restaurant and were greeted by the smiling faces of Ace, Morgan and Angel.

"Welcome to the 'Last Breakfast,'" Ace proclaimed loudly as Tommy and Becky approached the table, already topped for five.

"Hey, before we all scatter, whadya think of all that's happened recently?" Angel asked.

"Man, it scares me. Scares me big time," said Ace. "First there was Reggie, then Stewart. Then Goalpost. And now Miguel Zabala. Four dudes suspected of offing themselves. And I was connected somehow to all of them. Hope, for your guys' sakes, it's not contagious. I've just been a part of 'Four Funerals and a Wedding' – if any of you guys go, that line's ruined too."

"Aren't you ever serious?"

"Yeah, now I'm seriously scared."

"Me too."

Tommy interjected, "Hey, enough of the downer talk. I just got married."

"And that's enough of a downer for all of us," Ace added as the mood of the group swept upwards.

For the next hour or so they reminisced, chatted, gossiped, ripped on each other, joked, and talked about the future – the one they had imagined and the one they faced now. About the only person not mentioned was Jordan, somehow her sudden disappearance didn't seem right – especially to Angel. But hey, life goes on. And so were they.

Ace to England.

Morgan to New York.

Angel to her solo career.

And, as Ace stated, "Tommy to the 'hood' – parenthood that is."

Despite the jocularity and frivolity, an uneasy cloud of, not really gloom, but more like apprehension hung over the group.

Eight months ago they started with such unity, enthusiasm and optimism that success was a foregone conclusion.

Today, that unity, enthusiasm and optimism was tempered with a touch of despair, and a more reserved and guarded outlook.

Ten deaths, four of them thought to be suicides and six of them known to be murders, have a tendency to allow a creeping pessimism to encroach optimistic outlooks.

"Anyone heard from Sloan?"

"Who?"

"Sloan Dillard – the FBI chick?"

"She's on my voicemail," said Ace, "and you?"

"Never heard from her again."

"Me neither."

"Nor me – why just you, Ace?"

"Probably cause she's got a big trial coming up, and she wants me in case there isn't a hung jury," Ace joked, in a manner that was thoroughly unsuccessful in concealing his concern.

"Tommy, we should be going," whispered Becky softly.

And unwillingly and unceremoniously, Tommy, Ace, Morgan and Angel bid their farewells. Each left with tears welling in their eyes.

Becky smiled.

The cab ride from Dulles to Sloan's apartment near Georgetown was insufferable. The cab's antiquated air conditioner was no match for Washington's intense summer heat and humidity and Sloan could feel the unpleasant effects of perspiration.

Maybe it was the blast of furnace like heat when Sloan finally emerged from the cab, the daunting prospects of transporting bags and bags of clothing and gear to her third floor walk-up, or the grim reality of returning to an empty apartment with her heart half-a world behind; whatever it was, Sloan's eyes welled with tears as she stood by the curb and stared absent-mindedly at her brownstone.

Reluctantly, Sloan began the inevitable process of returning her belongings and life to some sense of normalcy. The unpacking went, as expected, extremely smoothly since Sloan had pre-planned every detail in advance. The life part was exponentially more difficult as the memories of John Mercedes, Miguel Zabala and the constant adrenaline ricocheted throughout her over-stimulated brain.

Sloan was looking forward to returning to work at the bureau's headquarters the following morning. The security of a routine was welcome, and the challenges of the office promised to occupy her and prevent – or at least postpone – the torturing game of "what if" which, despite her best efforts to prevent, she ceaselessly played.

Sloan arrived at the Pennsylvania Avenue Headquarters shortly before 7:00 AM. The early morning hours for Sloan had always been the most productive. Her long absence from the office meant that she would be facing a mountain of mail, packages, and, most dreaded, paperwork. She was surprised when she opened her office door and was surrounded by brightly colored helium filled balloons from various well-wishers congratulating her on the collar of Miguel Zabala.

Sloan was impressed by the display, but cognizant of the fact that an office filled with helium balloons was less than professional and might somehow diminish her well-earned credibility with her male counterparts.

"Fuck 'em," she said aloud, ever mindful of her previous language usage policy.

Though Sloan had done an admirable job of staying on top of her e-mail and voice-mail while she was away from the D.C. office, the traditional mail was quite another story. Sloan's assistant had neatly stacked piles of letters, brochures, magazines, etc. in chronological order according to the date of their receipt.

Sloan efficiently went through the mail, discarding, unopened, nearly two-thirds of the pieces. Somewhere towards the end of the pile, Sloan's attention was drawn to an 8.5 x 11 manila envelope with a curious and suspicious look. Sloan's cautionary nature precluded her from opening the piece, and she set it aside for later inspection and analyzation by the techs.

At precisely 8:30 AM, Sloan's catch-up was interrupted by sharp knocking on her office door.

"Excuse me, Special Agent Dillard."

"Come in."

"Good Morning, Ma'am. I'm Agent Schlitz, from Ballistics. Here is the report on the Pace bullets."

"Thank you."

Sloan took the rather lengthy report and scanned the information to get a preview of the conclusion. She was neither surprised nor dismayed to learn that the weapon type, caliber and bullets involved in the deaths of Reggie Beasley, Stewart Lindsey and Kevin Pace were, if not identical, exceedingly similar.

She was both surprised and dismayed, however, to learn that the bullet point of entry, for both the Beasley and Lindsey deaths were not consistent with self-inflicted fatal wounds; the Pace death was.

"But what does that mean?" Sloan queried herself, knowing full well the ominous implications.

Of the eleven deaths, nine were murders. Two were suspected suicides.

And she was clueless as to both the killer and the motive. Or the killers and the motives.

Chapter Sixty-four

Jordan Taylor was greeted by an overwhelming sense of despair upon her return to Los Angeles. Looming large in Jordan's mind were her two secrets, one of which, thankfully, wasn't discovered – and the other one, she didn't – couldn't, wouldn't – reveal. Since returning, Jordan's sleep had been fitful and restless as the photo of Becky at the concert was emblazoned in her mind.

Jordan prided herself on a number of key personal attributes – loyalty and honesty were at the top of her sacrosanct list. Becky's photo initiated a painful struggle as Jordan reluctantly recognized that, in this case, honesty and loyalty were mutually exclusive.

Professionally, Jordan had reached the apex of her career, yet a feeling of dissatisfaction perpetually gnawed at her. Jordan was hopeful that her languidness was the musical equivalent of the despair that a soldier feels when returning to civilization from a lengthy combat mission.

"Give it some time. You'll snap back. You've been through a lot recently. All that pressure, no wonder you're a little uptight. Time is a great healer. Relax. You'll be back to your old self in no time at all." A bevy of well wishers advised.

"Fucking bullshit, it's all fucking bullshit."

Jordan knew that her time with The Ungrateful had indelibly stamped her heart and soul and forever changed her.

"For better or worse?" she wondered to herself, knowing full well the answers. For, in The Ungrateful, Jordan once again discovered the power of innocence, the magic of dreams, the beauty of friendship, the eternity of love, the strength of commitment and the unity of diversity. The Ungrateful had awakened Jordan's dormant soul and stimulated every aspect of her life.

Jordan discovered her life, ironically, in death. For it was the death of the unfortunate victims of The Ungrateful that propelled Jordan to realize the power within her – her ability to manage, to lead, to negotiate, to facilitate, to mitigate, to accept, to challenge, to face uncertainty, to conquer fear, to produce, to win and to love.

And Jordan desperately missed all of that. And more. But still, the photo of Becky haunted Jordan's every waking moment.

Chapter Sixty-five

Sloan was beginning to settle into the comfortable joy of a routine. Each morning she would wake up, go into the living room and turn on the television and sit cross-legged on the couch, munching on cereal while watching the daybreak edition of the local news. Each morning, Sloan would watch as news of The Ungrateful murders dissipated and then, eventually, evaporated completely from coverage. For Sloan, this was bittersweet. The absence of coverage significantly lowered her umbrage, but the vacuum also demonstrated her inability to solve the perplexing series of murders/suicides.

After breakfast, Sloan engaged in her usual semi-serious round of physical conditioning. One hundred sit-ups. Fifty pushups. Leg lifts. Crunches. A contortion-like round of stretches. Modified yoga. And then the best part of her entire day.

Sloan would log on to her computer and check her e-mail. Usually, she was greeted by an increasingly warm message from John. Since he had returned to England, the e-mails had progressed from:

"Hi Sloan. Hope all is well. The word of the Miguel Zabala's arrest has made you a hero in England,"

... to

"Sloan, didn't think I'd think of you all the time, only most of the time, but it's all of the time,"

... to

"Sloan, I'm so sorry for how I left. It was unfair and selfish of me. You're too special to be treated that way. Sorry,"

... to

"Dear Sloan, each day I'm away from you, is one day closer to my being with you. I see your smile in the morning when I wake, and I smile. I imagine your softness and I become hard. I can't wait to see you again. To hold you. To love you. To love you forever."

Sloan's replies usually mirrored John's messages, both in length and emotion. It was, indeed, a happy way for Sloan to start her day, and one of her infrequent joys, since the pressures surrounding The Ungrateful deaths were mounting with each passing day.

Ironically, as John's messages became more supportive and expressive, Sloan's reception within the Bureau was becoming increasingly chilly. It was apparent to all the specter of the unsolved murders and suicides was weighing heavily on the minds of those both up and down the ladder, and Sloan was, ultimately, the agent in charge of the investigation that had, for all intents and purposes, stalled.

But as the leads became colder, Sloan only worked harder. For, truth be known, there really wasn't much else for her to do with John an ocean away. Sloan had always had a prodigious work ethic, but even her most-demanding standards were now obliterated by her ceaseless quest to solve the mysteries surrounding the deaths associated with The Ungrateful.

Sloan meticulously reviewed every aspect of the investigation and continuously postulated and speculated on various scenarios. In her customary manner, Sloan listed in neat, multi-colored bubble letters a chart with various potential killers and possible motives and conjectures for and against each. Sloan's task was considerably simplified since most of her original prime suspects were already dead – Thomas Puccini III, Reggie Beasley, Stewart Lindsey, Miguel Zabala. It had not escaped Sloan's attention that the killings had ceased with the death Miguel Zabala.

Included on Sloan's "living list" of suspects and motives were:

Dr. Fujimaro Chino:

Why he did – Despondent over loss of business. Desperately needed massive infusion of capital for legal and living expenses. Daughter Morgan was non-communicative and uncooperative. Tour deaths may have been an attempt to reach Morgan and access her money. Methamphetamines involved in certain deaths – had access to meth from diet formula. Known to be at each concert venue.

Why he didn't – Was loving father. Already was under government observation for role in diet deaths. Source of potential revenue would dry up if tour were canceled.

Becky Puccini:

Why she did – Protective of relationship with Tommy. Fearful of "competition" from others. Known to be, at least, in each concert city.

Why she didn't – Loving and supportive. Engaged. Pregnant. Little to gain if Tommy's career ended. No access to methamphetamines.

Kelly Puccini:

Why she did – Previously involved in suspicious deaths. May have been attempting to extort money to cover either husband's gambling debts or Paddy

O'Keane's requests. Known to be in each concert city

Why she didn't – Twenty years or more removed from Dublin and Belfast deaths. Not overly concerned with either her family life or her own life, for that matter.

The Rose Boys:

Why they did – Some sort of weird family thing. Closely connected to New York Yankees – easy access to cap.

Why they didn't – Little to gain from apparent random killings.

Jordan Taylor:

Why she did – Profited substantially from publicity surrounding concerts – both financially and professionally. Was at each venue. Knew exact details of concerts, timings, movements, etc. No close family ties. No close social ties. Was instrumental in separating The CDs from The Ungrateful. Whereabouts during concerts unaccounted for. Quick exit from Chicago problematic.

Why she didn't – Unlikely profile for a mass murderer.

Sloan double checked her notation and realized that an "unlikely profile" was the least compelling of all the reasons she had listed. Sloan noted that the crime annals and newspapers are filled with the most "unlikely suspects" possible who eventually are proven to be guilty – the society matron who shoplifts knick knacks, the catholic priest who molests young boys, the girl scout den mother who's running a house of prostitution on the side, the circuit court judge who's smoking crack in his chambers, the spinster church treasurer who's embezzling donations, the righteous, homophobic fundamentalist minister who is "outed," – the list was endless.

Sloan underlined Jordan Taylor's name. Then she underlined it again in a different color and continued.

Mickey Delaney:

Why he did – Jealous over the attention focused on The Ungrateful. Possible effects of latent drug induced rage. Desperate, theatrical attempt to stimulate even more interest in the sold out tour. In each venue, not on stage, when murder occurred.

Why he didn't – Reputation intact as rock and roll legend. Farewell tour and income boost has him set for life.

The Ungrateful:

Why they did: To gain notoriety and break through clutter.

Why they didn't: always on-stage, would need accomplices.

Paddy O'Keane:

Why he did – To extort money for the IRA.

Why he didn't – Under constant surveillance by Kevin Pace and John Mercedes.

Sloan reviewed the list and her observations. Though nothing revolutionary evolved from the exercise, Sloan prioritized her investigative activities.

Jordan Taylor's name was at the top of her list.

Chapter Sixty-six

Becky Puccini noticed that as the summer days gradually grew shorter, her stomach grew larger. For Becky, there was something oddly comforting in the combination. Becky and Tommy had settled into a relaxed routine, which, for Becky, was a welcome relief from the rigors of living with a rock and roll star on tour.

Becky was mindful of a gradual boredom descending upon Tommy. The thrill, energy, excitement and passion of performances were gone. Forever. In their place, Becky had created a structured schedule designed to, basically, deprogram Tommy from his rock and roll lifestyle. Early morning wake-ups replaced early morning bedtimes. A nutritionally correct breakfast replaced Mountain Dew and Doritos.

After breakfast, Tommy read the paper while Becky tidied up the kitchen, showered and came downstairs again to greet Tommy and the day with a bright smile. Midmornings usually found Tommy and Becky strolling through the neighborhood, hand-in-hand, talking, talking and talking. Tommy found the mornings boring, and Becky was pleased for boring, in her opinion, it was a vast improvement from the life of drugs, groupies, random sex, alcohol and only God knows what else – and if not God, certainly Sodom and Gomorrah that had awaited Tommy without her.

Lunches usually consisted of fruit, soup, maybe a salad and a turkey sandwich on whole wheat bread. Becky was exceedingly careful to eat correctly for her and the baby, and she was eager to introduce Tommy to healthy dietary habits. Though Tommy was less than thrilled with the lack of variety, he could actually see his body responding to "Camp Becky" and so he tolerated the culinary purgatory that he realized, he was forever subjected to.

After lunch, Tommy was in his prime. The pregnancy, the heat, the morning's activities and the exercise all combined to tire Becky, and so she napped. And while Becky napped, Tommy reverted to his musician's persona. Tommy played. And played. And played some more. And in music, Tommy found himself. For it was the playing, and not the performing, which Tommy realized was the foundation of his happiness. Each day, Tommy played a little more, and in doing so discovered new, divergent things about himself, his music and his life. Tommy was happy and so was Becky. But still, Tommy missed the friendship of Angel, Morgan and Ace.

Evenings, however, were less than idyllic for both of them. For, some time in the afternoon while Becky was sleeping and Tommy was playing, Kelly and Paddy emerged from the bedroom where they had been shacked up since stumbling in the previous night – morning, actually. Tommy had no idea where they went each night until 3:00 or 4:00 AM; his only hope was that they would go away. And never return. Curiously, Becky was conciliatory, reminding Tommy of his lineage and urging peace.

Dinner that evening for Tommy was delightful. Becky had prepared Tommy's childhood favorite dish, spaghetti and meatballs. Becky, for some unknown reason, could prepare the meal better than Tommy's paternal grandmother. Tommy had given up any hope of his mother ever preparing anything remotely delectable, and she obliged him at an early age by refusing to treat him to her impressive arrays of stews, boiled potatoes, cabbage and corned beef.

Tommy's Italian grandmother, however, captured the fancy of Tommy's taste buds at an early age. Recently, Becky surprised and delighted Tommy with the taste he remembered from many years ago and thought only resulted from hours standing over a stove, stirring a large pot and endlessly blending seasoning and spices until everything was *que bellisimo.*

Tommy knew that what made that dinner so special wasn't really Becky's spaghetti, it was Paddy's revelation that his visa was expiring and he was heading back to Ireland. Within days.

The plan, as Paddy detailed, was to have Kelly join him as soon as possible – once one little matter was cleared up. Kelly Puccini didn't have a passport. Or a valid driver's license. Or a state issued ID. And despite Kelly's searches, she couldn't produce her marriage license. It seems, like Tommy had wished so many times before, that Kelly Puccini, at least in the eyes of the government, didn't exist. And, unfortunately for both Tommy and Kelly, the government was in charge of issuing passports.

"Six weeks," said Paddy, "we'll get this little matter cleared up within six weeks. So, Becky me-lass. Grandma Kelly should be around to greet her little grandson."

Chapter Sixty-seven

Sloan was thoroughly unprepared when her director entered her office without knocking, early one afternoon. For Sloan, the meeting was as devastating as it was brief.

"Sloan, you are to be commended on the extensive work you have done to date on The Ungrateful murders. Since we are not certain whether or not Reggie Beasley, Stewart Lindsey, Kevin Pace or Miguel Zabala were involved, and since the progress on the investigation has stalled, I have decided that a fresh perspective is warranted. I've instructed your associates to immediately leave for Chicago and look at everything from a different angle. They will report all findings to me, through you. I'm hoping one way or another we can wrap this up and close the file. Thank you." And, with that, he was gone, along with her professional dignity.

From behind the closed doors, Sloan could hear the muffled sounds of laughter as Special Agent Kevin Flatly (also known to Sloan as "No One") and Special Agent Upton Lance (also know to Sloan as "One on One") basked equally in their newly found good fortune and Sloan's misery.

Sloan's heart sunk as she realized that the one thing that she least wanted to do in the world, was the one thing she had to do. Immediately. Sloan stood up from her desk and walked outside her office. Though she felt her heart sinking, her lips quivering and the world as she knew it tumbling down upon her, the "stupid fuckheads" were oblivious to her plight.

"I'd like to take this opportunity to congratulate you. I've been stumped as to what the final answer is, though I've got my strong suspicions. But I know that a fresh perspective is needed, so I'll spare you having to listen to my hunches. I've kept detailed notes and I'll forward the spreadsheet with all my activities. In the Chicago office, I've left duplicate notations of my work to the date of my departure. I wish you all the luck in the world," Sloan concluded as she shook their hands.

Left unsaid, after the wish of good luck, was, "'cause you're going to need it you chauvinistic, clueless bastards."

As Sloan turned to leave, a massive smile dominated her face. At the very instant when her professional career was spiraling downward, her spirits were buoyed by the partnership replacing her. FBI Special Agent Kevin Flatly and FBI Special Agent Upton Lance – K. Flatly and U. Lance. Sloan morphed their names into "Flatulence" and again smiled at the ironically exact description of their partnership.

Sloan returned to her office, gathered her purse and instructed her assistant that she would be out of the office for the balance of the day.

Many times, when Sloan was discombobulated, she would seek solace and comfort, not in herself, not in wallowing in self-pity and misery, but in helping others. But today was different, and a massive dose of "oh, poor, pitiful me" was planned for the menu as Sloan walked up the three creaky stairs to her apartment.

Sloan closed the door behind her, flung her coat on the couch and readied herself for a massive outpouring of tears. A banging on the door interrupted – no, temporarily postponed – the self-agonizing.

"Sloan, dear, something came for you."

Of all the people Sloan didn't want to deal with, it was her ever-chirpy elderly neighbor. Despite blindness, old age and various, sundry other infirmities, the widow Galin was always optimistic and cheery – the last thing in the world Sloan wanted now.

"Sloan, they're flowers. Roses, I think. Can't see them, but I'll never forget the smell. Sloan, dear, I bet that they are red. With baby's breath. And greens. Wrapped in a beautiful ribbon, I reckon."

Sloan opened the door and the tears poured forth, but these weren't the tears she had planned. They were tears of happiness.

The card read, "Sloan. I miss you. I love you. London is beautiful this time of year. Please come and see for yourself. Love, John."

Sloan hugged Mrs. Galin tightly, and then invited her in for tea.

Tea somehow, seamlessly, transitioned into dinner. Sloan made a simple, but delicious, meal consisting of homemade blueberry muffins, a garden salad and sour cream chicken breasts served with green beans topped with french fried onion rings. For a diminutive, elderly lady, Mrs. Galin exhibited a prodigious appetite and a bottomless stomach. After Sloan served, embarrassedly, a frozen cheesecake for dessert, Mrs. Galin stood up erectly, tightly hugged Sloan, and said matter-of factly, "Deary, that was the most special evening I've had in quite some time. You've made an old lady very happy. Now it's time for you to make a young lady very happy. And a man in London. You're not getting any younger, you know. Time is nobody's ally. Follow you heart."

With a kiss on the cheek and a squeeze of the arm, Mrs. Galin slowly felt her way out of Sloan's apartment and into her own. And Sloan struggled to remember how she had originally planned on spending the evening.

Sloan fell sound asleep, with John's card clutched tightly to her breast, and a resolve in her heart to accept his invitation.

Chapter Sixty-eight

In his twenty-two years of existence, Ace believed that he had pretty much seen, heard, or experienced it all. Growing up on the beaches of Jamaica, equi-distance from both abject poverty and lavish wealth, Ace had witnessed the polar opposites of wealth. And its impact.

Nothing in his wildest imagination could have ever prepared Ace for the circus he was experiencing as a potential impact player for a premier division English Football Team. Every move he made was chronicled by an all-absorbing press – every touch of the ball, every step over, thru pass, wall pass, dummy run, rocket shot, feigned injury, header, chest trap, everything.

Ace joked to a teammate, "Man, I fart, and they run behind me trying to figure out what I had for breakfast. What gives?"

"In England, we're serious about our football," was the universal response. "You think?"

Ace was familiar with his teammates on the field, for soccer spoke an international language that needed no interpretation. Because of the British influence in his native Jamaica, Ace was relatively comfortable with the Brits. Though more or less at home, on and off the field, Ace was lonely. Lonely for the fame and adulation that comes with being a rock star. Lonely for the camaraderie of the tour. Lonely for his physical closeness and nights of unbridled passion with Morgan. But more than anything, Ace was lonely for the security, laughter and friendship he so desperately missed with Morgan, Angel and Tommy.

When Ace first arrived in England, the original master plan called for him to train with the club and then play for the reserve team until he re-acclimated himself to the game and returned his legs to "match shape." However, Ace's unmistakable brilliance was obvious to all. Ace soon found himself starting on the field with ten other of the world's premier soccer stars, whose incomes dwarfed Ace's previous rock and roll pay.

And at the end of the match, their paychecks were deposited directly into their personal accounts.

With a little over four weeks until the opening friendly match, Ace was ready for his second bout of superstardom in recent months. If only England had Letterman.

Chapter Sixty-nine

Morgan's fame and fortune – well maybe misplaced fortune – meant nothing anymore. Not, at least, to the other models, creatives, photo directors, editors and fashion moguls. What mattered to them, pure and simple, was whether or not Morgan's looks, or look, could help them build their own personal and professional fame and fortune.

And fortunately for Morgan, she had the "look " – nearly six feet tall, 115 pounds, jet-black hair, distinctive features, high cheekbones, pouty lips, uncommonly expressive eyes, and, oh what a body. Completely nude, Morgan was stunningly beautiful. When she was clothed, Morgan somehow made the fabric more beautiful, the cut more elegant, the design more desirable. And it was Morgan's uncanny ability to enhance the fashion designer's creations that made her one of the hottest commodities ever to walk down a fashion runway or sit for a photo shoot.

Growing up, Morgan resented both her mother and father for forcing her to take ballet and dance. But somewhere in those lessons, Morgan learned how to carry herself with dignity, poise and sensuality. And fashion is certainly all about sensuality.

Morgan's whirlwind schedule – fittings, make-up, hair, photo shoots, rehearsals – kept her busy most days from early in the morning to late at night. But late at night, in the solitude of her room, Morgan knew that all the money and notoriety in the world could never replace the richness she had felt when she was with Tommy, Angel and Ace.

With thoughts of Ace, Morgan drifted off towards sleep, as her fingers drifted over the body that delighted so many.

Chapter Seventy

Angel's success as a solo singer was somewhat related to Morgan's success as a fashion model. Related, as war is to peace, hot is to cold, love is to hate and heaven is to hell. And hell is where Angel was.

Angel hopelessly missed performing. But more than that, she missed the emotional connections with Morgan, Tommy and Ace. She missed lingering over caramel cappuccino with Jordan, she missed rehearsing, and she missed the friendly trash-talking banter. She missed being a part of something. A part of someone. She was a "part" and desperately needed to be whole.

It wasn't being alone that so bothered Angel, it was the loneliness. From the time Angel was young, growing up in Cabrini, she was alone. But not lonely. For she had her dreams. Her aspirations. Her goals.

Angel was comforted in her solitude with frequent e-mails from John Mercedes and from Jordan. John talked about how much Angel's acceptance meant to him, how sorry he was for not being there for her childhood, how his absence may have been a blessing for Angel since she turned out so fabulously and how he probably would have screwed her up, and how they might go forward and continue to develop their relationship. John always thanked Angel for her forgiveness and told her how proud he was of her. And how much he loved her. John Mercedes also talked about Sloan. And love. John noted the irony in being alone for over twenty-two years, and now sharing his life and his love, mostly through cyber-space with two beautiful women, half a world away.

Jordan Taylor, in her e-mails, just talked. About anything and everything. About how, though her career was skyrocketing professionally, she was personally unfulfilled. About how much she missed Angel. And Morgan. And Ace. And Tommy. About her dreams, hopes, aspirations. About the future.

Somewhere in those e-mails, Angel convinced Jordan that she should resign and start anew as Angel's manager. Or maybe it was Jordan who convinced Angel that both of their careers needed reinventing and together they could make something special again. However it evolved, Jordan Taylor became the sole owner of Jordan Taylor Management. Angel was her only client.

Chapter Seventy-one

Sloan sat at her desk furiously tapping instructions on her keyboard. Fortunately, Sloan's computer wizardry, combined with the available software, made the task relatively effortless. With a final stroke, Sloan exclaimed, "*Viola!*" and silently congratulated herself. The vacation to London was booked – airfare and hotel. Sloan made some presumptuous assumptions – transfers wouldn't be required, one bed, king size, no need to pre-book a tour, for she was confident that she would have an indigenous lover to escort her through both the vibrancy of London and the eternally sleepy British countryside.

Sloan was somewhat disappointed that her director so readily approved her vacation request, saying only, "Be sure to stay in touch with your men in Chicago."

"Yes sir, I certainly will."

But Sloan thoroughly deserved the trip, and she was uncertain that she would be able to contain her excitement for another couple of weeks until the August 16 departure date.

Washington, DC's Dulles airport to London's Heathrow. First Class. Sloan envisioned departing from the plane, glancing furtively from side to side through the multi-ethnic crowds, finally spotting John and all of his ruggedly handsome beauty anxiously waiting, and then each running, almost in slow motion, with outstretched arms until they meet in a tight embrace and share a kiss that is tender at first, and then naughtily indecent. Sloan shook herself out of her reverie and mused that she had become sappier than a Harlequin novel.

Sloan's little scenario never accounted for customs, or the strict, almost quarantine-like, routing of arriving passengers, but hey – it was her fantasy and she would get off the plane and be greeted however she goddamned wanted. Sloan shuddered as she thought of what had become of her previously pristine vocabulary. "Fuck it," she thought with a self-congratulatory, gratifying smile.

Since her "demotion," Sloan had focused almost exclusively on tracing the money that disappeared from the custodial accounts of The Ungrateful.

That and analyzing the similarities and differences in the deaths of Thomas Puccini, Reggie Beasley, Stewart Lindsey, Kevin Pace and Miguel Zabala.

Sloan's professional opinion, somewhat substantiated by ballistics and forensics, somewhat substantiated by a thorough and meticulous review of all available evidence, (and partly unsubstantiated and based only on gut and instinct) was that Kevin Pace had murdered Reggie Beasley and Stewart Lindsey. That Kevin Pace and Miguel Zabala had committed suicide. And that Tommy Puccini was murdered by an unknown assailant.

Sloan's conclusions were founded in the similarities between Reggie's and Stewart's deaths. Killers are consistent in their modus operandi, and the staging of the suicides of Reggie and Stewart was definitely the work of a professional. Kevin Pace was nothing, if not the consummate professional. Sloan speculated that Kevin's role as a double agent, no a triple agent – as she remembered Kevin's dalliances with Mrs. Paddy O'Keane – had positioned him unwittingly in the role of Miguel Zabala's henchman. And hitman. Somehow, the drug deals had gone wrong, the money hadn't flowed as expected, the profits went into the arms, the double-crossing unfurled – whatever it was, Sloan speculated – was punishable in Miguel Zabala's world by the death penalty – and Kevin Pace was the executioner.

Sloan was totally certain that both Kevin Pace's and Miguel Zabala's deaths were, in fact suicides. In Kevin's case, the ballistics evidence was irrefutable. And his suicide note so implicated Miguel and left so many trails of clues to unravel and expose his operations, his death was a pre-ordained certainty anyway. There was no doubt in Sloan's mind that Kevin pulled the trigger that ended his life, and precipitated the end of Miguel's.

Sloan was equally certain that Miguel Zabala had intentionally ended his life, in the early morning hours of a solitary holding cell in Chicago. Because of Miguel's stature and reputation in the international law enforcement community, the incarcerating authorities had been circumspect in the processing and handling of Miguel. Though the expected allegations of police brutality and wrongful death accusations swirled in the frenzied media in the aftermath of his death, Sloan was assured that all proper protocol was followed to the letter. Miguel was stripped of his belt and shoelaces, was placed on formal "suicide watch" and was under constant video surveillance and personal visual inspection every fifteen minutes. The subsequent review of the tapes revealed that Miguel's intelligence enabled him to time the visual inspections and synchronize his well thought out, premeditated death plan. Though it never was, and never would be, revealed in the press, Sloan watched the tapes in horror as Miguel Zabala took his T-Shirt and stuffed it into his throat and down his esophagus. It was a ghastly, gruesome, repulsive finale as Miguel Zabala wretched on the cement floor of his cell and struggled to end his life as vomit filled his lungs and his desperate gasps for breath were thwarted by his overpowering will to die.

For Sloan, the death of Thomas Puccini was more problematic. Not as problematic as Thomas Puccini's death was to Thomas himself, but problematic nonetheless. Though Sloan couldn't entirely rule out Reggie Beasley, Stewart Lindsey or Kevin Pace as Thomas' murderer, she sincerely doubted if any of them were directly involved. First, Thomas's death was caused by two knife wounds – one plunged deep into his massive belly – and one grotesquely severing his carotid artery. The fact that he was murdered in close proximity suggested that he knew his killer. The fact that his death was passionately executed suggested a lack of emotional detachment that would characterize a professional execution.

Sloan was convinced that Thomas Puccini was killed by someone he knew very well. And someone who very badly wanted him dead. Sloan was also convinced that the secrets of The Ungrateful deaths were buried not with Miguel Zabala, but with Thomas Puccini.

Sloan had traced and retraced the money and had, at least, a pretty good idea of how it left. She knew where it went. She thought she knew where it was. She wanted to determine how to get it back.

When The Ungrateful started on the tour, Reggie Beasley was still their manager of record. In that capacity, Reggie though he had limited fiduciary involvement, he did have knowledge and access to social security numbers and, possibly, account passwords. Though Ace was not a citizen of the United States of America, and thus without a social security number, Stewart Lindsey undoubtedly had access to all of Ace's pertinent, personal information.

And so, Sloan speculated, with both Reggie Beasley and Stewart Lindsey beholden to Miguel Zabala, and with Miguel's knowledge of the intricacies of transferring money from account to account and nation to nation, the actual implementation details were perfunctory.

But Sloan knew that even the most proficient launderers left some scintilla of evidence. Somewhere. And she was determined to undercover it. But she couldn't do it alone. Fortunately for Sloan, she knew of someone in her line of business who would be more than willing to work closely with her – John Mercedes.

Sloan knew, from earlier investigations, that the money was originally transferred from the banks of the respective venues to the Los Angeles individual custodial accounts for each member of The Ungrateful. After the Chicago concert, each of the band members had approximately $1,250,000 in their account. Sometime not too far after Chicago, all of the money from each account was transferred from the original Los Angeles bank, to an offshore account in the Bahamas, and subsequently to a bank in Venezuela. From Venezuela, the money was split – $2,000,000 was wired to Kevin Pace's personal account at the Bank of London, and $3,000,000 was wired to an account jointly controlled by Kevin Pace and Mrs. Paddy O'Keane at the Central Bank of Ireland.

Retrieving the money from the Bank of London was to be a relatively simple matter of proving the identity of the rightful owners and waiting for the appropriate legal and governmental jurisdictions to coordinate their decisions. Having John Mercedes, in London, was invaluable. John worked closely with his fellow investigators at Scotland Yard to prove that the money in Kevin's account was illegally procured, and then with a sympathetic barrister from the British court to remove the money from Kevin's estate prior to probate. Sloan was able to expedite the re-transfer of the money back into the original custodial accounts. $500,000 to each account. No one was happier to learn of Sloan's recovery than Tommy Puccini. With the possible exception of Becky Puccini.

Tommy's first transaction was to repay Jordan Taylor for the wedding. And the ring. And the musicians. And the flowers. And the reception. And the honeymoon.

Sloan continued to focus her attention on the $3,000,000 in the Central Bank of Ireland. Sloan wasn't even certain if Mrs. Paddy O'Keane knew of the money's existence. Or of Kevin Pace's death. Sloan was reasonably certain that the account and Mrs. Paddy O'Keane were a conduit for the laundering of money for Paddy's insurgent Irish, for Miguel's international drug operation and for Kevin's illicit concubine.

But Sloan knew that more than speculation would be needed. And like the fiendishly simple plan that resulted in the arrest of Miguel Zabala, Sloan's scheme was brilliant in its simplicity. And in its deviousness.

On an overcast, dew covered morning, John Mercedes appeared, unannounced, on the stoop of Mrs. O'Keane's rustic, fieldstone house in the lush Irish countryside. John was straightforward, non-threatening as he stated simply, "Mrs. O'Keane, I am John Mercedes, an Investigator with Scotland Yard. It has been brought to our attention that a large sum of money has been transferred to your account. The origination of this transfer is an international drug smuggling operation controlled by Venezuelan Miguel Zabala. My former partner, Kevin Pace, who I believe you know – intimately – had informed me that you had been generously cooperating with him in the spirit of international détente in an attempt to stem the flow of illegal drugs which are ruining our youths.

"As you no doubt know, your husband is due to return home any day now, and I'm certain that you'll agree with me that if the existence of $3,000,000 in you account was known by either your husband or the international authorities investigating Miguel's operations, you would be find yourself in quite a dilemma – especially since Kevin Pace is dead and not available to vouch for your innocence."

Not surprisingly, Mrs. Paddy O'Keane accompanied John Mercedes to the Central Bank of Ireland and arranged for the transfer of the entire sum, in four equal installments, back to the original accounts in Los Angeles.

FBI Agent Sloan Dillard left the office for her London vacation.

Chapter Seventy-two

Becky Puccini stood, completely nude, in front of the full-length mirror in the bathroom. For the first time in quite a while, Becky could actually see her feet and her toes. Becky's appointments with her gynecologist had gradually increased in frequency, to the point now, when they were weekly. Becky showered, dressed in her favorite maternity shorts and top, and readied herself for the visit to the doctor.

As usual, Tommy accompanied Becky. Though customarily bored with the checkups and Becky's incessant chattering afterwards, Tommy had actually grown to anticipate the progress updates as the date of the birth drew nearer. Hell, Tommy even attended childbirth classes with Becky and was now well versed in state-of-the art breathing and pain management techniques.

Though he wanted to be surprised by the sex of the baby, Tommy was always relieved when Becky emerged from the office and assured Tommy that the pregnancy was progressing normally and everything would be perfect. Becky emerged from the doctor's office with a smile wider and more radiant than ever.

"Any day now, Tommy!" Becky proclaimed excitedly. "The doctor says everything's in order and the baby's head is in the birthing canal. Tommy, I've started to dilate! Two centimeters! The doctor isn't sure if she'll see me next in her office or in the hospital. Tommy, you're going to be a daddy. And I'm going to be a mommy. And we're going to be a family!"

In a famous Los Angeles recording studio, Jordan Taylor watched Angel put the "cans" over her ears, and step up to the recording microphone. It was so exciting to see the beginning of Angel's solo career – check that – to be such a major part of the start of her solo career. Cutting the deal with the label had been a cakewalk; Jordan had secured an obscene amount of money for a five-album deal, unprecedented, in fact, for an artist going solo. The album, self-titled *Angel,* was being recorded in an LA studio as quickly as possible to capitalize on the phenomenal interest in Angel and The Ungrateful. Some of the interest was morbid, but the majority of it was legitimate wonderment in the magical spell that Angel cast.

Though the recording sessions were grueling, Angel and Jordan ensured that efforts to expedite the release of what promised to be a chart-buster didn't compromise the artistic purity of the album.

Softly, Angel began to sing a song Jordan knew was going to be not only the first single of her solo career, but more importantly, the first hit.

I'm tired of being pushed
So tired of being pulled
Weary of this false sense of security
Into which I've been lulled

There have been too many tears
And days devoid of laughter
Now I realize that staying seems harder
That whatever might come after

Chorus:
And I know the shame is saying...not leaving
So I buried an old love today
And while Freedom can sometimes be deceiving
I've got to start making my own way

And this is what it has come down to
We both know it's time to make a break
Going through the motions, yeah that's what we do
And now love is a feeling, I can no longer fake
And I'm not afraid of being on my own
Leaving here, well it has to be done
So let me tell you something I've always known
The worst storms are still followed by the sun

Chorus:
And I know now the shame is in staying...not leaving
So I buried an old love today
And while Freedom can sometimes be deceiving
I've got to start making my own way
Yeah, baby, I'm going to start making my own way......

Angel held the final note, and then glanced over to Jordan for reassurance.

"Number one with a fucking bullet, baby!" Jordan exclaimed as she hugged her friend tightly.

Later that afternoon, Angel logged on to her computer. She smiled when she heard the familiar and much appreciated, "You've got mail" welcome.

Angel saw the e-mail was from Jordan who she had left only an hour earlier.

"Angel. Just spoke with Ace today. He called. Seems like his team is opening its season with a special exhibition game in the newly renovated London's Wembley National Stadium.

"Quite a big deal. 92,000 fans. The Royal Family, Queen Mother and all. I've booked your first gig! You've been selected to sing the United Kingdom National Anthem – 'God Save the Queen.' I did my best; they had originally picked Elton John, Sir Elton John! But that started a near riot with other British musicians - McCartney, Clapton, even Jaggar! Then their adopted daughter, Madonna, lobbied hard – Guy Ritchie even called Prince Charles himself. But it's you! Isn't that great? Only the pay's not so hot – well, actually there's no pay at all. But I needed a vacation and your career needed a launching pad – Here're the words:

God Save our gracious Queen,
Long live our noble queen
God save the Queen!
Send her victorious,
Happy and Glorious,
Long to reign over us;
God save the Queen!

O Lord our God arise,
Scatter her enemies
And make them fall;
Confound their politics,
Frustrate their knavish tricks,
On Thee our hopes we fix,
God, save us all!

Thy choicest gifts in store
On her be pleased to pour
Long may she reign;
May she defend our laws,
And ever give us cause
To sing with heart and voice,
God save the Queen!

Practice, baby, practice – This will be the largest live audience you'll ever play before. You kicked major ass in the studio today. See you soon. Love, Jordan."

Angel downloaded *God Save the Queen* from the Internet and practiced like she had never before in her life.

Morgan Chino returned home, late in the evening, exhausted. As was her custom, Morgan first checked her telephone answering machine for messages and then her e-mail. The note from Angel read,

"Hey, baby! Hope that hot little bod of yours has captured the hearts and minds of the entire fashion world. Am going to London. My first gig! Well, not really, ain't getting paid. Bummer. Love to see you there. Jordan's coming. Ace's first game. Wembley Stadium. Singing 'God Save The Queen.' Me and the Queen. Can you believe it? Little ghetto girl goes big time. Will be spending time getting to know John better. Looking forward to seeing your first cover. Hope to see you in London. Miss you. Love you. Angel."

Chapter Seventy-three

Sloan fidgeted in her seat in the international terminal at Washington's Dulles International Airport. Though she was actually quite comfortable flying, the prospects of a six-hour flight and the anticipation of who was waiting combined to ratchet up her apprehension level considerably.

Sloan's cell phone rang, and she eagerly glanced at the caller ID for an indication of the caller. Instantaneously, Sloan's mood soured considerably as she recognized the origination of the call – the Federal Bureau Of Investigation's regional field office in Chicago, Illinois.

In most instances, Sloan's near infallible, photographic memory served her extremely well. However, Sloan's memory, when it came to holding a grudge, snatched random bits of information in a vice-like grip that perpetuated information indefinitely.

Unfortunately, Sloan's still burned with the recollection of her jealous, incompetent cohorts referring to her as "Special Agent Titties."

"Special Agent Dillard."

"Er, um, hi Sloan. Um, er how are you?

"Just great, heading over to London. What's up?"

"Sloan, quite honestly, we're stumped. We've been at this for quite some time now. And we're no farther ahead than when we got here. Don't have a clue if it was Reggie, Stewart, Kevin, Miguel – or someone else. We've gone over everything. And all roads lead to the same dead end. Any suggestions? Please."

Sloan took interpreted the "please" to mean, "Sloan, we're so sorry for ever challenging you. You have been right all along. We humbly beg your forgiveness and hope, no pray, that you can find room in your heart to forgive us. And enlighten us."

Sloan was nothing if she was not forgiving. And so she started, "Here are my thoughts, I think that Reggie Beasley and Stewart Lindsey were murdered by Kevin Pace. I think Kevin Pace took his own life. I know that Miguel Zabala did. Unfortunately, I saw Miguel's death on tape. And the autopsy confirmed that Miguel was beginning to experience the ravages of Acquired Immunity Deficiency Syndrome. AIDS. He knew he was going to die. Soon.

Maybe it was the lifestyle. Maybe it was the needles.

"My intuition is that whoever killed Thomas Puccini was also involved, somehow, in the Ungrateful deaths. I've got hunches, but no proof. Mickey Delaney's a long shot. Jordan Taylor's a possibility. So is Becky Puccini. And Kelly Puccini. I'm not sure about the Rose boys. Dr. Chino's got a strong motive. I never even checked on Ace's parents – just assumed that they were in Jamaica. All my notes and my findings are in the desk drawers. And be sure to check the bottom drawers. I'll be available on my cell, and via e-mail. Good luck. I sincerely mean it. Thanks for the call. I've got to board."

"Thanks Sloan, just one more question, please."

"Go ahead."

"Thomas Puccini was bladed. One in. One across. The death at the Fleet Center in Boston was a massive overdose of methamphetamine. One died in New York at Madison Square Garden as the result of another, involuntary, massive overdose of methamphetamine. One in New York was pushed into the path of an oncoming, speeding taxi. The Philly death at First Union was strangulation. Two at the MCI Center in DC were shot. Two in Chicago were shot. That's eight deaths, Sloan. And four different MO's. Could there be more than one killer?"

"Oh fuck," is all that Sloan could think as her mind raced, the plane's door closed and the flight crew readied for a trans-continental journey. 38,000 feet above sea level, heading toward England, Sloan's mind was still in Chicago. And in Boston, New York, Philly, D.C. and Cleveland.

The fact that her vocabulary was deteriorating appreciably was not lost on Sloan, but, hey, she thought, "What the fuck."

Chapter Seventy-four

"The captain has just advised me that we have been cleared for landing at London's Heathrow Airport. The temperature in London is a balmy sixty-six degrees. The flight attendants will be going through the cabin shortly to collect any items you may wish to discard. In preparation for landing, please return your seats to an upright position and make sure that your tray tables are secured to the seat in front of you. We realize that you have many choices in air travel, and we thank you for choosing British Airlines. We hope you had as much fun flying with us as we did in serving you. We will be on the ground shortly. Thank you and enjoy your time in London."

Sloan had been engaged in deep concentration since the beginning of the journey. For the first time since the plane took off more than five and one half hours ago, Sloan spoke to the person in the adjacent seat, "Excuse me, do you have any idea when we will be landing?"

"Shortly."

"I sure hope the weather is nice in London."

Becky Puccini awoke in bed with a smile on her face. For Becky, life was good, and each new day brought with it the promise of a better tomorrow. Becky yawned, stretched her arms out and readied herself for her less than graceful exit from bed when she noticed an unusual warmness between her legs. Instinctively, Becky's hands raced to the area and she felt both warmness and wetness.

Becky reached over and started to shake Tommy vigorously.

"Tommy, Tommy, wake up! Wake up Tommy! It's time. My water broke! Call the doctor. Call the hospital!"

Tommy shook the sleep from his eyes and bounded up, still somewhat foggy, but vaguely aware of what was happening. Tommy had somewhat prepared for this time, but Becky's first muffled scream of pain more than slightly unnerved him.

"Let's go to the hospital, now!" Tommy said.

"Oh, Tommy, hurry!" Becky said as she hastily dressed.

In all of Tommy's "baby arrival" scenarios, he never really thought out the transportation to the hospital. For neither Tommy nor Becky had an automobile. Never really needed one with the constant traveling and living in downtown Chicago.

Kelly Puccini was awakened by the clatter and knocked on the door. "Everything all right?"

"It's Becky, Mom, her water broke, and she started her contractions. The first one was really strong."

"Relax, Tommy, this sort of thing has happened before. Not to worry. You can take my car to the hospital. But no speeding. Drive carefully."

Tommy and Becky were out of the house before Kelly had completed her admonitions about obeying the posted limits, coming to a complete stop at signs and making sure to yield the right of way, when appropriate.

Tommy opened Becky's door and helped her as she uncomfortably slid into the too-small front seat. Tommy struggled to adjust the seat belt around her too-large stomach, then raced around to the driver's side door and entered Kelly's 1990 GEO Prism.

Tommy thought Kelly's speeding lecture was slightly humorous, as he doubted if the rusting, baby blue Prism was capable of breaking the speed limit even in a school zone. With children present. And a child was going to be present quickly if he didn't get Becky to the hospital shortly.

Though it seemed like an eternity, Tommy and Becky arrived at the hospital's emergency room door in less than ten minutes. The emergency room nurse calmly assisted Becky into a wheelchair. Tommy was instructed to park the car in the visitor's lot and then check with admissions prior to joining Becky on the maternity floor. Somehow the relaxed, assuring demeanor of the nurse significantly diminished both Tommy's and Becky's apprehensions.

Tommy kissed Becky tenderly on the cheek and watched as the elevator doors closed, and then hurriedly parked the car and returned to the admitting clerk. Though somewhat annoyed with the multiple signatures required, Tommy was thankful that they had pre-registered.

A short time later, Tommy was in the elevator on the way to the maternity floor. For the first time since that fateful day as he waited for the curtain to rise at the United Center, Tommy was a bundle of nerves. Butterflies. Agitation. Nerves. Then Tommy remembered the breathing exercises that they had so faithfully practiced. Deep breath in. Deep breath out. When the door opened, Tommy was greeted by the floor nurse who chaperoned him to the birthing room. Tommy didn't really need her accompaniment as Becky's shrill screams readily identified her location.

Tommy was warmly welcomed by a pair of elderly, matronly shift nurses who instructed him to thoroughly wash his hands and change into the scrubs. Tommy emerged from the restroom, nattily attired in hospital blues, complete with fancy little footsie-like shoe covers, funky headpiece and mouth shield with an elastic band. Tommy caught a glance of his profile in the mirror, and though he wouldn't be mistaken for *ER*'s Dr. Carter, he liked the look – needing only a stethoscope dangling around his neck to complete it.

Tommy was instructed to position himself at the head of the bed, directly behind Becky. Becky's contractions were getting stronger and stronger, and more and more frequent. Tommy was amazed that his modest, private wife was lying on a hospital bed, partially nude, with her legs spread wide, her ankles in stirrups in the company of relative strangers who poked, prodded and inspected her continuously. He was even more amazed that this didn't faze her at all.

"Okay, honey, the doctor will be here shortly, you're seven centimeters dilated. You're doing excellent. You're going to want to push. But resist the urge. You're doing great."

Tommy was mesmerized by the entire scene, but he was bolted back to reality by another of Becky's piercing screams. Knowing that he should be doing something, but not sure quite what, Tommy took the lead of the maternity nurse and offered words of encouragement and reassurance.

Dramatically, the doctor entered the birthing room, inspected Becky's fully dilated cervix, announced that the baby's head was crowning and proclaimed Becky ready to deliver.

Three intensely painful contractions later, and one massive final push, a black head of curly hair emerged, followed by a gasp of joy from Becky, and a lusty and reassuringly loud cry.

The doctor gently laid a beautiful, healthy baby boy on Becky's stomach and asked Tommy if he wanted to cut the umbilical cord.

With large tears of happiness streaming down his face, Tommy tightly squeezed Becky's hand, whispered "I love you" into her ear, and tenderly picked up his son who was warmly wrapped in a blue receiving blanket, "Hi, I'm your dad. I love you,"

Chapter Seventy-five

"Everything is in order," the British government agent who inspected Sloan's passport and entry documents proclaimed. "Welcome to London, are you here on business or pleasure?"

With an uncustomary twinkle in her eye, Sloan replied, "Pleasure, definitely pleasure." Sloan's voice trailed off as she spotted John Mercedes across the concourse with the largest bouquet of multi-colored roses she had ever seen.

Their greeting was almost exactly as Sloan had earlier envisioned it – the outstretched arms, the tight embrace, the tender first kiss transitioning into a passionate one – although she hadn't anticipated the warm round of applause from the delighted and charmed airport travelers.

Sloan Dillard waited impatiently at the luggage carousel for her prince to bring around her carriage. John returned a short time later and escorted Sloan to his sleek, dark blue, BMW sedan. John opened the door and Sloan sunk into the deep leather seats. John put on his sunglasses and sped away from the curb. Sloan was confused. She wasn't actually sure if she was with John Mercedes or James Bond. But whoever it was, he was driving on the wrong side of the road. Very fast.

"I'm sure you're exhausted after the flight," John started.

Sloan was thrilled when he had reached over and intertwined his fingers with hers, but somewhat alarmed and concerned with his one-handed driving technique. Effortlessly, John wove in and out of traffic, seemingly never taking his eyes off Sloan. Though she very much appreciated the attention, she was hoping to postpone it until a more appropriately safe time.

"We'll get you checked into your hotel, and then I've made arrangements to have a sort-of homecoming dinner. Nothing fancy, but Angel's in town for Ace's first game. Hope you don't mind. Then tomorrow, we'll catch the game and play it by ear from there."

For Sloan, the idea seemed absolutely perfect. She was wondering how their relationship was going to unfold, apprehensive if things would be forced, uncertain – but hopeful – that her strong emotional and physical feelings were going to be reciprocated.

"Yes," Sloan thought. "The easing into thing was ideal."

Sloan's hotel was exactly as she had envisioned it. From the time she was greeted by the Beefeater uniformed bellman, to the ever-so-proper and polite desk clerk, to her quaintly perfect room featuring a canopied, four poster bed with oversized pillows and a goose-down comforter, Sloan was thrilled. Unpacking, while John waited near the fireplace in the lobby below, Sloan felt a little like Mary Poppins, a little like Liza Dolittle, and a lot like the happiest woman alive. Her happiness magnified when she entered the bathroom and found heated towel racks and a freshly scrubbed, old fashioned, cast iron bathtub.

Sloan freshened up and met John in the lobby for what was sure to be another wildly exciting ride on the wrong side of the road.

Sloan's curiosity was piqued as John informed her that dinner was at his place, and she speculated just what type of place "his place" was. A stately English manor, at the end of a tree lined, winding driveway? A stale smelling, messy two room apartment with ripped furniture and littered with scattered newspapers. A small bungalow cottage with a well-manicured lawn? A penthouse apartment with a stunning view of the city?

John seamlessly wove his car in and out of the slow moving traffic. As the car headed towards London's West-end Theatrical district, Sloan's inquisitive, conjectural mind raced into overdrive. John finally parked his BMW behind a century-old warehouse, opened Sloan's car door, and proceeded to escort her to a large green steel door with wire mesh covering a smoky window. John opened the door for Sloan, placed his hand under her elbow and pulled the gate of the freight elevator down. Apprehensively, Sloan joined John and the "lift" slowly lumbered up to the third floor. John opened his apartment door, and Angel rushed to hug him. Sloan looked in amazement at John's ultra modern, spacious loft, tastefully decorated exclusively in complimentary shades of white.

Angel mentioned that Jordan couldn't join them for dinner as planned, since her flight from LA had been delayed.

Sloan silently thanked God, for the thought of sharing dinner with a possible mass murderer was less than appetizing.

The dinner was exquisitely perfect. In addition to being an international man of mystery and intrigue, John was also a gourmet cook and wine connoisseur. More than once during the meal, Angel noticed the loving looks that John and Sloan not so secretly exchanged over flickering candles.

"I'm going to be heading back now," Angel announced.

Sloan found herself unsuccessfully fighting off more frequent urges to yawn, but was still startled, and mildly disappointed, when John said,

"Angel, I'm taking Sloan back to her hotel shortly. Yours isn't much further. I'll drop her first. Then you."

The Beefeater doorman smiled as John tenderly kissed Sloan goodnight. "See you at noon, sharp. Dress casually. I love you."

Hours later, a smile still creased Sloan's lips in sleep, as she dreamed of those three words, "I love you."

Chapter Seventy-six

Tommy Puccini was up late into the evening, putting the final touches on the nursery. Once his funds became accessible, and money wasn't really an object anymore, Tommy had purchased duplicates of everything – blankets, sheets, stuffed animals, mobiles – to ensure that their baby would enter family life in an appropriately colored room.

Tommy found himself excited with the prospects of family life and was getting increasingly comfortable with his new role as a daddy. Tommy realized that, in their haste to get to the hospital, they had brought along the bag with baby clothing and Becky's personal things and toiletries, but Becky had nothing to wear home from the hospital. Though Becky and the baby weren't going to be home until later in the day, Tommy wanted time to ensure that everything was perfect upon their return.

Carefully, Tommy selected a sun dress from Becky's closet, assuming that it would fit comfortably and that she could brag, years later to her grandchildren, that she was in such excellent shape after childbirth that she didn't have to wear maternity clothes home from the hospital.

Tommy laid the sundress on the bed, and guessed at the appropriate foundation garments and jewelry. Realizing that it would be inappropriate to bundle the outfit, underwear and accoutrements under his arm for transport to the hospital, Tommy went down into the basement to locate Becky's suitcase.

Tommy carried the suitcase upstairs and was surprised by the clanging within. Tommy opened the suitcase and removed a large brown paper bag with "Dominick's" written in bright red script letters.

Tommy's face was ashen, he shook uncontrollably and shivered as he peered into the bag and saw hypodermic syringes, needles, a shiny bright knife, a blood splattered knife, a .22 caliber handgun, assorted wigs and a New York Yankees baseball cap.

For the second time in less than twelve hours, large tears welled inside of Tommy's eyes and streamed down his cheeks.

Tommy's life didn't flash before his eyes, the future life of his son did. In less than a nanosecond, Tommy knew exactly what to do. For himself. For his son. For his son's future.

Tommy dialed the Chicago Regional Office of The Federal Bureau of Investigation.

"I'd like to speak with Special Agent Sloan Dillard."

"I'm sorry, she's unavailable. May I take a message, or may someone else assist you?"

Moments later, Sloan's assistant was on the telephone and bewildered with joy at his good fortune.

"Thank you very much for calling, please be sure not to touch anything. We'll be there within minutes."

Tommy stood on the porch and watched forlornly as the agents from the FBI sped away with the evidence and marveled at the stupidity of their departing instructions, "Please do not share this information with anyone else. Please go about your regular routine as if none of this happened. We'll dust the evidence for fingerprints and see if anything matches. Remember, act normally."

"Fat fucking chance of that ever happening, you dim-witted mother fucking bastards," Tommy said as he walked back into the house that he shared with a mass murderer.

The hours that followed were nothing but a blur for Tommy. He walked in circles. He paced. He stood and stared. He cried. And he cried some more.

Tommy picked up his guitar and played. And playing, he prayed. He prayed for strength. For compassion. For forgiveness. For understanding. For the wisdom to accept what he would never understand. For himself. For his son. Mostly Tommy prayed for his son.

Hours later, with strength and resolve from above and a peaceful sense of resignation to make the best of whatever the future held, Tommy Puccini pulled the GEO Prism into the hospital's parking lot to pick up his wife and son. Tommy had carefully placed Becky's going-home wardrobe in a Jewel Foods bag.

As the nurse once again doubled checked to ensure that the wristbands of both Becky and the baby matched, Tommy secured the child seat and positioned the sun shield to block the rays from disturbing the sleep of his beloved son.

Kelly Puccini greeted Tommy and Becky at the door and squealed with delight at the sight of her grandson. Kelly and Becky busied themselves in the nursery, and Tommy returned to the car to complete the unpacking.

Tommy knew that it was inevitable and this moment would eventually come, but not this quickly – not today.

The FBI agents met him in the driveway and said solemnly, but without any real compassion, "The prints were a perfect match. Sorry, Tommy, We're bringing her in. We've got no other choice."

Tommy followed them into the house. Kelly and Becky emerged from the nursery, each with a surprised, panicked look on their faces.

"Mrs. Puccini, you are under arrest. You are charged with nine counts of first degree murder. You have the right to remain silent. You have the right to an attorney…"

Becky screamed, "No! No! No!"

The agents roughly pulled Kelly Puccini's arms behind her back and tightly secured the cuffs.

Tommy looked on incredulously. And silently.

Chapter Seventy-seven

Sloan Dillard stood, along with 92,000 others, as the warm summer sun shone brightly on Angel.

Angel was standing on a platform directly in front of the royal box. To her left stood eleven of England's finest soccer players. To her right, stood Ace and ten of his teammates. Directly in front of Angel was the entire royal family.

Just as she had practiced so many times, Angel's beautiful voice began *God Save the Queen*. But never in her innumerable rehearsal session had Angel anticipated the energy she could draw from 92,000. With each note, she grew stronger, more passionate and the melodious tones of her sweet voice resonated throughout the stadium. The excitement of the crowd became increasingly palpable, and even the usually reserved, stoic royal family was infused with the crowd's energy.

Ace stood and rocked uneasily. His excitement grew too, as he thought about the incredibly beautiful musician

92,000 cheered wildly as Angel's final verse of *God Save the Queen* echoed throughout their souls, and then unfortunately faded away.

Ace watched as Angel walked off the platform and was greeted by a passionate, congratulatory kiss.

"I'll be goddamned." Ace smiled, jealously and surprisedly.

Sloan's memory of the actual game and the rest of the day would be forever overshadowed by her moment by moment recollection of what was, quite possibly, the most wonderfully pleasurable evening anyone had ever spent. Sloan was reasonably certain that Ace's team won the match 1-0, and that Ace scored a spectacular goal on a bicycle kick. But after that, everything was just a haze until she met John Mercedes in the lobby of her hotel at 7:00 PM.

John took Sloan by the hand, and they followed a path of carefully strewn rose petals out the side door of the hotel. The London evening was warm, and brilliant stars illuminated the sky. The driver of the all white, horse-drawn carriage was an authentically British character, seemingly extracted directly from a Dicken's novel. As the carriage slowly clanked over the cobblestone streets, the driver regaled Sloan with charming bits of London lore, as John held her hand tightly.

The restaurant was nestled off the main road, and was as eloquent as it was small. Even on a warm night, the flames dancing in the stone hearth fireplace seemed entirely appropriate, and their table was adorned with a bouquet of freshly cut flowers and a singular. tapered candle. John pulled Sloan's chair out for her, and on the seat was a beautifully wrapped jewelry box, festively decorated with multi-colored ribbons.

Sloan started to gently protest, but John silently put a finger to her lips. Sloan opened the package and inside found an enchanting string of lustrous, alabaster pearls. Without a word, John kissed Sloan's fingers, then her hands. John stood behind Sloan, kissed her gently on the cheek, on the collarbone, and then flawlessly fastened the pearls around her neck. Sloan had never before felt such a powerful surge of sensuality race throughout her body and she felt herself becoming warm as her entire body poised in anticipation of what Sloan could only hope would happen immediately.

John returned to his seat with a satisfied smile of contentment, and Sloan watched his eyes dance through the flickering flame. Without a word, or any apparent signal from John, the waiter arrived with an appetizer of Lobster Fondue, and the sommelier followed shortly with two glasses of a perfectly complimenting Chardonnay.

A tuxedo clad waitress appeared with two small cut crystal bowls, each with a single scoop of lemon sorbet.

Palettes properly cleansed, the soup followed shortly, then a delightful salad with a uniquely delicious vinaigrette dressing. Mysteriously, after a perfectly timed interval, the main course arrived. With a theatrical presentation that was worthy of applause, the wait staff removed the sterling silver domes and presented two artistically arranged plates of, appropriately, Beef Wellington. The sommelier arrived shortly thereafter with a 1982 Bordeaux that made each mouthful even more delicious.

Somehow, John had known that Sloan would never be able to eat dessert after such a wonderful meal. As the classical music trio gently played beautiful background music, John and Sloan stood up to leave. Only then did Sloan realize that they had the entire restaurant to themselves. As Sloan re-entered the still-waiting carriage, she saw the restaurant re-open to the public.

John kissed her passionately, and the driver headed, with an appreciated degree of urgency, directly to Sloan's hotel.

Once inside Sloan's room, John was tantalizingly deliberate. Sloan had waited for months for this moment, yet John was leisurely, unhurried and seemingly intent on lightly kissing every inch of Sloan's passion inflamed body.

And then, the magic moment finally arrived. For Sloan it was erotic. It was sensual. It was sexual. It was everything she had ever imagined. And more. By an exponential degree of infinity. Her fingers dug deep into John's back, her back arched, her eyes rolled, her breath quickened, her gasps became audible.

For John Mercedes, it was even better.

Sloan Dillard awoke early in the morning with her arm around John and her head resting comfortably on his chest. Sloan still tingled with excitement at the memory of last evening's rendezvous. Carefully and silently, Sloan gently covered John and crept from the room.

The London Daily Mirror had been slipped under her door, and the headlines screamed: "The Ungrateful Dead Murders Solved! It's Mommy Not-So Dearest!"

Sloan read with rapt attention every word of the article about Kelly Puccini's arrest, filled with annoying puns like "Mum's the Word No Longer" and the "Mother Lode of All Mass Murders."

Sloan awakened John and asked him to take her immediately to Heathrow. John glanced at the paper and understood Sloan's urgency.

Angel quietly got up and softly kissed her sleeping lover's hand. Angel stood in front of the large picture window in her luxuriously appointed penthouse suite atop London's prestigious Connaught Hotel and slowly opened the drapes. A brilliant sunshine filled the room and softly, warmly and slowly awakened Jordan Taylor.

Angel saw the headlines of *The London Daily Mirror*. She read the article in its entirety. And then re-read it. Curiously, Angel's attention was drawn to the small advertisement at the bottom of the page. The headline boldly proclaimed, "Lose Ten Pounds in Ten Days or Double Your Money Back!" The slim, curvaceous body of Morgan Chino was unmistakable. Morgan - the product spokesperson for Dr. Fujimaro Chino's newly formed "European Pharamacal Company."

Chapter Seventy-eight

FBI Special Agent Sloan Dillard's flight landed shortly after 4:00 PM. Immediately upon arriving at Chicago's O'Hare International Airport, before clearing customs, Sloan used her cellular phone and called the FBI's regional office.

"I'll be arriving in approximately two hours. Please have all the evidence used in securing the arrest warrant available for my inspection. I would like to review any new evidence you have accumulated since my departure. Please understand, I am not in any way insinuating that anything is amiss. However, as the agent in charge, I would have appreciated a courtesy heads up, before the arrest was made. Now, I just want to cover all the bases and take a look at things from a fresh perspective."

Over the next three hours, Sloan meticulously examined the evidence and a sickening feeling gradually enveloped her. It was nearly 11:00 PM local time and Sloan had been awake for more than twenty four hours. Fatigue was fighting nausea, and Sloan was certain that, unfortunately, nausea was going to be the initial victor. Sloan excused herself and returned from the women's restroom looking pale and weak.

"Let me play it back for you to see if I've got everything right, okay? Tommy discovered the bag inside of Becky's suitcase. Within the bag were hypodermic syringes, needles, a .22 caliber handgun, a clean knife, a blood splattered knife, and a New York Yankees baseball cap. Right so far?

"You took the evidence back and matched the prints to the ones found on the drinking glass in the Zip-lock bag in my bottom left hand drawer, marked 'Kelly Puccini.'

"You found matching prints on one of the knives, the handgun, and the baseball cap. Based on this evidence, you arrested Kelly Puccini."

"That's correct."

"You've been set up, you fucking idiots."

Early the next morning, Sloan Dillard and her slightly embarrassed assistant investigators were interviewing Kelly Puccini. Fortunately, she waived her right to have her attorney present, sobbing, "I haven't done anything, I've got nothing to hide."

The answers to the questions were exactly as Sloan had anticipated.

"Yes, Becky handed me a gun once, told me I might need protection after the first two young women had been murdered on the tour."

"Yes, Becky was wearing a glove at the time, which I thought was unusual, but never really gave it a second thought. I thought a lot of things Becky did were unusual."

"Yes, that same day, right after the gun, Becky gave her the Yankees cap, said it was a gift from her brother who was in the Yankee farm system."

"Well, yes, Becky still had the glove on."

"No, I never handled any syringes or needles."

"The knife was a part of the set that Becky gave me for Mother's Day."

"That's all I can remember. I swear I'm innocent. Can't you please help me? Please?"

"Yes, Mrs. Puccini, I think that I can."

"What tipped you off?"

"First of all, it was too perfect. Too neat. Secondly, while I was on the plane I poured over everyone's background for clues after you pointed out the radically different MO's of the killings. Only Becky had all the bases covered. Becky was an expert outdoors enthusiast who 'could drop a whitetail from seventy-five yards or flawlessly fillet a twenty-six inch walleye.' She was a biology major and readying herself for medical school, she had knowledge and possibly access to the drugs. And then there was the photo of Becky someone anonymously sent. But it was the baseball cap – it had never been worn. And then I went back and revisited her father's death. The death certificate read 'heart attack,' but the coroner I tracked down and spoke with a short time ago suspected it was a poisoning. Only he was from the small town of Oregon, in Wisconsin, without much support. And the Rose boys were local heroes. And Becky was an orphan. So he didn't press for further investigation. It's something that's bothered him immensely since. Things just didn't add up. There was just too much perfection – and too much suspicion surrounding Becky."

Tommy Puccini answered the door, holding his son. Both Tommy and Sloan shuddered when the single gunshot erupted from the rear room.

FBI Agent Sloan Dillard cautiously opened the room's door.

Becky Puccini lay motionless, with her brains scattered on the walls behind her. Dead, just as Reggie Beasley and Stewart Lindsey had died.

Sloan Dillard immediately left and proceeded directly to O'Hare in hopes of catching the next available flight to London's Heathrow airport. As her luck would have it, she was successful. Sloan boarded a London-bound flight at approximately the same time as John Mercedes settled in for the long London-to-Chicago trans-Atlantic flight. Thus again delaying the much-anticipated replay of their night of passion.